A HERO IN THE STRIFE

LADY ELIZABETH WAS CALLING HIM UP. (PAGE 48.)

A

HERO

IN THE

STRIFE

A TALE OF THE SEVENTEENTH CENTURY

BY

LOUISA C. SILKE

ILLUSTRATED BY

J. F. WEEDON

PUBLISHED BY

CURIOSMITH
MINNEAPOLIS
2010

Published by Curiosmith.
P. O. Box 390293, Minneapolis, Minnesota, 55439.
Internet: curiosmith.com.
E-mail: shopkeeper@curiosmith.com.

Previously printed by THE RELIGIOUS TRACT SOCIETY in 1892.

ISBN 9781935626046

CONTENTS

———◇———

"Sigh not the old heroic ages back;
    The heroes were but brave and earnest men;
Do thou but hero-like pursue thy track;
    Striving, not sighing, brings them back again!

The hero's path is straight, to do and say
    God's words and works in spite of toil and shame;
Labours enough will meet thee in thy way,
    So thou forsak'st it not to seek for them."

Mrs. Charles

CHAPTER I

A VISIT TO LONDON

HURSTWOOD MANOR, the seat of Sir Richard Devereux, was, at the time of the Restoration, a pleasant, spacious, and substantially built old country house, in which already generation after generation of the family of Devereux had lived and died. Numerous additions to the original building had been made from time to time, but little had been done since the days of Elizabeth, when a new wing had been added.

Its owner was a staunch royalist, as his father had been before him. But the latter's loyalty had cost him dear, for he had lost his life in one of the battles with the Parliamentarian troops, while his coffers had suffered considerably from the demand made upon them in the king's cause.

Still, the present Sir Richard possessed a fair income, and was able to exercise a considerable amount of hospitality, for which, indeed, he was famed; while his wife, the Lady Elizabeth, was no less noted for her goodness and kindness to the poor around.

On a fine day in the early part of April, in the year of our Lord 1661, Sir Richard and his lady might have been seen pacing slowly up and down the broad terrace walk which skirted the lawn on the south side of the house, from which an extensive view of the surrounding country might be obtained. For Hurstwood was situated near the top of a long steep hill in one of the most romantic parts of Sussex.

Thick woods clothed one side of the valley, extending almost close up to the house, and sheltering it considerably from the wind. The other side was more open, sloping gently upwards, until the gracefully rounded outlines of the downs melted off into the clear blue sky.

Nature had not yet fully donned her beautiful spring garment of softly-tinted emerald hue, but she had awakened from the sleep of winter, as many a bud and shoot testified; while the birds were rejoicing over sunnier skies and more balmy breezes.

However, the two who were pacing up and down the terrace were just then too deeply engaged in conversation to take much note of the beauties around them. They were talking over what was in those days a great and rare event to dwellers in the country—a visit to London. For the state of the roads was such that travelling was attended by many dangers. The ruts were so deep that there was the risk, nay, almost certainty, of a coach being overturned sooner or later; for, except in fine weather, the mud usually lay deep on the right and left of the road in a sort of quagmire, leaving only the centre available for a wheeled vehicle. It was a common thing for a coach to stick fast until extra horses or a team of cattle could be procured to drag it out of the mire.

"In some parts of Kent and Sussex," we are told, "none but the strongest horses could in winter get through the bog, in which at every step they sank deep."

Added to this there was always the risk of being attacked and plundered by highwaymen, who were a constant terror to travellers, while the Government seemed unable to put them down. Thus a journey, even to London, was not lightly or very frequently undertaken by country gentlemen in those days, more especially accompanied by the ladies of the family.

But it was just this which Sir Richard was proposing, feeling that the occasion was unusual enough to justify the unwonted proceeding.

The occasion was no less an event than the coronation of his Majesty King Charles II., which was to take place at the end of the month; and Sir Richard, with his ardent notions of loyalty, wished—or, as he said, thought it fitting,—not only to be present himself, but to afford his wife and eldest daughter the same gratification also. For he was a kind-hearted man, and though he and Lady Elizabeth were almost as widely sundered in disposition and tastes as the two poles, yet that did not prevent him from reverencing his wife's saintly character, and entertaining a true affection for her. Then too Dorothy was his special favorite, "and," he argued, "it would be a rare treat to her to witness the gay doings; while at the same time she would be company for her mother."

Lady Elizabeth at first shrank from the idea. She knew

something already of the tone of morals at the court, and felt that the world of London would be pretty sure to follow the example set at headquarters. Thus she dreaded the thought of bringing her young daughter in any way into contact with influences so likely to be hurtful.

But Sir Richard scouted the notion of there being any danger. Would she not be there herself to shield the child from all harm?—if harm there was, though he could not himself see where it lay; and a fine girl like Dorothy could not be kept in rigid seclusion all her life; he would not have her turned into a little Puritan.

Had Sir Richard spoken out all his feelings on the subject, he would have had to own to a lurking desire to show off Dorothy's beauty, of which he was very proud, not pausing to reflect whether it might prove a dangerous possession to her in the new surroundings into which he wished to introduce her.

Lady Elizabeth felt she must resist no longer; evidently his heart was quite set on the plan, and she had better yield with a good grace. So she thanked him for his kind wish to give Dorothy and herself this pleasure, inwardly rejoicing that he did not desire also to include her little Cicely in the party.

"Then I will see about making the necessary arrangements, and I will leave you to tell Dorothy the good news. I see the two girls yonder in the lime walk, but I must not stop longer. Be sure you make your own preparations in good time, and be ready by the 18th."

Lady Elizabeth, thus left alone, was turning to seek her young daughters, when they forestalled her by hastening towards her.

There was a good deal of difference in age between the sisters, two brothers who came after Dorothy having died in infancy. The latter, who was now eighteen, was a tall and decidedly handsome girl, with regular features, a wealth of dark glossy brown hair, and beautiful dark eyes shaded by long silky lashes. Her complexion was clear, with the glow of health upon it, and her small head was well set on her shoulders. Her mouth was firm, and as well as her chin showed strength of character. There was something proud and independent in her bearing, but her countenance was open and her manner frank, though wanting in the graciousness that characterized Lady Elizabeth.

Cicely, who was scarcely twelve, was a fair-haired girl,

altogether on a smaller scale than her sister, and by no means equaling her in good looks. But she had a sweet, trustful little face, and her gentle ways made her very winning.

"We saw you and father walking up and down for ever so long, but you seemed in such grave talk that we did not venture to draw near," said Dorothy.

"Has anything happened, mother?" asked little Cicely, slipping her hand into that of Lady Elizabeth. "Anything sad, I mean?"

"No, dear; rather something is going to happen, and it can scarcely be called sad—at any rate I do not think Dorothy will so regard it. What say you, daughter, to going with your father and myself to pay a visit to the great capital?"

"Go to London, mother!" exclaimed the girl, half incredulously, but with her eyes sparkling at the mere notion; "do you really mean you are going to take me to London? Oh, such a thing seems too good to be true. You are not joking, mother mine?"

"No, my child; your father has proposed it, and though I own I would rather have kept you still longer in the retirement of our simple life here, yet, as his heart is set upon it, I cannot say nay."

"Oh, how delightful! I have so often longed to see London, especially since Eugene has been there, and I have never yet been away from home at all. I hope we are going soon" cried the girl, clasping her hands in her excitement; "it will be difficult to wait till the day comes."

"And am I going too, mother?" asked Cicely's soft tones.

"No, dearest; you are too young, so you must stay quietly and happily here with good Owen. And when we come home we will tell you of all our doings. It will be pleasant to meet after our absence, and I shall be very glad to be back with my little Cicely again."

A slight cloud of disappointment swept over Cicely's face, but it soon dispersed. She had a happy, sunny nature, and her mother's will was law for her. Moreover she did not share Dorothy's love of change and excitement. The pleasures of home were enough for her for the present; and she was not at all sure that she would like to encounter the risks of travelling.

"I hope you will all come back safe and sound," she remarked, with an anxious look in her blue eyes. "It would be dreadful to think of your being attacked by highwaymen."

"But you needn't think of such things, you foolish child," interrupted Dorothy. "Shall we not have father and the serving men to protect us?"

"We shall have better protection than that, dear one; even the protection of Him 'who never slumbereth nor sleepeth.' And you, my Cicely, will be in the same keeping."

The little girl responded by a bright smile, showing that her mother's words comforted her; and then the coming event was still further discussed between them, Dorothy having endless questions to ask, and going into fresh raptures on hearing that the object of the visit was to witness the king's coronation.

"What a grand sight it will be! Poor Cicely, I wish you were coming too; and yet I am not sure that you would enjoy it. You are such a quiet, timid little being that I know you would be in a fright half the time from one cause or another. Whereas I like a little adventure, and only think it fun."

The short time that intervened before the day fixed for departure passed all too quickly for Cicely, who could not but feel the parting from her mother, who had never left home before within her recollection.

Lady Elizabeth herself looked forward to this coming visit to London with mingled feelings. Eugene, her only son, had recently, through the influence of her brother, the Earl of Burnham, obtained a place at court, much to the gratification of his father. The Devereux family, which was an ancient one, had always served their king; and though Sir Richard already began to see that he must not look for much, or indeed any reward for past services, Charles not being troubled with superfluous feelings of gratitude, regarding as he did all the sacrifices made on his behalf as proceeding from self-interested motives, yet it seemed to the loyal knight to follow as a matter of course that his son should in his turn devote himself to the service of his royal master.

But Lady Elizabeth regarded the matter in a very different light, and dreaded exposing her son, with his weak, pleasure-loving nature, to the evil influences of court life. Rumors came that the young man's handsome face and gay disposition were rapidly advancing him in the king's favor; but while the news gratified the father, it only added to the mother's anxieties.

Lady Elizabeth, however, had long ago made the sorrowful

discovery that, much as she loved her husband, she and he thought alike on scarcely any subject whatever. While his hopes and aspirations were bounded by earth's horizon, hers had become fixed on heaven; while he lived for things present, she felt that nothing short of things eternal could satisfy her spirit. Thus a great gulf severed them; and the two lives, though lived under the one roof at Hurstwood, yet ran in widely diverse channels.

Sir Richard spent his days, as did most country squires of the time, in hunting, hawking, and shooting, watching the sports of racing and wrestling, and looking after his estate. He kept an hospitable table, and was always good-naturedly ready to do a kindness for a neighbor; but beyond this his ideas soared not.

Lady Elizabeth, on the other hand, passed much of her time in her boudoir or closet, or in visiting the poor; leading a saintly life, in spite of the absence of all outward helps to devotion. The Bible and one or two religious books were her constant study, and from them she drew spiritual comfort and teaching, of which she got none from the rector of the parish, who was fonder of horse-racing and hunting than of attending to the duties of his calling: a thing by no means uncommon in those days among the country clergy.

Thus, regarding matters as she did, it was little wonder that, as the 18th drew near, Lady Elizabeth, while looking forward to the meeting with her son, was yet full of misgivings as to the effect she might find his new life had had on him. Would the meeting be all joy, or would there be an intermingling of pain? What grief it would be to her to see him following the licentious customs and ways that seemed to be prevailing since the king's return!

But there was no one with whom she could share her anxieties. Her husband could not even understand them; and though little Cicely was strangely thoughtful for her years, and love made her quick to discern when aught was troubling her mother, yet she was too young to be taken into confidence.

A very close tie bound these two together, Cicely being the only one of the family who resembled Lady Elizabeth at all in character or tastes; but she was wonderfully like her mother in sweetness of disposition and in her love for sacred things. It was her delight to steal into the latter's chamber, and there, seated on a footstool at her feet, she would listen while Lady Elizabeth read to her the gospel story, until the Savior of whom it told had become to her a living reality, and was enshrined in her inmost heart. If there was a tinge of gravity about the child, who did not care much for the merry-makings that pleased Dorothy, she yet always seemed to dwell in an atmosphere of quiet, deep-seated happiness.

But though the days before the 18th went all too quickly for Cicely, to Dorothy's impatience they passed far too slowly. At last, however, the morning of their departure dawned, to her great satisfaction, and at an early hour the family coach, a large lumbering vehicle with four horses, drew up at the door. It was not as an evidence of wealth nor from a desire for show that so many horses were employed, but from simple necessity; as with fewer there would have been the danger of constantly sticking in the mud. Even six horses were not always sufficient.

They spent a couple of nights on the road, for the rate of travelling was slow in those days. We are told that when a royal prince visited one of the stately mansions of Sussex in wet weather, he was six hours in going nine miles, and men had to prop up his carriage on either side, while several of the coaches which conveyed his retinue were upset and injured.

Fortunately for our party the weather was fine, and the sun was shining brightly when at length they entered London, which, previous to the Great Fire, was very different from the city as we see it now.

"It was then a strange network of buildings, chiefly of wood and plaster. Narrow streets of lofty houses with gabled roofs and lattice windows, with oddly imagined symbols of trade dangling over each shop door, and not unfrequently shields with armorial bearings indicating that the trader had superseded some noble family," all gave it a picturesque appearance. The residences of the merchants in the city were often most handsome, almost as much so as those of the nobility—of stately dimensions, with richly carved pillars and porticos at the entrance, spacious rooms and staircases, and the whole frequently much decorated.

The shops or booths were distinguished from one another by painted signs, such as Royal Oak, Golden Lamb, Blue Bear. It would have been almost useless to number them, few of the errand boys, porters, or coachmen being able to read.

The state of the city then was what we should call intolerable in these days. In rainy weather the gutters became torrents, which often bore along the refuse from the stalls of butchers and greengrocers; while passing vehicles bespattered the pedestrians, whose only chance of avoiding the mud was to keep as far as possible from the carriage road. At nightfall most of the streets were left in profound darkness; and the danger of walking about was increased by the number of thieves, as well as by the fashion prevailing among certain young gentlemen of swaggering about the town breaking windows, upsetting passengers, and indulging in other amusements of a similar character, to the terror of the inhabitants.

However, when Sir Richard Devereux and his party entered London it was broad daylight. Bright sunbeams were lighting up the quaint old streets and playing around each ancient device, casting broad shadows here and there, which only served to throw into deeper relief the projecting portions of the irregular old buildings.

Dorothy was delighted with all she saw, and gazed, eagerly on the novel sights, nothing seeming to escape the observation of her bright eyes, while her exclamations of wonder or of admiration were unceasing.

CHAPTER II

A NEW ACQUAINTANCE

"It is a weary task to school the heart,
Ere years or griefs have tamed its fiery throbbings,
Into that still and passive fortitude
Which is but learned from suffering."—MRS. HEMANS

THE following afternoon, between the hours of three and six, the broad aisle of the nave of St. Paul's was thronged by a goodly company of people of various classes and degrees. It was called "Paul's Walk" in those days, and formed a fashionable meeting-place where the busy and the idle, the aristocrat and the rich merchant, the professional man and the indolent loiterer were accustomed to mingle and elbow one another. On this particular day the common topic on the lips of almost every one was the approaching ceremony of the king's coronation.

Standing near one of the pillars was a little group consisting of a gentleman in a handsome but comparatively plain doublet and cloak, such as country squires in those days wore, a lady in a soft-colored gown of tabbinet trimmed with point lace and a plain hood, and a young maiden whose fresh beauty and simplicity of costume seemed to proclaim her a dweller in the country but recently come to town.

They were evidently on the look-out for some one they were expecting to meet there, and after a while a gay young cavalier approached them, dressed in a close, tight-fitting satin doublet which, as well as his short cloak, was edged with deep gold lace. He also wore a falling band of richest point lace round his neck, bows of ribbons above the knees with lace ruffles beneath them, while his low-crowned broad-brimmed hat was adorned with a bunch of feathers. His features were good, but the expression told of a weak, self-indulgent nature.

"How late you are, Eugene; we have been here almost three

quarters of an hour awaiting you," remarked the girl with a touch of impatience in her tones.

"Forgive me, sister mine, though I doubt not you have been well entertained meanwhile in watching all this goodly concourse of people. And, mother, I pray you excuse my lack of punctuality, for I was hindered. Everybody one meets has so much to say about tomorrow's ceremony."

"It is going to be very grand, is it not?" said Dorothy eagerly. "I mean the procession from the Tower to Whitehall."

"Yes, I can promise you it will be mighty fine,—such a spectacle as will dazzle your unaccustomed eyes, that have only hitherto looked upon country sports and maypoles."

The girl's face grew bright with anticipation.

"And you will secure good places for us, so that we may see it well?"

"Yes, yes," he answered. "You will be in a balcony from which you can look down upon the whole cavalcade as it passes below. You may think yourself fortunate to possess a brother who has been able to arrange this for you, for I warrant you every window and balcony from which a view of the procession can be had is in tremendous request, and people are willing to pay any price for them. In fact, they are scarcely to be had for love or money."

"Then how have you managed to secure this for us?" asked Lady Elizabeth. "Have you undertaken that we shall pay some fabulous sum for just an hour's entertainment?"

"Nay, mother mine, I have managed so cleverly that it is offered as a personal favor, and no price is to be paid save that which my fair sister will contribute by her good looks towards enhancing the attractions of the group assembled there, among whom she is to shine as a star," said the young man lightly, speaking after the manner of the gallants of the day.

"Cease such foolish tattle, I beg you," interposed Lady Elizabeth hastily, and even sternly for one so gentle, "and fill not the child's head with such nonsense, or I shall regret having agreed to bring her up to town."

Further remark on the subject was prevented by the approach of the well-known Mr. Evelyn, who was an old acquaintance of Lady Elizabeth's, and who now advanced with outstretched hand to greet her.

"This is an unexpected pleasure, for I did not know that you were in London."

"We only arrived yesterday; but I was hoping we might see you during our stay."

"I suppose Sir Richard has come too?"

"Yes; he was with us a few minutes ago, but he espied a friend in the crowd and went off to speak to him. He will doubtless rejoin us shortly."

"And is this Mistress Dorothy, whom I knew as a little child when I was visiting you at Hurstwood several years ago?"

"Yes; she has grown into quite a young woman now," remarked Lady Elizabeth, as Mr. Evelyn and Dorothy exchanged greetings. "And my son you know?"

"Yes, I have met him once or twice at court lately. I should know him from his likeness to his father. He has quite a Devereux face—"

"But the fashion of his garments is very different," remarked Lady Elizabeth, who, though no Puritan, could not help regarding with disfavor the bejeweled and extravagant costume of her son. "These are the new modes, I suppose."

"Yes; the king has introduced them, and naturally the young gallants copy them," said Mr. Evelyn, as he and Lady Elizabeth turned a little aside, leaving the brother and sister to entertain each other for a while.

The two elders conversed for a time on different topics of interest, and then Mr. Evelyn pointed out to his companion some of the more remarkable characters who were mingling in the throng.

"Can you tell me who that tall young man is yonder who has just entered?"

Mr. Evelyn, following the direction of Lady Elizabeth's glance, found her eyes were fixed on a young divine in a plain black doublet and cloak, with narrow white bands round the neck, the dress of a Puritan clergyman. His hair was what we in these days should call long, instead of being closely cropped, after the fashion which had won for his party in days gone by the name of Roundheads; but which custom was by no means universally or even generally adopted now. His face, pale, refined, and intellectual, was lighted up by large dreamy-looking eyes. The features were good, and bore the stamp of nobility upon them. But it was the rare purity and sweetness of the expression which made the countenance so attractive, causing it at the same time to present a marked contrast to the dissolute looks of most of the young cavaliers around.

"That is Dr. Stephen Willoughby, the great preacher at St. Benedict's. All the world goes to hear him, whether of his persuasion or not. He is a learned man—wonderfully so for one so young; and he makes himself beloved as well as respected by his devoted, blameless life."

"He has a most striking face; just such a one as might serve a painter for a model were he wishing to depict one of the holy martyrs or saints of old."

"I quite agree with you. The face is singularly pure and guileless, while the broad massive brow betokens intellect, and you can see by a glance at the mouth and chin that there is plenty of strength of character there also. Stephen Willoughby is a very fine fellow."

"He looks very different from most of those around," remarked Lady Elizabeth.

"Would you like me to introduce Dr. Willoughby to you?" asked Mr. Evelyn. "I think you and he would have much in common."

"Pray do: I would fain make his acquaintance, and as St. Benedict's is not far from where we are staying, I shall hope to go and hear him preach on the first opportunity."

The unconscious object of their remarks was at that moment bidding adieu to a gentleman with whom he had been conversing, when he found himself hailed by Mr. Evelyn, and led by him to be presented to Lady Elizabeth Devereux.

The latter gave him a gracious greeting, and then turned to introduce her young daughter to him.

Dorothy's manner was a little cold and haughty. Puritan divines did not possess much attraction in her eyes, and yet, in spite of herself, she felt there was something out of the common in this grave-looking young man, who was of a type different from any she had ever met before. His bearing was perfectly polished and courteous, but yet totally unlike that of her brother and his friends.

Lady Elizabeth would also have presented her son to the stranger, but he had frustrated her intentions by turning away with a supercilious glance at the new-comer and joining a group of young gallants a few paces off, who apparently were diverting themselves with witticisms at the Puritan's expense, and their laughter, if not the sally that caused it, could be heard by Lady Elizabeth, causing a flush to mount into her cheek.

With redoubled graciousness of manner she continued to converse with Dr. Willoughby, until another old friend coming up claimed her attention.

The next few days were full of delight and enjoyment to Dorothy. This being her first visit to London everything possessed the charm of novelty, and her excitement was great in witnessing the grand doings of the 22nd, when the streets through which the procession was to pass were strewn with flowers and hung with tapestry, while the magnificent cavalcade on horseback was as rich as embroidery, velvet, cloth of silver and gold, and jewels could make it.

The imposing ceremony of the coronation took place on the following day, good seats for which they had obtained through the interest of their relative, the Earl of Burnham. Moreover, the admiration and flattery which she met with from the young gallants who thronged around this new star, and, according to the custom of the times paid her the most extravagant compliments, were almost enough to turn her head. The rich color in her cheek deepened, and her dark eyes glowed with additional brightness as she listened, even while her good sense told her that it was most of it mere empty flattery.

Foremost among her admirers was her cousin, Robert Hay, Lord Burnham's son, who professed himself her devoted servant; but Dorothy for some reason or other did not seem more disposed to favor him than did her mother, who looked with evident disapproval upon the free manners and extravagant attire of the young cavaliers who formed her son's principal acquaintances.

"I shall not be sorry when we are back in our own quiet home," she remarked one day when visiting Dr. Willoughby's mother, with whom she had already made acquaintance—an acquaintance that was rapidly ripening into friendship. For the two ladies, though belonging to different parties in the State, as well as to opposite sections in the Church, had yet much in common, inasmuch as they both loved and served the same Master in heaven, and had the same hopes and aspirations with regard to unseen things. Thus Lady Elizabeth found herself opening her heart with its fears and anxieties to her new friend, whose sympathy drew her out; and very pleasant to both was the intercourse they had together.

Dr. Willoughby, though belonging to the Puritan party, was

by no means extreme or narrow in his views; but his mother
was a little more rigid in her sentiments. Her dress showed
which side she took, consisting as it did of a plain gown of sad-
colored grogram, with a simple white kerchief which was not
even edged with lace, though such vanities were not discarded
by all Puritans, for we are told that even Cromwell's mother
used to wear such broad point lace on her kerchief that nothing but the lace could be seen. Mrs. Willoughby, however, was
more severe in her tastes. A close-fitting cap or hood tied under
the chin surrounded a face which, in spite of a certain stern-
ness when in repose, was a pleasant one when it relaxed into
a smile.

The house was plainly though comfortably furnished, but
no unnecessary adornment was to be seen in it. It almost ad-
joined the church of St. Benedict, which was situated only a few
minutes' walk from St. Paul's, on the side towards the river.

On this particular afternoon Lady Elizabeth, having seen
Dorothy start off under her father's protection on a round of
sight-seeing, had availed herself of the opportunity of paying a
visit to Mrs. Willoughby.

"I shall not be sorry to be at home again," she had remarked,
"London society in these days is not what one would choose for
one's daughters."

Mrs. Willoughby shook her head solemnly. "We have indeed fallen upon evil times, and if we live we shall see worse
ones. The ungodly abound in the land."

"But happily all are not bad," rejoined Lady Elizabeth with
a smile. "Your son, for instance. One glance at his face is enough
to show that he lives in and breathes a higher atmosphere; and
it has been a rare treat to me to have the opportunity of listening to his preaching. But beyond that I have no interests here.
I feel I have little in common with this gay world, and it only
saddens me."

"The less we have to do with it the better," said Mrs.
Willoughby briefly.

"Yes. But yet it is possible to be in the world and not of it.
In whatever position God places us, He is able to keep us true
and faithful and unspotted, is He not?"

"Yes, doubtless, if we seek it."

"And it is not only at court that there are dangers and temptations; they meet us everywhere. I am thinking of Eugene, as

you will guess," said Lady Elizabeth, a look of sorrowful yearning passing over her sweet face. "He causes me many a sleepless night, and oh, how gladly would I remove him from the influences that surround him, but his father thinks differently."

"I can well understand your feelings," responded Mrs. Willoughby, her somewhat stern face relaxing into an expression of true sympathy. "To any one like yourself it must be a source of perpetual anxiety to see him thrown into the company of the dissolute and ungodly followers of the king. But do not limit the Lord's power. He has before this singled out witnesses for Himself even in wicked Ahab's court, as well as in the household of Caesar. And His arm has not grown weaker, nor His power feebler."

"No, it is one's own faith that is so weak."

"I hope your daughter, Mistress Dorothy, is like to be a comfort to you," said Mrs. Willoughby gently.

"She is a dear girl, warm-hearted and true, but a little willful and wayward at times. Just now she is a good deal excited with this her first glimpse of London gaieties, and all the admiration she has received."

"Vanity of vanities! it is all vanity!" murmured Mrs. Willoughby, the gentleness of her companion restraining her from giving utterance to more severe sentiments. "I doubt not you would fain see her setting her affections on things above."

"I do indeed long for it; but for the present they seem fixed on things around. Life to her, with her high spirits and buoyant nature, seems one long holiday, and she never appears to give a thought to the future. You see she has never known any trouble or care; but it cannot always be thus. Clouds must some time or other arise; the brightness must be dimmed sooner or later in this changing world, and then perhaps, when earth fails to satisfy, she may turn to the only true source of joy, and find her delight in God Himself. I often fear that with her strong nature she may have to pass through deep waters, that for her the furnace may have to be heated hotter than for some; but if only the gold come out purified, all will be well."

Little did Lady Elizabeth know how true her presentiment was, nor how scorching would need to be the refiner's fire that was to separate the dross from the true metal; it was mercifully hidden from her eyes.

CHAPTER III

ST. BARTHOLOMEW'S DAY

"Well may Thy own beloved, who see
  In all their lot their Father's pleasure,
Bear loss of all they love, save Thee,
  Their living everlasting treasure."—A. L. Waring

"I bow myself beneath His hand:
  That pain itself was wisely planned
I feel, and partly understand."—Whittier

ON August 17, 1662, the Sunday before St. Bartholomew's day, London presented an unwonted spectacle. During the last year or two the city had witnessed many a pageant and splendid procession; had almost gone mad with joy over the king's restoration, and had ransacked its brains to do honor to his coronation.

But on this day it bore a totally different aspect. It was a day of sadness and gloom,—known indeed for years afterwards as "the Black Sunday;" for on that day two thousand ministers of Christ, we are told, were taking their leave of two thousand congregations; and mourning and lamentation were deep and widespread.

The Act of Uniformity had passed, and was to come into force on St. Bartholomew's day; and a number of ministers who were neither incompetent nor disloyal, nor averse to a moderate episcopacy, nor to a liturgical service, subject to certain revisions, but who had scruples about wearing the surplice, using the sign of the cross at baptism, and kneeling at the Lord's Supper, felt themselves compelled for conscience' sake to decline to take the oath, and were in consequence ejected from their livings.

"Some might think they made too much of these things; but

what might seem trifles to others were in their estimation the marks of a ceremonial as opposed to a spiritual Christianity. They believed that in the defense of the Gospel they were acting as they did."

And they acted thus with a full knowledge of the consequences,—the parting from their flocks, and the going forth, in most instances, to a life of poverty and hardship. Whatever we may think of their views on certain points, we must acknowledge that they were grand men, and the Church of England could ill afford to lose them.

And thus on that day, so unlike other days, many hundreds of ministers were at the same moment taking leave of people devoted to them, amid deep silence or stifled sobs. The churches were thronged long before the time for service, and overflowed into the streets or churchyards.

Dr. Willoughby was one of those who for conscience' sake that day said farewell to those among whom he had lived and labored with such devotion and singleness of purpose, and who on their side were bound to him by the closest ties of love and gratitude. Were not many of them his spiritual children? Had not many felt their zeal and love quickened by his fervor, and their worldliness rebuked by his spirituality? Had he not in countless instances stood by the death-bed of their dear ones, pointing them to Christ, and cheering them as they passed through the dark valley? Had not their own sick beds or hours of bereavement been soothed by his tender ministrations? Was there one who did not owe him something, if not their own selves, yet a debt of gratitude for kindness received or sympathy, counsel, or encouragement ever freely given out as the occasion required?

Sorrow was plainly depicted on each countenance upraised towards him, as for the last time he mounted the pulpit to give his farewell address. He was pale, and his lips were firmly compressed, while in his eyes was a deep look of earnest resolve. No vacillation, no weakness was visible, even as he confronted that sorrow-stricken crowd; the tenderness of his expression as he gazed upon them was mingled with a look of grave steadfastness of purpose, such as we might imagine Abraham's face to have worn as he went onward to the spot where he was to offer up his son.

And Stephen Willoughby was laying *his* Isaac upon the altar; not grudgingly—though the pain was felt to the full, and would probably leave its scar to his dying day—but bravely, unflinchingly did he make the sacrifice which he believed his Heavenly Master demanded from him.

He said very little of a personal nature, and uttered only sentiments of loyalty and moderation.

"I beg you will not interpret our Nonconformity," he proceeded, while the people hung in breathless silence upon every word that fell from the beloved lips, "to disloyalty. Let him never be accounted a sound Christian who doth not both fear God and honor the king. We will do anything for his Majesty but sin. We will hazard anything for him but our souls. We make no question, however we may be accounted of here, we shall be found loyal and obedient subjects at our appearance before God's tribunal."[1]

Then he continued, seeking to comfort his sorrowful people, from whom many a sob had broken forth: "Your ministers may be banished, may be imprisoned, but there is a Comforter that abides for ever. If Christ can comfort His people in the absence of Himself, He can surely comfort them in the absence of all other comforts. When He denies the means, He can comfort us without; when He dries up the stream, He can make us drink at the fountain. They may keep your ministers out of the pulpit; they shall not take the Comforter out of your hearts. So that when I shall not preach any more to you I shall pray the Father that He shall send you another Comforter, even the Spirit of truth, that He may abide with you for ever."[2]

Many of his hearers that day wished in their secret hearts that their young minister's conscience had been of a more elastic nature, so that it might have allowed him to remain at his post. But there were others who felt that when he had preached to them in days gone by of single-hearted following of Christ, of the need of taking up the cross and giving up all for Him, of the impossibility of serving two masters, and the absolute necessity of making a choice between Christ and the world, he had meant what he said, and was now putting into practice the truths which he had sought to teach. In his steadfast determination to follow that which he conceived to be the right course, they saw in him the spirit that had animated Joshua and Caleb of old, and felt that the words spoken of them would not be

---

1 Robert Atkins.
2 Cradecot.

inapplicable to Stephen Willoughby—"for they have wholly followed the Lord." And their spirits were stirred within them to go and do likewise, to imitate his singleness of aim and noble purity of motive.

Great things had been predicted of Dr. Willoughby by his admirers, who had looked forward to his winning many a coveted honor and distinction. Such things, however, had been far from his own thoughts. He felt he had a message to proclaim, and he would use every power he possessed to aid him in proclaiming it effectively; but for reward he looked higher than earth, or aught that earth could afford. Like his namesake of old, the eye of his faith seemed to pierce the veil that shrouds the unseen world, and his ardent soul was ever seeking to soar higher and higher. He had the spirit of the martyr in him in his readiness to do or dare anything in his Master's cause, and yet the lowliness and simplicity of a child equally characterized him. While others spoke of his saintly life, he in deepest self-abasement deplored his own shortcomings and imperfections. Falling thus so far below his own ideal, the praises of men fell almost unheeded on his ear.

The next step, which, indeed, followed as a necessary consequence, was the leaving the rectory, which had been the home of Dr. Willoughby and his mother for some years, but which must now be vacated in favor of his successor. A small house was taken in Knightrider Street, which before the Fire of London ran parallel with Thames Street, and had several good houses in it. But the one in which Dr. Willoughby established himself was of the most unpretending nature.

His wants were few and simple, and easily satisfied, while his mother, with her sterner creed, had always set her face against show and luxury of every sort. For the present, however, it was more a question of obtaining the necessaries of life than of putting down superfluities; for Dr. Willoughby, though of a good old family, had no private means, and now that the regular income which he had derived from St. Benedict's was no longer his, poverty might in one sense have been said to stare him in the face.

But more than one member of his late congregation had come forward and offered to employ him as tutor to their sons, so that he might reasonably hope to earn sufficient for the daily needs in that manner.

"And the rest—indeed, everything—we can leave in God's hands, can we not, mother?" he remarked, as they were sitting together at the close of the day on which they had taken possession of the new dwelling. It was a warm, sultry evening, and the small rooms felt close and stifling after the more airy, spacious ones to which they had been accustomed.

Mrs. Willoughby was hot and tired with her exertions in settling and arranging their simple belongings, and getting things into order, but she responded without hesitation to her son's remark, "Yes, we can trust Him. He has never failed us yet, nor ever will. And the more we are brought to see the vanity of things below the better for us. I would rather see you, my son, a poor man, wanting even a crust of bread, than in the king's palace yonder, feasted and caressed; for the ways followed there are the ways of death."

"Then you fully approve of the course I have taken, mother? It has pained me to think that you would of necessity be involved in the sacrifice."

"I not only approve, my son, I honor you for it," she said, with a softened look in the eyes which met his questioning ones. "Could you have acted differently, you had not been son of mine. What!" she went on with kindling face, "would it have been possible to have taken the other alternative—go against your conscience, and forswear yourself for the sake of a few paltry loaves and fishes! You could not have acted thus, Stephen;" and the speaker's tones grew indignant at the bare idea of such a thing. "Do you think I am so wedded to creature comforts that I would have my son sell his soul to purchase them for me?"

"Nay, mother," he answered gently, "I know you would never wish me to swerve from the path of duty. And, whatever views others may hold, I have no shadow of doubt what was the right course for me. I blame not those who have acted differently, and have found it possible to bring their consciences to take the oath. I only feel that it would have been wrong in me; and Christ my Savior is so precious that I dare not risk losing His company by turning aside into paths in which He does not lead."

"And if further suffering come," he went on musingly, "as I misdoubt me it will, for I dream not that our enemies will give us no further molestation, still whatever comes, I have Him, and if I can truly say, 'The Lord is the portion of mine inheritance,' what more can I want?"

"Things have come to a pretty pass when they turn out such men from the churches, and fill their places with base time-servers, or papists in sheep's clothing," said Mrs. Willoughby bitterly, but in a low tone.

"Nay, mother, I trust they do not all merit such a description," returned her son, smiling at her warmth. "There are numbers of most godly men who see no harm in episcopacy, and yet hate the Church of Rome almost as you hate it. Their not agreeing with us on certain points does not prove that they are not true men. The minds of all are not cast in the same mould. Let us be ready to give the right hand of fellowship to all who are truly following Christ; that is the touchstone. All objects, let us remember, do not reflect the same rays of light, and yet every ray proceeds from the same source."

A few weeks had passed by, and the little household, consisting of Mrs. Willoughby, her son, and their one faithful servant, Tabitha, had settled down into the routine of their altered life. Mrs. Willoughby, when they moved, had intended dismissing Tabitha, fearing they might not be justified under their changed circumstances in incurring the expense of keeping a servant; but Tabitha had refused to be dismissed, saying she was willing to serve them for nothing, but leave them she would not. So her mistress, nothing loath, had retained her, for a time at least.

One morning towards the end of summer, as the mother and son were sitting at breakfast, Tabitha brought in a letter which she handed to Dr. Willoughby. He took it in silence and at once opened it. But he had not read far when his face turned ashy white, and his brow became knitted as by sudden pain.

Mrs. Willoughby, watching him, could keep silence no longer. "Have you had bad news, my son?"

He lifted up his head from the letter, over which he had been bending forgetful of her presence. His look startled her, so changed, so haggard was the usually calm, sweet face. He gazed at her for a moment with a dazed expression in his eyes, as if he had received a blow which had stunned him, and he opened his lips as if to speak; but apparently they refused to do so, for rising from the table with the letter in his hand he silently left the room.

Mrs. Willoughby longed to follow him, and hear what the news could be which had so affected him, but she felt he wished to be alone, and she must not intrude. So she had to restrain her impatience as well as she could; but as she remained seated at the breakfast table, her mind too much discomposed to allow her to proceed with the meal, her thoughts were busy seeking to conjecture what this new trouble could be.

"I expect it must be in some way connected with Rosamond," she said to herself. "I never fully liked or trusted the girl. But as Stephen's affections were so firmly set on her, I tried to hope she was all he thought her, and would make him a good wife. Oh, I hope—I trust—she is not playing him false!" And Mrs. Willoughby's heart almost stood still, while her face grew pale with apprehension, as the thought presented itself to her mind.

"Poor Stephen! it would be indeed a bitter blow to him. With his trustful nature he has believed her to be all that is good and true; but I have had my doubts. And of late she has certainly been very cold and changed. Poor Stephen! if it is so, God help him, for none other will be able to comfort him! With his tender loving nature such a wound as this will take long to heal."

The mother's intuitions were correct; and when at length, after nearly an hour's absence, her son returned to her, pale and worn-looking, like one who has been going through some exceeding bitter struggle, and yet with the calmness of one who has come off victorious, she needed not to put him to the pain of an explanation; one word sufficed, and she understood that her worst fears were realized.

Her heart was deeply moved, and very tender was the sympathy she gave. She yearned to comfort him; longed to bind up the bleeding wound, and yet knew how powerless she was to do so. He placed the letter in her hands, for his mother had always been his confidant. He knew well the depths of tenderness concealed beneath the outer shell which to others sometimes seemed harsh and stern. And he could not with his own lips have uttered the words that would have proclaimed her who had been enshrined in his heart—false and a deceiver.

Yet such was the fact. In Rosamond Brown's estimation the ejected minister, reduced to earning his daily bread by teaching, or by any such occupation which he could obtain, was a very different person from the gifted popular preacher at St. Benedict's, whose praises had been on everybody's lips, and whose chances of promotion had appeared so sure. But now the only sure thing about him seemed to be his poverty; and moreover, as he belonged to the unpopular party, there was now no prospect of his rising. And poverty was a thing she hated, while to be obscure and looked down upon was equally distasteful to her. What she liked was to be envied and flattered, and to live in ease and luxury.

While such thoughts were dwelling in her mind, and gaining more and more power over her, another suitor came across her path, and he offered her wealth and position. Such tempting baits proved too much for her. So she broke off her engagement with Stephen Willoughby, casting from her, apparently without thought or compunction, as true and faithful a heart as ever beat; one too true to suspect unfaithfulness in her; one who in his unworldliness had never dreamed that the fair exterior was only outside glitter concealing a nature heartless and selfish.

She perhaps deceived herself as much as she deceived him when she said she felt she was not worthy to be the wife of a minister, adding that their union could not have brought happiness to him, for she was not suited to him; nay, she even owned that she was not all he thought her, and that therefore it was better they should part, that she should leave him free.

As Mrs. Willoughby read the letter, seeing through the false excuses, and the hollowness and pitifulness of the whole thing, burning indignation took possession of her. Bitter words were on her lips, the love she bore her son only deepening the anger she felt at seeing him thus treated, and that by one so worthless. But her speech was stopped by a deprecating gesture from him.

"Mother, say no more, I pray you. I may have been deceived; I may have been blind, foolish, but I cannot hear her spoken against. It has all been a mistake—a painful mistake on my side; I was not suited to her—that was not her fault. Better that she should have found it out now, rather than later on."

"Better indeed! especially when one considers what it is that has opened her eyes. It is matter for deepest thankfulness that you have escaped being tied to her for life," said Mrs. Willoughby, letting her indignation get the better of her.

"Mother, if you please, we will not mention her name between us again," said Dr. Willoughby gently, but firmly, as with a weary, absent air he resumed his seat at the breakfast table, and then pushed from him the remains of his unfinished meal.

"I would not have the things removed, hoping you would take something more," said Mrs. Willoughby, approaching and standing beside him. "Will you not try to eat something? You look as if you needed it."

"No, thank you; I cannot eat just now."

"Oh, my son," moaned the mother, with a burst of tenderness and sympathy that would not be repressed, as she laid her hand on his head and looked down into the pale worn face, "what can I do to comfort you?"

"Your love comforts me," he murmured, as he took her hand in his.

"Trouble after trouble has indeed come thick upon you, my poor Stephen!"

"But not one too many, mother. The God we serve loves His children too well to send them a needless pang or a single unnecessary sorrow. He leads us by the 'right' way; we feel that, do we not? He can make no mistake, and He shall have the ordering of my life. I would take this stroke as from His hand, and bow before it.

"Mother," he added, as he raised his eyes to hers, for no response came from her, "we would not have things otherwise than as He appoints them, would we?"

"I trust not, my son; but it needs God's grace to enable us always fully to submit," said Mrs. Willoughby, feeling at that moment, as so many have felt at times, that it is harder to see those we love suffer than to suffer ourselves.

Her heart was deeply touched to see him so sorely stricken and yet so entirely submissive. In silence she stooped and printed a lingering, almost reverential kiss upon his brow.

After a few moments Dr. Willoughby rose, and pulling his tall figure up to its full height, with the air of a warrior bracing himself for the conflict, said, "It is time for me now to be off to my work, for I have three hours' teaching this morning." Giving his mother a farewell salutation, he departed.

The days and weeks went by, and in silence Stephen Willoughby wrestled with his sorrow, never once again referring to that fatal letter or the sender of it. Nor did Mrs. Willoughby dare to do so, though often sorely tempted to transgress and give vent to her feelings in words, as she watched her son's face growing paler and thinner, and noted the listlessness and weariness which he tried to conceal and resolutely fought against.

He did not mean to nurse his sorrow, or allow himself to be crushed or soured by his disappointment; on the contrary, he strove to carry his cross bravely, as a man and a Christian. Still, none the less an exceeding bitter drop had been added to the cup of the young minister already suffering for conscience' sake; and the full bitterness of it none knew but himself. To have lost the object of his affections by death would have been a light trial compared with this. But now his faith in womanhood itself seemed shaken; and but for his mother, whose character commanded his deepest reverence and respect, he might have been in danger of morbidly shunning all womankind as treacherous and deceitful under a fair exterior.

His dream of earthly love thus over, he felt he had henceforth no aim but to devote himself afresh to his Master's service, and to follow Him with increasing singleness of purpose.

CHAPTER IV

THE SERVICE OF THE KING

"Oh, Love unspeakable! that Thou shouldst be
  Patient amidst the night's chill falling dews,
While I Thy proffered fellowship refuse,
  Slothful to rise and ope the door to Thee."

W. R. NEALE

TOWARDS the end of April, 1665, Sir Richard Devereux again brought his wife, accompanied this time by both Dorothy and Cicely, up to London, there to remain for a few months while he went abroad on some errand for the king. It was on Eugene's account that the plan had found favor in Lady Elizabeth's eyes; for she longed to see more of her son than she had done of late, his visits home having been few and far between. Being within reach of Whitehall would, she hoped, afford them opportunities for frequent meetings. And then they would be on the spot to welcome Sir Richard back, when it was probable he would be detained in the city on business for some little time.

They took up their abode in Aldersgate Street, where at that time were many mansions inhabited by the nobility and others. The Duke of Lauderdale's town house was there, as was also that of the Earl of Peterborough. Milton also dwelt there in a house standing back in a garden, to avoid the noise of the road.

Having established his family in lodgings, Sir Richard departed, little dreaming of the terrible calamity that was about to overtake the doomed city.

One of the first to pay Lady Elizabeth a visit and renew former acquaintanceship was Mr. Evelyn, who came bringing his wife. They were received with a warm welcome, for Mr. Evelyn was a general favorite. Even Dorothy was very partial to him, and Cicely, who had not seen them before, lost her heart to both of them on the spot.

"We hope you will come with your daughters to see us at Sayes Court some fine day," said Mrs. Evelyn addressing Lady Elizabeth.

"We shall be very pleased to do so. I have heard so much about the gardens and grounds there that I should much like to see them."

After a little more conversation on different subjects Lady Elizabeth, turning to Mr. Evelyn, while Mrs. Evelyn was talking to Cicely, inquired of him after Dr. Willoughby, saying one enjoyment she had promised herself in coming to London again was the opportunity of again hearing him preach.

"Ah, do you not know that he is no longer at St. Benedict's? When the Act of Uniformity was passed his conscience would not allow him to conform, so he went out."

"I am sorry to hear that. And what is he doing now? Is he still in London?"

"Yes; he has moved into a small house in Knightrider Street, and supports himself mainly by teaching."

"Such a man as that must be a great loss to the Church."

"He is indeed; for he is one who commands respect from all parties, not only on account of his learning and abilities, but from his personal character."

"It seems to my way of thinking a pity he has these scruples; though of course one cannot but honor him the more for his conscientiousness," said Lady Elizabeth.

"Yes, for he has had to sacrifice much. But I believe he would lay down his life sooner than go against his conscience."

"The being ejected from his living," continued Mr. Evelyn, "is not the only trial that has befallen him since you were last in London."

"Indeed. I hope there is nothing the matter with his mother. I have a great esteem for Mrs. Willoughby, and was hoping to renew our acquaintance."

"No; it is not that. Mrs. Willoughby is well, and has all along fully approved of the course taken by her son. But the young gentlewoman to whom he was engaged before his ejectment threw him over soon after the change in his fortunes, and in no great while bestowed herself in marriage upon Sir John Grant."

"How could she! She would find it hard to meet with Dr. Willoughby's equal."

"Ah! madam, tastes differ. With some, wealth and position are the chief things sought in marriage, and those she obtained. Happiness I should fancy she has scarcely found, judging by the character Sir John bears, and the look her face has worn whenever I have chanced to meet her."

"I am truly sorry for Dr. Willoughby; but it is well he has escaped being united to one who evidently was unsuited to him. Does she still live in London?"

"Sir John has a fine place in the country, where they chiefly reside, but he also has a house in the Strand, and they come up pretty often. I fancy my lady prefers town to country. They are here at present, for I saw her in the distance yesterday. I do not visit them, though I happen to have known something of them both for a good while. I was acquainted with Lady Grant's father, who was a great friend of Mrs. Willoughby's husband. He was a good old man, very different from his daughter, of whose conduct he would have highly disapproved. But both he and the mother have been dead for years."

Another to pay a speedy visit was Robert Hay, dressed in the extreme of fashion in satin and laces, plumes and jewels. He had seen nothing of Dorothy since she had last been in London, but he had meantime done his best to console himself in the society of other fair ladies. Now, however, he hastened to pay his respects with his usual air of gallantry, and a familiarity of manner which Lady Elizabeth much disliked.

Dorothy's bright eyes seemed to give him a silent welcome, or at any rate so he interpreted her look, and it served to increase the apparent ardor of his devotion.

"How has my fair cousin managed to exist all this time, buried in the depths of the country?" he asked, with an admiring glance at Dorothy's handsome face, on which the color deepened under his gaze. "Has she not been sighing to taste of the delights of town life again?"

"I trust Dorothy has been making herself happy and contented," interposed Lady Elizabeth, answering instead of her daughter. "We lead a busy life, and the country has its pleasures as well as the town."

"I am glad you find it so, aunt; but I fear I should feel unutterably bored. I would as soon go to gaol at once as be forced to vegetate at Burnham Castle year after year. What say you, Dorothy?"

"Oh, I like London much the best, and I wish we always lived here."

"Oh, Dorothy!" exclaimed Cicely half incredulously; "can you like it better than our dear old home, where everything is so quiet and peaceful, and not noisy and bustling as it is here?"

"It is just the noise and bustle, as you call it, that I like. There is plenty of stir and life here, and plenty of people, but at Hurstwood there is scarcely anybody to speak to," said the girl in a half-defiant tone, as if conscious that her words would not be approved by her mother.

"Oh, Dorothy!" again burst from Cicely, who in her innocence was about to remind her sister of the many cottagers round about to whom they so often paid visits with their mother, and for whom there was always something to do in the way of making warm garments, carrying them hot soup, or inquiring for their ailments; things which to her simple nature made life full of interest, when Robert Hay, not noticing her exclamation, hindered further remark by saying,

"And so my fair cousin is forced to 'waste her sweetness on the desert air' with absolutely nobody to appreciate her good looks save country bumpkins and clodhoppers! Such a thing ought not to be allowed. I call it monstrous! But here it is not so. There is one at least who has eyes to admire the beauty of Mistress Dorothy Devereux, and is ready to do homage to her charms."

But here Lady Elizabeth interposed, cutting short her nephew's rhapsody.

"Robert, I like not such foolish talk. I beg you not to let me hear more of it. The only beauty that is worth anything is the beauty of pure and noble deeds, of a life spent in the service of God. And of that beauty I fear me you see little in the ungodly court of the king, and among his ungodly followers."

"My good aunt appears to deem us a sad set of scapegraces," said the young man with a good-natured shrug of his shoulders. "Ah," he went on as the door opened, "here comes Eugene. Let him share in the rebuke, for he deserves it as much as I. If I am a sad dog, so is he."

A look of pain crossed Lady Elizabeth's face at these words, which her nephew had uttered carelessly, as was his is wont. Good-natured, but utterly thoughtless, was Robert Hay; living, like so many of the young cavaliers of that day, just for the present hour in pleasure and self-gratification, and giving no thought beyond. And Eugene was much the same, only a trifle more reckless and headstrong.

"What slanders are these that you are uttering? And what rebuke is it that I deserve?" asked Eugene, advancing into the room. "I am much obliged to you, my good cousin, for taking away my character thus behind my back."

"One can scarcely take away from a man that which he does not possess," laughed Robert; "so I have done you no wrong, fair sir. I did but wish for a companion in disgrace, not feeling equal to facing your lady mother's censures all alone. She thinks us a sad set of reprobates."

Eugene looked annoyed, for he perceived the shade of sadness that had come over his mother's face, and he always hated to bring that look there; it reproached him more than words could have done. But there it always ended; he did not like to see her pained, but any real reformation was far from his thoughts.

"We cannot all be saints like yourself, mother mine. Young fellows must have their fling. But when we have sown our wild oats, who knows what we may turn into! Perhaps into canting Puritans, spending all our days in conventicles, thinking it sinful to laugh, and going about looking as if we were to be hanged;" and Eugene drew down the corners of his mouth, in imitation of the long face which was supposed to be characteristic of the party.

Dorothy broke into a laugh, but Cicely cried, "I am sure they are not all like that—not a bit. Look at Dr. Willoughby;—he has the nicest face I ever saw."

"And when had my young sister the privilege of looking upon this paragon of perfection, seeing she has so recently come to town?" asked Eugene in a mocking tone.

"He came in here yesterday to see mother," quietly answered Cicely.

"Eugene," said Lady Elizabeth, speaking gravely but gently, "cease jesting for a moment. It is a solemn thing to talk as you do about sowing your wild oats, when one thinks of the crop that must be the inevitable result. Do you not know that 'what a man soweth that shall he also reap,' both in kind and in degree? And if you sow, and go on sowing to the end, the seeds of ungodly deeds, of a profane, dissolute life, the reaping will be death—the death of the soul. Would it not be wise to pause and think of these things while still the door of heaven stands open, and an invitation comes to each of us to enter?"

Her tones were soft and persuasive, and the sweet graciousness of her manner made her appeal the more telling. Both young men were awed for the moment into silence. In her gentle presence neither of them could summon up the scoffing jest with which they were accustomed to meet any serious remark.

"That door will be shut some day," she went on, "and many then will beat upon it in vain, entreating, when too late, to be permitted to enter. But now there standeth One among you whom ye know not; even the King Himself; a discrowned King, it is true, when He was on earth, but now crowned with many crowns. And to each of His followers He offers a crown and a kingdom eternal in the heavens. Oh, will you not take service under this King? Can his Majesty Charles II. give you rewards such as these?"

Eugene had turned away and was gazing out of window, but Robert, with a blank look on his face of wonderment and perplexity, said,

"Good mine aunt, I conceive not of whom you are speaking. I know of but one king of this realm."

"He of whom I speak is no earthly king, but King of all kings, and His kingdom is a heavenly one, though here it is set up in the hearts of men. They are His throne. Have you never heard, Robert, of the Son of God, who, laying aside His glory, came down to earth, and took the form of sinful man that He might die in the sinner's place, and thus win pardon for all who should seek it? He died for you, and 'greater love hath no man than this, that a man lay down his life for his friends;' and now He stands pleading with you by the great love He bears you to forsake all sinful ways, which lead to death, and follow Him in paths that lead to glory."

"To glory!" echoed Robert, who had been listening with a puzzled look. "Why, this I suppose is He whom these Puritan fellows profess to follow, but I don't see they get much glory by it—rather ridicule and contempt."

"The glory comes hereafter; the cross often has to be borne here. When the veil that hides the other world from our eyes shall be torn away, we doubtless shall see that many who here have been the most despised will there be the highest in honor.

'Then shall the righteous shine forth as the sun in the kingdom of their Father.'"

Eugene made no remark all this time. Trained and taught by such a mother as his, he was not in ignorance of these things like Robert, who, brought up in utter worldliness and forgetfulness of God, had never perhaps in his life before listened with patience to so grave a discourse. Would either heart open to receive the King? or would both remain barred against Him?

"Mother," cried Dorothy, a few days later, entering Lady Elizabeth's chamber, where she was sitting reading, "Robert has come with an invitation for me from Cousin Alicia to accompany her to a masquerade which is to be held at Whitehall a week hence. You will give me permission, won't you, sweet mother?" said the girl coaxingly, while her eyes pleaded for an answer in the affirmative.

Lady Elizabeth shook her head decidedly.

"My child, do you know what it is you are asking?" she said, with a sterner look than Dorothy ever remembered to have seen on her gentle face.

"I am only asking to go and look on," returned Dorothy, with a little pout on her rosy lips, as she began to foresee the downfall of her hopes. "Cousin Alicia would take care of me. She is invited, and can bring a friend. So she offers to take me. Oh, it would be so delightful! Dear mother, do let me go! It is only just for this once."

"I would as soon you begged me to let you put your head into the jaws of a hungry lion 'just for once,' as ask me to let you set foot within the precincts of yonder sinful court."

"But, mother, what harm could come to me?" persisted Dorothy.

"Dear child, I cannot explain to you all the evils and perils lurking there, to which I would not for worlds expose you. It is enough that I know, and will do what I can to shield you. Cannot you trust me? I am not wont to deny you anything that is for your real happiness, am I, my Dorothy?"

"But, mother," she returned, dashing away the tears of disappointment which had sprung into her eyes, "you don't know how much I want to go. Robert has been telling me how grand it will all be, and I may never have such a chance again."

"I sincerely hope you never may," said Lady Elizabeth, with a sort of shudder. "Nay, my child; it pains me to refuse you anything on which you have set your heart, but in this case I cannot consent. And now say no more about it."

But a rebellious look came into the girl's face, and with a little defiant toss of her shapely head she murmured, "If father were here, I am sure he would let me go."

No sooner were the words uttered, however, than she seemed half frightened at the sound of them, as well as at the grieved look which they called up on her mother's face.

"Dorothy," said the latter reproachfully, "would it be true love in me if you were to ask my consent to ruin yourself body and soul, and I gave it? if I saw you were about blindly to walk over a precipice, and never held out a hand to hinder you? if, knowing that a deadly fever was raging, I sent you into the midst of it? You are dazzled with the idea of going to court and getting a glimpse of the splendors and gaieties there, but they are but as a mask concealing much that is foul and hideous. Your inexperienced eyes would not be able to detect the false from the true; your unwary steps might be entrapped in some snare before you knew where you were treading."

"But, mother," persisted Dorothy, "Cousin Alicia goes."

"Alicia has had no mother to watch over her, and I fear me she has been misguided and foolish, if no worse. At any rate, it is plain that she has made shipwreck of her happiness in this hasty marriage with my Lord Castleton,—a man of evil repute as he is. My child, I would fain save you from any like fate. Your welfare is so dear to me that I cannot imperil it by suffering you to breathe the impure air of the king's court at Whitehall."

There was silence when Lady Elizabeth paused; Dorothy remaining standing erect with averted face, as if still unwilling to yield.

"Would you rather be in Alicia's case with no mother to restrain her?" asked Lady Elizabeth in a pained tone, which went to Dorothy's heart. "Is my child longing to spread her wings and fly away from the home nest?"

"Nay, mother, please don't talk so," sobbed Dorothy, vanquished at length, as she threw herself down on the ground beside her mother and buried her face on her shoulder. "You know I love you dearly, and I will try not to vex you any more. You shall choose for me."

"My own Dorothy," murmured Lady Elizabeth fondly,

folding her arms around her young daughter in a tender embrace. "I know it is hard for you to have your wish denied, but some day you will understand the reason better. And now, dear, I suppose Robert will be getting impatient for an answer. You had better go down to him."

Robert received his aunt's decision with an exclamation of annoyance and disappointment.

"I call it a horrid shame that you should be kept shut up like this! I had counted on your coming, and had planned it all so nicely. It was I who made Alicia ask you. I thought you would have enjoyed it so, for you have never seen anything of the sort."

"I should have enjoyed it immensely; but it cannot be. Mother will not give her consent."

"Then go without it," said the young man in a low tone. "You could surely contrive to slip out, and we would be waiting for you outside."

"Robert!" broke from Dorothy in tones of indignation, "how can you think of such a thing! Do you imagine I would do anything so mean and deceitful? However much I may wish to go, I should be ashamed to behave like that."

Robert gave a low whistle through his teeth, while a look of discomfiture came into his face.

"I didn't know my fair cousin was so very straitlaced in her notions. We are not accustomed to such high-flown virtue at Whitehall, and I thought you liked a bit of fun as well as the rest of us."

"So I do, and no one would have liked going better than I, if I could have got mother's consent. But I will not go without it. I have never deceived her yet, and I think it would break her heart if I were to do such a thing as that you proposed."

"Well, I own Lady Elizabeth Devereux is not like other people, and I can understand your not liking to vex her. I almost believe I should have been a different fellow myself if I had had her for my mother. There is something in her that makes a fellow feel ashamed in her presence of things he thinks no harm at all of at other times," added Robert candidly; and Dorothy, mollified by this praise of her mother, allowed her indignation to subside.

CHAPTER V

THE DISTEMPER

"Not for a soul like thine the calm
  Of selfish ease and joys of sense;
But duty, more than crown or palm,
  Its own exceeding recompense."—WHITTIER

ON a hot sultry day in the month of June, 1665, Mrs. Willoughby was seated in a straight high-backed chair near the front parlor window of the little house in Knightrider Street. It was seldom she was idle for a moment, but now her work lay unheeded on her lap, as from time to time she bent forward to take a look up and down the street, as though watching for some one. Her thoughts appeared to be of an anxious nature, judging by the lines on her face.

At length the door opened and Stephen Willoughby entered the room.

"You are late, my son. I looked for your return more than an hour ago."

"I was delayed unexpectedly," replied the young man, as he sank down with a weary gesture upon a plain oak settle which stood at the farther end of the room. "I am sorry to be behind time."

"You look tired," said his mother. "I fear you have no good news to impart. Is the distemper still increasing?"

"Alas! yes; it appears to be gaining ground rapidly. Many are dying of it. I have just come from the death-bed of one of its victims."

Mrs. Willoughby turned her head quickly, as if startled, and looked at her son with a glance half searching, half uneasy.

"You are not affrighted, mother?" he said in questioning tones, for her cheek had blanched a little.

"Nay, but I had not expected it to come thus nigh our

door so soon. Verily, this plague appears to be growing apace. Nevertheless," she added in a different tone, "I trust the Lord will keep me from all foolish fears. He is my refuge and defense, a very present help in time of trouble, and under the shadow of His wings we shall be safe. If I feared, it was not for myself, but for thee."

The momentary tremor was gone; the voice was firm and the grey eyes shone with a steadfast light.

"The people are flocking out of town as fast as they can go," remarked Stephen. "The streets and thoroughfares are quite blocked with coaches and waggons conveying the people and their goods away from this infected place. Quite a panic seems to have set in, and almost everybody who can go is making preparations for departing."

"And you, Stephen? What do you intend to do?"

"Mother," he answered deliberately, "my mind is made up as regards myself. I stay here in the midst of the sick and dying, to minister as far as I may to the souls of the flock that was once committed to my charge. It may be that in the hour of sorrow or need I may gain admission, and be able to deliver God's message where in the time of health and happiness the door has been shut against me. I have laid the matter before God in earnest prayer for direction, and the answer seems to be, 'Remain at your post.'"

"And the Lord be with you, my son, and His mighty arm round about you to protect you!" said Mrs. Willoughby solemnly. "Far be it from me to say aught to deter you, or turn you aside from the path of duty, even if it be also the path of danger. We have but one life; it is right that it should be spent in God's service, and even laid down in His cause, if so He wills."

The speaker's face kindled, and her voice faltered not as she thus sanctioned her son's giving himself up to a work in which he must be prepared to run every risk of infection among the plague-stricken people, and carry his life so to speak in his hand, ready to yield it up at any moment. For so deadly was the disease, and often so sudden in its attacks, that men and women frequently fell down dead in the streets; or perhaps were taken ill while out on some errand abroad, and were only able to crawl to some doorstep and die.

"You have counted the cost, my son?" she continued interrogatively, as she scanned his countenance keenly.

"Yes, mother; but life is not so dear to me as to some; in offering it up, I fear I am not offering a very costly thing."

Mrs. Willoughby winced at his words, showing as they did that not even yet was the wound inflicted by Rosamond's hands healed. He had never referred so plainly to it during all the time which had passed since the day her letter had been received, and it pained her to think the old sorrow was still there.

"Still, such as it is," he went on, "I doubt not God will graciously accept it, if He has need of it. Mother, I would crave your blessing," he added, as with a sudden impulse he crossed the room and knelt down before her.

Her voice trembled a little as, laying her hand on his head, she said slowly, "The blessing of the Lord God Almighty be upon you, and if it be His will, may He preserve you in your going out and coming in! May He grant you many souls for your hire, and satisfy you with His goodness!"

Tears sprang into her eyes as she uttered these last words, but her resolute nature speedily forced them back. Not so easily, however, could she still the emotions that were stirring within her. Her son, she knew, felt he had bidden adieu to all dreams of earthly bliss, and held his life but cheaply. Whether he were right or wrong, at any rate that life was very precious to her. He was her last tie to earth, the only one of her children left to her, and she lived but for him. Still, dear as he was, her brave spirit was ready to give him up to any service to which the Lord might call him, even if that service meant death.

There was silence for a few moments, and then he spoke.

"And you, mother? Will you let me send you away to a place of safety, out of reach of infection?"

"Nay," she answered promptly; "where thou stayest I will stay. Let them flee away who know not what it is to put their trust in the Lord of hosts, and to lie hidden in the hollow of His hand. But let those who do rest calmly in His almighty keeping, if so be they are in the path of duty."

"But, my mother, though I shrink not myself from facing the danger, I would fain not be the means of exposing you to the same. I would gladly feel you were away, and well out of this pestilential atmosphere."

"My son, say no more. My mind is made up. I stay and share your peril, and will do what in me lies to minister to you while you minister to others. How could you get on without some womenfolk to look after you, I should like to know?" she added with a smile. "But I must tell Tabitha she is free to depart, if so it liketh her; for if she is timid and fearful it would be better for her to be gone."

"If she goes at all she had better do so speedily, for soon it may be too late."

But nothing was farther from Tabitha's intentions than deserting her master and mistress, and so no more was said on the subject of departing. The question was considered as finally settled.

"Have you seen Lady Elizabeth Devereux lately?" asked Mrs. Willoughby, as she and her son sat together over their evening meal.

"Yes, I saw her yesterday."

"And is she thinking of fleeing?"

"No. She is expecting Sir Richard back soon, and would not like to be unable to welcome him as arranged. Besides, they could scarcely travel without an escort, being all ladies. Moreover she feels that our times are in God's hands, and has no foolish fears. Still, I dare say they will depart as soon as Sir Richard arrives."

The weeks went by, and still the plague continued its ravages, which did but increase as the weather grew hotter, until there seemed not a breath of air in the narrow streets. Now house after house was shut up having a red cross a foot long upon the door, with the inscription, "Lord, have mercy upon us!" showing that the plague had attacked some of the inmates. The streets were deserted, grass began to grow in them, and fires were burning in all parts, with a view to purifying the air. Few sounds were to be heard save the cries and groans of the infected, and the dreadful call, "Bring out your dead."

Many had fled, among them doctors, surgeons, and numbers of the clergy. "The Nonconformists," we are told, "a far more earnest set of men, felt it a shame that the thousands still left in London should be deprived of all spiritual privileges, and so undertook the duties of the vacant parishes, visiting the sick and preaching in the empty pulpits."

Among these latter was Stephen Willoughby. His successor at St. Benedict's had fled, and Dr. Willoughby with his heart deeply touched by the needs of his late flock, felt that all minor considerations must be waived,—for did he not stand as a dying man amongst dying men and women, and must he not while life and breath remained do what in him lay to point perishing souls to the Savior of the lost? So he mounted the pulpit in which he had thought never again to stand, and crowds thronged to hear him.

There, as Moses of old had pointed the smitten and dying Israelites to the serpent of brass, so he held up to them Christ crucified, and bade them look and live.

One awful feature of the times was the hardening effect which the terrible familiarity with death produced in many, who tried to stifle thought by plunging only deeper and deeper into vice and debauchery. But it was not so with all. There were some devout souls who saw in all this fearful judgment the "finger of God," and humbled themselves under His chastisement; while others found that the Savior, whom in days of health and prosperity they had ignored and despised, was ready in their extremity to open His arms of mercy, and in His divine long-suffering willing to extend to them the pardon they sought.

Lady Elizabeth frequently formed one of the crowd that pressed to hear Dr. Willoughby at St. Benedict's, and Cicely often pleaded to be allowed to accompany her mother. Young though she was, she dearly loved to listen to the earnest words of the great preacher, and to the loving invitations he gave in his Master's name to all, whether young or old, rich or poor. Her heart kindled as he spoke in glowing words of the glories of heaven and the bliss of the redeemed; of the contrast between this life, with its sorrows and partings, its sickness and death, and that land the inhabitant whereof shall no more say, "I am sick," and where God shall wipe away all tears from off every face.

Often while Dorothy was surrounded by a group of young gallants in the withdrawing room, Cicely would steal away to the quiet of the chamber the sisters shared together, and there ensconced in the deep window seat she would open and read the little Testament her mother had given her, or ponder over words of Dr. Willoughby's which had stirred the depths of her being.

Dorothy once coming up unexpectedly to fetch something found her thus engaged, to her great surprise.

"Why, Cicely, whatever are you doing? Why are you moping up here?"

"I am not moping; I am very happy," returned Cicely, lifting up a bright peaceful face, which certainly did not look either *triste* or moped.

"You have strange ideas of enjoyment," said Dorothy. "What an odd child you are! What can there be to make you happy in poring over a dull book mewed up here all by yourself?"

"It isn't a dull book, Sister Dorothy, and if you would read it for yourself you would say so too."

"Thank you," said the other contemptuously; "but I have no wish to turn into a little Puritan like yourself. You may go to your conventicles if you like, and sit and hear preaching by the hour, but don't ask me to go too. I prefer things of a different sort. However, there is not much gaiety to be had now; and it is getting dreadfully dismal staying on in this deserted place. I would rather go home if it goes on like this."

"But then father wouldn't find us here to welcome him. I wish he would come, though, for it would be very nice to be back again in our dear old home."

"Oh, as to that, if it were not for this distemper that is going about, London is far better than the dreary country, where there is scarcely a creature one cares to speak to, and, as Robert says, all one's good looks are quite thrown away," said Dorothy, with a candor that was one of her characteristics, as she arched her graceful neck and gave a glance at her handsome face in the mirror. "One might as well be as ugly as a scarecrow when there is no one to see the difference."

"You certainly are very pretty, Doll," remarked Cicely innocently, casting a look of admiration at her elder sister, "but I can't fancy that being admired can make one as happy as thinking about the beautiful home above, and all the wonderful love of God. I don't think there is any one I love so much as Jesus," she went on simply, "not even my own dear mother; so of course it makes me happy to think about Him and read what He says in His Word. Oh, Dorothy, I wish you would love Him too, and then you would know how happy it makes one."

The young speaker's face glowed, and an earnest light shone in her eyes, making Dorothy feel that, little as she could understand these things, they were very real to her young sister, and certainly made her very happy, for there was scarcely ever a cloud on the bright sunny face, while Dorothy herself was conscious of often feeling discontented and dissatisfied. She made no reply, but over and over again in days that followed did she seem to hear the echo of those pleading words.

As time passed by the dullness of which Dorothy complained did but increase in the plague-stricken city. Sir Richard had not yet come, but even if Lady Elizabeth had seen her way to leaving, it was now rendered impossible by an accident which Dorothy met with through the overturning of a coach, and which laid her up for several weeks, during which time her mother and sister were her devoted attendants.

Eugene and also Robert Hay were now absent with the court at Oxford, and very few people came and went. It was deemed safer to keep as much as possible within doors.

By the time Dorothy was about again August had come, and the hot weather did but swell the number of the victims.

CHAPTER VI

PASSING THROUGH THE VALLEY

"They saw the smile
He passed away in, and they said, 'He looks
As he had woke and seen the face of Christ,'
And with that rapturous smile held out his arms
To come to Him."—JEAN INGELOW

ONE close morning in August Dr. Willoughby was passing down Aldersgate Street, thinking as he walked of Lady Elizabeth, and hoping all was well with her and her little party. For though he had seen her and Cicely at church on Sunday, there was no telling from day to day who might have been taken away.

As he drew near the house in which they were lodging he heard his name called in a sort of hoarse whisper. It was no uncommon thing for people to call loudly for help out of the windows upon the passers-by, when house after house was shut up, with a watchman stationed before each, to prevent any from going in or out; a regulation that was made in hopes of hindering the spread of the contagion, but which often caused great misery to those shut up in the infected dwellings.

On looking up Dr. Willoughby perceived the face of Lady Elizabeth at an upper casement, and found it was she who was calling him, and was also making signs to him to come up to the room where she was. There was as yet no red cross on the door, which moreover he found was standing a little ajar, so he was free to enter. He did so, meeting no one on the stairs, for indeed the house seemed deserted, and knocked at the door of the chamber from which Lady Elizabeth had beckoned to him. She opened it, locking it behind him the moment he had entered, and then sank down on a couch.

Her looks struck a chill to his heart, so pale and livid was her face, while on a bed in a corner of the room was a motion-less form covered with a sheet. She noticed his glance, and said briefly in sorrow-stricken tones, "My sweet Cicely!"

"What! taken with this terrible malady?" said Dr. Willoughby aghast.

"Yes, and dead in a few hours. She was taken ill in the night and was gone at daybreak."

Her voice was unnaturally calm. "You are not afraid to come into the midst of the infection, are you?" she went on. "It is what you are doing every day, is it not?"

"Yes, I go wherever I can be of any use or comfort."

"I knew that, and therefore I did not scruple to call you in when I saw you passing. I had prayed God to send you, for I am in sore straits. The serving maid we brought with us has fled, or disappeared somehow, and the people of the house have done the same. I went in search of help when Cicely became ill, and found there was not a creature left, save a maid-servant who was lying dead in the attic. I heard some cries in the early part of the night, which doubtless was when she was taken ill or was dying, and then I suppose they all fled, before it should become known and the house be shut up."

Dr. Willoughby seemed too much shocked to speak for the moment, and she went on, "I immediately locked the door upon Dorothy, and thus confined her to her room, to prevent her having any contact with us, and thus spare her all possible risk. I hear her every now and then beating on the door, but I have called to her from the outside, and bid her stay quietly there until I send to release her. I would fain keep my Dorothy from the infection if I could;" and the mother clasped her hands, as if to still her pain.

"And you have been alone all these hours with no one to share your watch?"

"God has been with me," she answered simply, "There was no means of sending for good Dr. Barwick, who I know would have come; and I could not go myself to fetch him, for how could I leave Cicely? But I knew what remedies to adopt, and did what was possible."

Dr. Willoughby's face showed the deep sympathy he felt.

"And yourself? I fear you are ill?" he said, alarmed at her own ghastly looks.

"Yes, I am attacked too," she quietly answered.

"Then, my dear madam, let me go at once for the doctor."

"Wait a moment," she implored. "I have many things I want to say to you; let me say them before I become too ill. It might be too late by the time you returned."

"It is about Dorothy," she continued. "If I should be taken, she will be left utterly unprotected, with her father abroad, and even Eugene away at Oxford with the king. Though he would be but poor protection even were he here. Is it too much to ask if Mrs. Willoughby would give her a shelter until Sir Richard returns?"

There was agonized entreaty in the tones, as well as in the look with which Lady Elizabeth scanned Dr. Willoughby's face.

"I know of no one else to whom I could entrust her with any satisfaction," she went on. "But with your mother she would be under good influences, and might learn to seek better things. That is the one thing for which I long: that my Dorothy might seek her portion in God. Oh, Dr. Willoughby, you will not refuse me? Teach her to love God. It is the thing I have prayed for all her life,—have watched and waited for. Surely the answer will come. Surely God will be gracious, and will not cut her off all unprepared as she is, but will soften her heart through this chastisement, and in His own good time draw her to Himself."

Dr. Willoughby's heart was not made of stone,—on the contrary, it was a very tender, sympathizing one; and though Lady Elizabeth's request was about the last for which he was prepared, and as distasteful to him as it was unexpected, he found it impossible to steel himself against such pleading, from one moreover towards whom he had ever been most strongly attracted from the moment he had made her acquaintance. The sweetness and gentleness of her disposition, joined to the deep spirituality of her character, had won his reverence and love; and during this period of her stay in London they had enjoyed many times of holy communing together about heavenly things, which had much refreshed his spirit.

Could he then refuse her anything, even though the thing she asked was a hard one, because, as far as it was possible for his gentle nature to harbor such a feeling, he had conceived a distrust of womankind in general, his mother and Lady Elizabeth being the two notable exceptions? It was this feeling which had caused his momentary hesitation; the perceiving which hesitation, though without knowing its source, had led

Lady Elizabeth to press her request with the greater urgency.

But he hastened to put from him this feeling of reluctance. Was not this a solemn bequest, as it were? Might there not be a work for God to be done in that young soul through his mother's influence? Besides, in common hospitality how could they possibly refuse a shelter under their roof to one so utterly unprotected?

"It shall be as you propose," he answered; "that is, if Mistress Dorothy will consent to become an inmate of our poor home."

"Oh, she must, she will. Tell her it is her mother's dying charge to her. How can I ever thank you, Dr. Willoughby! You little know what a load you have taken from my heart, or how grateful I feel to you and your mother. And ask Mrs. Willoughby from me to bear with my poor child; she is willful and wayward, I know, at times; but oh! how I shall bless you and your mother when we meet hereafter in heaven above, if Dorothy too is there, led home by you!"

The pressing need for speech had kept Lady Elizabeth up, and given her strength for the time being, but now she sank back exhausted, and could scarcely repress a moan of pain.

"I will hasten now for Dr. Barwick," said Stephen Willoughby; and she gave a mute assent.

But rousing herself as he was leaving the room she said, "Will you be so good as to go to Dorothy's door, and without opening it beg her to remain content for a little while longer? Tell her it is a message from me, and that she shall soon learn the reason."

Dr. Willoughby, feeling there was no time to be lost, did as he was requested, and then emerged into the street, where to his great joy he met Dr. Barwick before he had gone many paces.

The good doctor at once turned to follow him, much concerned at the news that Lady Elizabeth Devereux was apparently to be one of the victims of this dread plague.

Dr. Barwick lived at that time near St. Paul's, having chosen that locality that he might be able to attend the daily service, where, we are told, he was present as often as three times a day during this period. He remained in London all through the plague, devoting himself to the sick and dying, and showing great liberality to the poor. He had been introduced to Lady Elizabeth by Mr. Evelyn on the occasion of Dorothy's accident, and it was little wonder that the two kindred spirits had been mutually attracted to each other.

"As sweet a soul as ever breathed," he remarked, as they turned to walk back together; "so gentle and guileless, so ripe for heaven. Ah, well, we must not wish it otherwise. When the grain is ready for the sickle, the great Husbandman loves to garner it in. Our turn, Willoughby, will come some day, and then we shall be gathered in too."

The sadness vanished from Stephen Willoughby's pale face as it kindled into a radiant look in response to Dr. Barwick's words; and then they passed into Lady Elizabeth's chamber.

She greeted them with a sweet smile. "How good of you to come," she said, addressing the physician; "but I do not think there is much you can do. It will not be long now, I feel assured. The golden gates seem almost open. I can well nigh catch the angels' song; and I long to rise and go to my Beloved, since He calls. It is not wrong to be glad to go, since it is He who thus appoints it?" she added in a questioning tone, looking towards Dr. Willoughby.

"Nay, surely; how can it be? Does not the Father like to see His children glad to reach their home when He sends for them? To wish to go before He calls is a different matter."

"But my poor Dorothy," said Lady Elizabeth, with the look of agonized yearning again coming into her eyes; "my poor child! It seems selfish to be content to leave her; and it almost breaks my heart to go without one farewell word. But I would not expose her to the risk of infection for the world."

"You are right," said Dr. Barwick gently; "and I could wish all would be as unselfish and thoughtful. If it had been so in every case, it is scarcely likely the disease would have made such frightful ravages."

There was little to be done. Dr. Barwick's practiced eye saw, as Stephen Willoughby's experience had told him, that it was a hopeless case, and had been so from the first. All he could do was to wish the parting soul God speed.

It was a hallowed hour. Both men felt it a privilege to stand beside such a death-bed, illumined as it was by light from the other world; and together they knelt and joined in prayer as Dr. Willoughby commended the passing soul into the hands of its faithful God.

Then the good doctor took his leave. Others were waiting

for him who sorely needed his aid, and though he would have liked to linger in the room which seemed irradiated by heaven's own sunshine, he had duties towards the living which must not be put aside. But the other remained. He could not leave that gentle spirit to die untended, and this was a kind of ministration to which he was called almost daily now.

After a while Lady Elizabeth seemed to revive a little, the waning strength appearing to flow back for a brief space. "My darling Cicely," she murmured, "my happy child; taken away from the evil to come, and safely sheltered in the home above. Just gone before me for a few hours, and then we shall be together for all eternity."

"Did she know she was going? Was she conscious?"

"Yes, and her face lit up as she went through the valley. It was not dark to her; the Savior whom she had loved was there, and joyfully, trustfully she rose up to go with Him. It seemed to fill her with unutterable gladness that she would so soon be allowed to gaze upon the glories of the heavenly city of which she had so often read. It was a brief and blessed passing."

"We thank and bless Thy holy name for all Thy servants departed this life in Thy faith and fear," said Dr. Willoughby slowly and solemnly, with bent head, using the words of the Liturgy which he knew Lady Elizabeth loved; and with fervor in her tones she added, "Amen."

Once more she roused herself. "I cannot thank you now as I would for promising in your mother's name to shelter my beloved child, but I ask that blessings may descend upon your head abundantly. And one more favor I would crave. If ever you have the chance, befriend my poor Eugene. I fear he is indeed a wandering sheep. Oh, if you can ever stretch out a helping hand to guide him back to the fold, do it, I pray you, for his dead mother's sake,—nay, for the sake of Him who died for us."

"And tell Dorothy from me that I wish, I command her, with my last breath, thankfully to accept the temporary home provided for her, and to show her gratitude by being docile and obedient to Mrs. Willoughby. What her future will be I know not; nor that of my poor Eugene. I leave it with God; He is faithful; I can trust them to Him."

"He is able to keep that which you have committed to him," said Dr. Willoughby.

She scarcely spoke again, save to murmur once or twice

the names of her beloved; but the last word on her lips was, "Jesus."

In spite of her sufferings, an expression of holy peace rested on her face, which did but grow brighter as the end drew near. When past speaking she still continued to give a grateful look from time to time into Dr. Willoughby's face, and then with an upward glance she was gone.

It was all over in so short a space of time that it almost seemed like a dream to Stephen Willoughby; and yet he had seen many a similar case during these last few painful weeks. Reverently and sadly he closed her eyes and drew a covering over her. Then for some moments he knelt in silent prayer. Was he wondering who would be the next to be called?

Rising up, and locking the door behind him, so that Dorothy might not be able, in a fit of willfulness, to insist on going into the room, he proceeded to the latter's chamber, and knocked at the door. He would rather have had almost any other task imposed upon him than this of confronting the proud young beauty.

Dr. Willoughby turned the key in the lock, and Dorothy on hearing the sound at once opened the door, when the two stood face to face. The young clergyman had never felt so like a coward before; had he followed his impulses, he would have turned and fled. But he could not do that. Dislike the task as he might, he must go through with it. "But suppose she utterly refused to come with him," as he thought was not improbable, "what was he to do then?" was the question he was debating in his mind.

The girl's eyes were red with crying, and at this moment they were also flashing with anger.

"So it is you, Dr. Willoughby! You have been my jailor!" and the tones expressed annoyance. "And pray why have I been shut up in this manner like a prisoner? Will you tell me, if you please?" she demanded imperiously.

"It was your mother's doing; it was she who locked the door upon you; and now she wishes you to come with me."

"With you! And whither, pray? To one of your conventicles?" she asked scornfully.

"Nay. But do not stay to argue now. I will tell you all when we get outside. It is Lady Elizabeth's desire that you don your walking habit and accompany me without loss of time."

"I will go and get my orders from my mother herself," said

Dorothy, endeavoring to pass Dr. Willoughby; but he prevented it.

"Nay, Mistress Dorothy, she will not see you; her one desire is to get you out of this house; and that as speedily as may be. You will not disobey her?"

"Why does she want me to leave the house? Oh," she cried suddenly with a shriek of dismay, "it is then as I feared; the plague has come, the dreadful plague!" and the girl's face blanched while her eyes dilated with horror.

"Yes, there has been a case," said Dr. Willoughby, seeing it was best to work on her fears, "and therefore Lady Elizabeth wishes you to be removed at once out of the infection."

Dr. Willoughby added no more, fearing that if Dorothy knew whither she was to be removed she would resist with all her might. Nor would he tell her yet of Lady Elizabeth's death. It would, he felt, be better to defer the painful scene until he should have placed her under his mother's care.

"Let me go to my mother first," persisted the willful maiden.

"Nay, she will not see you. I beg you to hasten, and to come immediately. We shall find it difficult to leave the house if we delay too long, for after the watchmen once shut it up they will not suffer people to pass out. Let me urge you to follow me at once."

"Come then, I am ready," said Dorothy, her movements quickened by this new fear. "Let us make haste and get out of this dreadful place," she added, as with feverish haste she tossed on a hood and drew a cloak around her. "But where are mother and Cicely? Have they gone already? Oh, why did they not take me with them?"

"I will tell you all later on. For the present, what we have to do is to escape while we may," returned the discreet Dr. Willoughby.

Like one half stunned Dorothy followed her guide down the stairs and out into the open air. Urged by fear, she walked as swiftly as he could desire. In silence they passed along the deserted street, which was silent too save for a cry that now and then broke on the stillness from some one in mortal pain or bitter anguish.

They walked in the middle of the road, as people did at that time, by way of avoiding contact with other passers-by. Every here and there great fires were burning, in spite of the heat of the August day; but it was ordered, as it was considered a means of purification. They scarcely met any one save now and then a watchman going on an errand, and one or two miserable objects with haggard faces, who apparently had had the plague and were slowly recovering, or had been driven to the verge of despair by poverty and wretchedness.

Most of the shops were closed: no business or traffic seemed to be going on. Here and there were empty houses with windows standing wide open, all the occupants being dead or having fled in a panic.

Dorothy shuddered as she went along. She had not, been out of doors now for some time, her accident having first of all confined her for some weeks, and since her recovery it had been deemed safer to keep within doors, save for the purpose of going to church, whither Dorothy had not cared to accompany her mother and Cicely.

She seemed too much appalled to ask any questions as they went along, or perhaps it was that Dr. Willoughby's quiet decision of manner a little overawed her. Once or twice she glanced at the face beside her. It was calm, with a look of abstraction on it, as if his mind and thoughts were far away. Even at that moment she could not help inwardly owning it a beautiful face; but there was something in the firmly closed lips that prevented her from breaking in upon his reverie.

He almost seemed to have forgotten her presence until they reached his own door, and then he paused for a moment with a half-startled glance at his companion.

CHAPTER VII

AMONG THE PURITANS

"Instead of looking upwards,
    And seeing the face divine,
So full of the tenderest pity,
    For weary hearts like mine,
I only thought of the burden,
    The cross that before me lay,
So hard and heavy to carry,
    That it darkened the light of day."

The Changed Cross

T HE door was opened by Tabitha.

"Where is thy mistress, Tabitha? Is she within doors?"

"She is in the front parlor," returned the old servant, giving an astonished and half-suspicious glance at her master's companion. Who might this young maiden be in rich attire of a fashion that proclaimed her of the Cavalier party, and was so different from the plain Puritan dress which alone was worn in that household? But Tabitha had to keep her surmises to herself, for Dr. Willoughby vouchsafed no explanation.

"Come with me," he said, turning to Dorothy; and silently she followed him into Mrs. Willoughby's presence. She understood then where she was; for though she had never been to the house before, she knew Mrs. Willoughby by sight, and had exchanged a few words with her once or twice, when the latter had come to see Lady Elizabeth, and Dorothy had happened to be present; on which occasions, however, she had always made a point of leaving the room on the first opportunity.

Mrs. Willoughby raised her head from her work to greet her son with a welcoming smile, but the smile died away in a look of unfeigned surprise as her eye fell on Dorothy. Dr. Willoughby placed a seat for the latter, and then said, turning to his mother,

"I have brought Mistress Dorothy here by Lady Elizabeth's request. She begs you to receive her as your guest for the time being."

Mrs. Willoughby was unconscious that a look of something very like dismay passed over her face, but Dorothy with her quick eye noticed it and resented it.

"Do you mean that she intends me to stay here?" she cried, starting up, as much dismayed at the thought of remaining in that Puritan household as Mrs. Willoughby could possibly be at being called upon to receive such an inmate. "No, no; take me back to my mother. I did not know you were bringing me here. I insist on going back!" she added, with the petulance of a spoiled child.

"Nay, nay, calm yourself, Mistress Dorothy," said Stephen Willoughby, gently but authoritatively, "and hear me out. I pray you be seated again, and listen while I explain to you and my mother how matters stand."

"Is it the plague?" asked Mrs. Willoughby, in an awed voice and with a look of consternation.

"It is, I grieve to say. The first case was that of a maid servant belonging to the people of the house, who was taken ill yesterday evening."

"And the second?" demanded Dorothy impatiently. "Oh, Dr. Willoughby has mother got it? Then I must go to her. Oh, you must not keep me back! Mother ill, and I not with her! I could not bear such a thought!" cried the girl, clasping her hands in her distress, and apparently forgetting the terror she had previously shown at the very mention of the dread disease.

"Nay," said Dr. Willoughby, slowly and gently; "she does not need your help. And if she did she would have none of it. Her one desire was to keep you away from the infection."

"But how can you say she does not need my help? She must have some one to nurse her, and I have heard that people often get so frightened they run away and leave those who are attacked to die alone. Let me go to my mother; my place is beside her," said Dorothy imperiously, rising to her feet with a determined gesture.

"Nay, Mistress Dorothy; as I said, she no longer needs your help. Do you not understand?" said Stephen gently, looking compassionately at the girl before him, and feeling how impossible it was to soften the blow, though he would gladly have done so if he could. It was indeed terrible news which he had to break. "She no longer needs your help because she has done with pain and suffering for ever, and has passed into the land where there is no more sickness or death."

Dorothy gazed at him for a moment, as if trying to comprehend his words. Then, as their meaning dawned upon her, a look of anguish came into her face, as she cried with an exceeding bitter cry,—

"Dead? My mother dead? Is that what you would tell me?"

Dr. Willoughby bowed his head in sad but silent assent; while his mother uttered an exclamation of dismay and sorrow.

Dorothy resumed her seat like one stunned or turned into stone. All color had forsaken her face, which looked as if chiseled in marble. For some moments there was silence in the room. Then in a hollow voice came the words, as if she dreaded to put the question, "And where is Cicely?"

"She is with her sainted mother. She went first, and now they are in bliss together."

"And have left me! Oh, mother, mother!" wailed the girl in tones that went to the hearts of the others; and then, in sorrow too deep for utterance, she turned her face away and hid it in the cushions of the couch on which she was seated.

Again silence prevailed; for what words could touch grief such as this? Dorothy with all her faults had never shown a want of heart; on the contrary, the warmth and depth of her affection for her mother had been the one thing that had enabled Lady Elizabeth to exert the influence she did over her, and had made her commands law to the high-spirited girl, who would not brook control from others.

Mrs. Willoughby glanced from time to time at the crouching figure with a look of deep concern on her face, while Dr. Willoughby, leaning back in his chair with his eyes fixed on the ground, seemed lost in thought.

Deep sobs shook Dorothy's frame from time to time. At length Mrs. Willoughby approached, and laid her hand gently on her shoulder as she said, "The kindest thing I deem will be to leave thee, dear child, to thyself for a time. I know it is too soon to comfort thee, and yet I would fain bid thee raise thine eyes above to the heaven where thy sweet mother and sister have gone, and think of their blessedness. The God in whose presence they are now rejoicing will be thy God too if thou ask

Him. He is able to make thee fit to rejoin them some day, never to be parted more. I pray God you may follow them, Mistress Dorothy, in the path they trod till it bring you at last to the same blessed bourne."

Dorothy's only reply was another deep sob. Then Mrs. Willoughby left the room to go to prepare a chamber for the unexpected guest, and her son at the same moment rose to follow her. They turned into the little apartment at the back, which was Stephen's study.

"My son, these are heavy tidings."

"Yes; these are terrible times. But if any one seemed ready for the home above it was Lady Elizabeth. We must not grudge her the happiness that is now hers," said Dr. Willoughby, with a wistful look. "She is now with Him whom she loved,—no dark mists of earth between, no more clouds of sin or unbelief to obscure His radiance. She gazes with undimmed vision upon the King in His beauty. 'Blessed are the dead who die in the Lord.'"

"Yes. And blessed are they also who amid the shadows and dimness still patiently seek to follow in His footsteps; still go about on His errands, doing the work He appoints them, and still day by day lay their will, their all at His feet. Blessed are such servants, my son; and it is no small honor to be called to such service. Don't let us sigh for the rest before the day's work is done."

"Nay, that would be selfish indeed," responded Stephen, with a smile and look that thanked her for her words. "And now I must be off again, to minister if I may to other poor creatures; and to bid the dead cart go tonight to fetch the bodies," he added in a low tone, and with a sort of shudder at the thought of such a burial for the sweet and honored lady and her no less sweet young daughter.

But by this time it had grown impossible to bury the dead in the ordinary way; coffins could not have been supplied in sufficient numbers, nor could the grave-diggers have prepared anything like the number of graves required. So large pits had been dug, into which they were obliged to put the bodies promiscuously. Funerals had had to be abandoned; and now the "dead cart," as it was called, went its rounds every night, with the mournful cry, "Bring out your dead." Collected thus from house to house, they were conveyed to the common burying-ground. But to the Christian that was after all a small matter. Would not He to whom they had committed their souls watch over their dust until the Resurrection Day?

"Then, mother, you accept Lady Elizabeth's charge? For her sake you will shelter and be kind to this young maiden until her father's return?"

"I must, since it is for her sake," returned Mrs. Willoughby, with an emphasis upon the last two words which seemed to imply that for no other motive could she have consented to undertake such a charge. "I loved the mother," she went on, "but the daughter is so different. However, I feel deeply for the poor girl. Still, I hope Sir Richard may soon return."

"It seemed a solemn charge put into our hands, mother, and one we could not refuse; though, as far as I am concerned, I would as soon have been asked to shelter a young savage from the wilds of America. I should have known how to deal with him better, I believe," said Stephen Willoughby with a smile.

And then he proceeded to relate all that had been said by Lady Elizabeth, and told how bright and blessed had been her end.

The days and weeks went by, and still Dr. Willoughby continued to visit the sick, the dying and the sorrowful, moving about like a ministering angel in their midst; shrinking from no scene, however painful, where he could be of use; hazarding his life from day to day in infected houses, and beside the beds of plague-stricken people. His countenance through it all wore a calm, unruffled look, while frequently a light of deep quiet happiness shone in the large dreamy eyes. It often seemed to sorrow-stricken and despairing hearts as if a ray of heaven's own sunshine had come into their room with Dr. Willoughby's entrance; and many a dying one who but for him might in all probability have gone down to the grave in darkness and gloom heard from his lips words that encouraged them to lift their eyes to the Savior on the cross, and pass away with the smile of hope on their faces.

"Nay, mother," said Stephen once, when she was commiserating his tired looks and begging him to rest, "I need no pity. Never have I known so much of what the joy of the Lord is as during this terrible time; never have I so uninterruptedly tasted of the sunshine of His presence. It is almost as if I lived with Him, as John did of old during those years of His ministry on earth; as if I lay on His breast, only leaving it to do His bidding, and then returning to tell Him all and receive further commands. Nay," he added reverently, "it is something better still, for when I go on His errands He goes with me. I seem to hear Him say, 'Come, let us visit this sick person, let us carry the Words of Life to that dying soul.' And so we go together; I just the mouthpiece, and He the power behind."

"Verily, my son, you are richly blest; and in the great harvest day what rejoicing will be yours over souls that have been won for Him!"

And so in that little household there was no gloom, no foolish fear, no selfish shrinking from duty; for Tabitha was a close follower of the example set by her master and mistress. It was a solemn time; for all when they rose in the morning felt that ere night the summons might have come for them; but there was a chastened gladness too, for who could tell how soon they might be allowed to pass into the presence of the King, to see Him face to face, and go no more out?

The new-comer was the only exception, the only one out of harmony. Poor Dorothy! they pitied her much, and bore with her patiently. At first the sympathy she felt helped Mrs. Willoughby to overlook the many points of friction between them. But Dorothy showed no gratitude for her sympathy, seemed rather to repel it, and shutting herself up in proud reserve abandoned herself to grief and discontent. Her face wore a stony look of misery, and she would sit for hours at a time doing nothing, idly gazing out of window, brooding over her sorrow, while inwardly chafing against the restraints of her new life.

The long family prayers night and morning were irksome to her; the severely sober garments of the two female members of the household were hateful to her; the absence of all grace and taste in the rigidly plain appointments of the house grated on her sense of beauty and love of pretty things. A greater contrast than that which the little house in Knightrider Street presented to her beautiful home at Hurstwood could scarcely have been found. These were small things, but they jarred upon her, even while she wondered at herself for noticing such trifles in the midst of the overwhelming sorrow that had come upon her.

She saw but little of Dr. Willoughby. He was out a great deal, and only joined them at meals, always retiring afterwards to his study, whither Mrs. Willoughby sometimes followed him. Few words were exchanged between himself and their guest; in fact, he took but little notice of her beyond seeing that her wants at table were supplied, and every little attention rendered that courtesy required. His conversation was chiefly directed to his mother. But meantime Dorothy observed him narrowly, and often wondered at the serenity of his face and the cheerfulness of his demeanor in the midst of so much that was gloomy and depressing.

And then she came by degrees to understand something of the cause. She had before her a living exemplification of the words, "He that dwelleth in the secret place of the Most High shall abide under the shadow of the Almighty:" words that Dr. Willoughby frequently chose for reading aloud at prayers. At first she paid little attention, but gradually the words laid hold on her, and she would ponder over them, thinking that here she had found the explanation of the calmness and fearlessness in the midst of danger which characterized those about her. They, were possessed of something which she had not; something which it must be grand to possess, if it removed all fear and imparted the courage which she so much admired, and in which now she feared she was wanting.

She used to think herself brave and courageous, and had often laughed at Cicely for her timidity; but even that young sister had, according to Dr. Willoughby's account, found the secret of this strange courage, which had enabled her to face death itself and the unknown world without shrinking. While she, Dorothy, felt terribly afraid to die, and could not bear to contemplate such a thing. She tried to put away such thoughts, but could not succeed in banishing them altogether.

She was sitting alone one day in the front parlor, Mrs. Willoughby having gone to attend to some household duty, when Dr. Willoughby, re-entering the house, came into the room in search of his mother. He noticed the look of intense despondency on the face that was raised to see who the new-comer might be; while the heavy eyes, that used to be so bright, bore traces of recent tears, and the whole attitude told of listless dejection.

"Do you know where my mother is, Mistress Dorothy?"

"She was here a little while ago, and I expect she will be back soon, as she has not put by her work, you see. I do not think she has left the house, or I should have heard her."

He was about to depart, but before he reached the door he turned back, for her look of misery touched him.

"Mistress Dorothy," he said gently, "it is hard work trying to bear our sorrows and our burdens alone; and I fear me that is what you are doing."

She looked up at him in surprise. "I don't know what you mean," she said coldly. "I have no one to share my sorrows now. Those who would have done so have been taken from me;" and the tears rushed into her eyes, in spite of her proud attempts to keep them back.

"Nay," he returned gently, real sympathy showing itself in his face and manner, "there is One who loves you, and feels for you, and stands even now inviting you to cast your burden upon Him. He knows the full weight of your sorrow, and all the pain of loneliness, and His heart is very pitiful. He longs to see you turn to Him, that He may comfort you with His love. And His love, Mistress Dorothy, transcends all that heart can conceive: those who know what it is possess a priceless treasure, and one that can never be taken from them."

She had fixed her large eyes on his face, and was listening with a dreamy look, as if she only partially comprehended his meaning. She said nothing when he paused.

"Will you not make trial of this love? Will you not take your mother's God for your God, and let His love fold you in its embrace?"

"You tell me He loves me," replied Dorothy, with a hard look coming into her face, "and yet He takes from me that which I loved most, and leaves me desolate and dreary. A strange way of showing love! Oh, why did we ever come to this dreadful place?" she cried passionately. "If we had stayed at home, we might all have been happy still."

"'What I do thou knowest not now, but thou shalt know here-after,' says Christ. We must wait a while for the full explanation of His dealings with us. But meantime we do know something of His meaning in it all. He often causes earthly fountains of happiness to dry up, that we may be led to the one true source of joy, and quench our thirst in life-giving streams. Oh, why remain longer outside in the cold and the darkness when you might come at once into the warmth and brightness and glory of His own presence?"

"Mistress Dorothy," he went on, as she did not speak, "you would like to meet your sainted mother again, would you not?"

"How can you ask such a question?" she returned impatiently.

"Do you intend to do so?"

She looked a little startled. "Intend?" she echoed in an interrogative tone.

"Yes; it rests with you whether you will spend eternity together or not."

"With me?"

"Ay, it is even so. For God offers to be to you all that he was to her. He offers to adopt you into His family—of which she is a member—and it is left with you to accept the offer or reject it. He is willing to make you a child of God; and the children of God will spend the long ages of eternity together in the home He has prepared for them. Lady Elizabeth has but gone on before; you may follow after if you like, and find her there waiting to receive you."

A wistful look came into the dark eyes. "Oh, to see her once more! I would give the whole world if I might have her back!" cried the girl, clasping her hands as if to still the yearning pain at her heart.

"That cannot be. She cannot return to you, but you may go to her. It was ever the deep longing of her heart that you would give yourself to God, and with almost her last breath she said how much she hoped this sorrow would bring you to Him. Then turn to Him. Why should you be lonely and desolate when He offers to be to you a Father? ay, and more,—for His love has all the tenderness of a mother's as well. Listen to what He says, 'As one whom his mother comforteth, so will I comfort you.' Don't seek comfort elsewhere; there is no true joy apart from Him. But He can comfort. I am speaking of that I know, and have proved."

Dorothy looked up at him with a searching glance, as if taking his measure in her mind, and then, half averting her face, she said, "You have never lost a mother—such a mother as mine—and a sister all at one stroke. You cannot understand."

"There are other sorrows in this life, and even harder ones to bear."

Again that quick keen glance from the dark eyes.

"Yes, Mistress Dorothy, there are some sorrows which cannot be talked about, but compared with which the seeing a dear one pass from us to go right into the presence of the Savior seems a joy rather than a grief. Not that I would make light of your trouble. I know how heavy it is, and therefore I urge you not to reject the help and comfort you might find in God."

At this moment Mrs. Willoughby suddenly re-entered the
room; and the scene she witnessed much discomposed her
maternal mind. Her son and their young guest in close conversation, the latter leaning back in her chair with her face
upturned, while Stephen was standing looking down upon her
with sympathy—even if nothing more tender—plainly written on his countenance! Her motherly fears were aroused. Was
this girl beginning to have designs upon him? Was she putting
forth her arts to bring him to her feet, just to cast him off as
Rosamond had done? And was he already being drawn into her
toils? Hitherto they had seemed so utterly indifferent to each
other, and the gulf between them was so great, that her mind
had been at ease upon that score; but she had suffered too much
from seeing her son once trifled with, not to be easily alarmed
at the slightest indication of the possibility of such a thing hap-
pening again.

Henceforth, unconsciously to herself, her manner changed
towards Dorothy. All that the latter did she now viewed with
prejudiced eyes, and her great object was to keep her son as
much apart from her as possible. Stephen would have smiled,
had he known the new anxiety that was preying upon her mind,
for he could in all honesty have assured her that her fears were
entirely groundless. But, not knowing or suspecting the cause,
he sometimes wondered a little at his mother's manner, which
was occasionally almost stern towards the young maiden.

He ventured once on a mild remonstrance when he found
himself alone with her. Mrs. Willoughby, whose patience had
been sorely tried by Dorothy's listless ways, feeling strongly as
she did how much better it would be for the girl herself if she
were to exert herself and turn to some useful occupation, instead
of idly dreaming away the precious hours, selfishly nursing her
sorrow and brooding over it, instead of seeking to lay herself out
for others, had been making some remarks to that effect.

"We mustn't be too hard upon her," he said gently. "We must
make allowances for difference of temperament and bringing
up."

"With such a mother as Lady Elizabeth she cannot have
been brought up to think of nobody but herself," returned Mrs.
Willoughby, her face wearing a severe look. "And whilst I am
nearly driven off my feet and Tabitha too in attending to the
many claims for help in these times of terrible distress—she sits

with her hands before her and never offers to assist in any way whatsoever."

"You must remember, mother, she has been accustomed to have servants to do things for her, and not to do them herself. Our plain life and ways must present a great contrast to all that she has hitherto known."

"I had not looked to find you taking her part, and upholding idleness and indolence in a young thing who is strong and healthy, while your old mother has to put her shoulder to the wheel, with the extra burden of an additional inmate at such a time as this."

"Nay, mother, I uphold her not, and I grieve to hear she gives you not the aid she might. It is wrong to be so engrossed with our sorrow as to be oblivious of the needs of those around."

"It is very unlike you, my son; it is not so that you would have acted," said Mrs. Willoughby in softer tones as she looked at the face before her, on which hard work and incessant toil had traced fresh lines of late, but on which, in spite of all, heaven's own peace ever rested. "But I must not, I know, expect all to be alike."

CHAPTER VIII

AN UNEXPECTED MEETING

"Faithful and just art Thou,
　　Forgiving all;
Loving and kind art Thou,
　　When poor ones call;
Lord, let the cleansing blood,
Blood of the Lamb of God,
　　Pass o'er my soul."—H. BONAR

DR. WILLOUGHBY one day came in a little late for the evening meal, and when he took his seat it was with an air of abstraction, as if his thoughts were elsewhere, while his pale countenance seemed to bear traces of some recent mental conflict. His mother felt as she glanced at him that he must have been going through some painful ordeal, but she forbore to ask any questions, at any rate until they should be alone.

Dorothy also noticed something unlike his ordinary manner, and it set her wondering what the sorrows could be to which he had referred the other day as being worse than even losing friends by death.

He was evidently trying to throw off whatever it might be that was oppressing him, and to enter into conversation as usual; but that it cost him an effort so to do was more apparent than he was aware.

"Is the plague still as bad as ever? Are the people still dying in the same dreadful manner?" asked Dorothy abruptly.

It was a topic that was never willingly brought forward before her by either Dr. or Mrs. Willoughby.

"It depends on what you mean by the word 'dreadful.'" said Stephen slowly. "To many death has been but as the angel of light, setting open for them the door into heaven itself; and they seemed, even before they went, to have obtained a glimpse of the brightness and glory awaiting them. Others have rejoiced to hear the voice of their Beloved calling to them to come up higher, and have gladly risen up to go. There was nothing 'dreadful' in that. But with some," he went on in a lower tone, "it has all been darkness and despair. And some have been taken so suddenly they had scarcely time to realize that the summons had come for them before they were no more.

"Do you not think those blessed, Mistress Dorothy," he went on, "who, having made their peace with God and sought refuge in Christ, have no need to fear when the death-angel knocks at their door? He is then to them but as the messenger sent to bring them into their Father's presence. The whole question turns upon whether we are sons and daughters of the Lord or not. To the children death means going home; to those who are not children it means banishment from God, the only source of light and happiness."

"Have you been at many death-beds today?" she asked with strange persistence.

"I have been at one," he replied, with something in his manner which forbade further questioning; and then silence fell upon them.

When the other inmates of the little household had retired to rest, Mrs. Willoughby repaired to her son's study where she found him for once sitting unoccupied, with his book lying unopened beside him.

"You have been witnessing some painful scenes today I fear, my son."

"Such, alas, are of daily occurrence," he returned evasively. Then after a pause, "But today has been unlike any other day. Mother," he went on in lower tones, and slightly averting his face, "I have been standing beside *her* deathbed."

She knew at once to whom he referred. "Rosamond's?" she exclaimed in startled tones.

He bowed his head in assent, while mingled thoughts and feelings surged through Mrs. Willoughby's mind, and kept her silent. She knew not what to say. Perhaps it was best to say nothing, and yet she longed to hear more, and it would seem unsympathetic to show no interest. But she was afraid of touching the wound with unskillful hand, lest she should cause pain where she only longed to soothe.

"Did you know she was in London?" she asked at length, hoping to draw out more information.

"No. It was quite by accident that I came upon her. A watchman pointing to a certain house said he had believed it quite empty—all the inmates having apparently fled during the night—but he had within the last hour or so heard sounds, cries or moans, which made him think some one must be left behind. I told him I would go and see. I entered the house; it all seemed silent and deserted; I went into several rooms, all spacious and luxuriously furnished, but saw nobody. So I passed up the stairs and looked into one chamber after another. As I opened the door of one, the handsomest of all, I thought I discerned a figure lying on a bed, but ere I could advance a step I was greeted by a piercing shriek. Mother, it was she— Rosamond—lying there deserted by everybody and stricken down to death."

He covered his face with his hand, apparently unable to proceed. He could not tell all, or relate how on catching sight of him she had exclaimed, "Stephen Willoughby, what brings you here? How is it you have found me out? Have you come to call my sin to my remembrance—the sin that I committed when I sold myself for gold, turning away from you and all that was good and true, and deliberately choosing the lower and baser things that money could procure?

"That downward step has cost me dear," she went on, as Stephen stood, too overcome with astonishment and conflicting emotions to find words come readily. "Oh, I have had my punishment, even in this life, and now I go to that which awaits me in the other world. But it has begun here, in the pangs of remorse, in the bitter reaping of that which I so madly sowed. Then leave me; the sight of you brings back all that might have been—all that I cast from me—and I cannot endure it!"

The looks and tones were those of utter despair, while the feverish eyes glowed like fire, and the intense excitement had brought two crimson spots on the hollow, livid cheeks.

A great contrast was the calm countenance of Dr. Willoughby, on which the light at that moment fell, revealing it in all its manly beauty. Still he seemed at a loss for words.

"You do not speak," she went on excitedly. "You say nothing. I suppose you consider me beneath reproach; you can only regard me with loathing and contempt. Oh, I know it well.

Then go and leave me. I know not what brought you here; but I shall breathe more freely when you are gone. The very sight of you is a reproach to me."

She turned her face to the wall, as if to shut out the vision of purity and goodness before her. But after a moment's pause she added in softer tones, "And yet I would fain hear you say you forgive me before I go."

"That I did long ago," was the grave, tender answer, and the accents of the well-known voice sent a thrill through her. "But, Rosamond, it is the forgiveness of Another which it behooves you now to seek, and to seek without delay. The moments are passing. Have you made your peace with God? Have you sought His pardon?"

"It is too late," she returned bitterly. "I have forsaken Him, and He has forsaken me. I chose the ways of sin, and when at length I came to hate them I was too weak to turn from them. There is no hope for me."

"It is Satan who whispers that lie in your ear," said Stephen earnestly. "The voice of Christ still says, 'Come unto Me, and I will give you rest;' and 'Him that cometh to Me I will in no wise cast out.' Will you not listen to His voice, the voice of God, and cast yourself at His feet?"

"I am too vile, too polluted. You do not know how low I have sunk; how I have chosen darkness rather than light; how when I might have trodden the path to heaven beside you I cast in my lot with one who was pursuing the other road, and he has dragged me down with him—down—down—deep into the mire!"

"You cannot have sunk too low for Christ's hand to reach you; He can draw you out. Only cry to Him. Only come just as you are, with all the leprosy of sin upon you, and see if He will not put forth His hand and say to you, even you, 'thou clean.' He never yet turned away from the repentant sinner; it is only the proud and self-righteous who have no part or lot with Him. But to be vile and sinful is to have the only passport needed to admit you into His presence. Such are those He came to save, those He invites to Him."

The large feverish eyes were turned on the speaker with a wistful look of intense longing.

"Oh, if I could take those words of His as spoken to myself! Does He, against whom I have so sinned, indeed say to me 'Come?'"

"He does. He stretches out His arms towards you. Only trust Him. Look to Him hanging on the cross. Hear Him saying, 'I have seen thy ways, and will heal thee.' It is with the full knowledge of all the past that He offers forgiveness. And His forgiveness is so full and free that His promise is, 'Their sins and their iniquities will I remember no more.'"

"Can it be true that He offers me this, at this very minute, though I have only a few hours or moments left of life, and can bring Him nothing, do nothing for Him?"

"It is even so. One marvels at such grace, but then He is God. It is His divine nature ever to have mercy and forgive. Try Him. Cast yourself at His feet."

"I will. Pray for me, Stephen. Ask Him to receive me, vile as I am."

"And so, mother," went on Stephen, who had briefly narrated some of the foregoing conversation, "I fell on my knees and prayed that He would put forth His hand of Divine power, and cleanse and heal that soul. And then—it was almost as if I saw Him do as He did to the leper of old—He seemed to stretch forth His hand and lay it upon her; and healing came with the touch. The agony passed; the bitterness of despair changed into the joy of pardon; and so, with deepest self-abasement, but in a rapture of gratitude, and lost in wonder at such goodness, she passed into the other world—one snatched as a brand from the burning."

"Marvelous are His ways, and infinite His long suffering; His compassions fail not, they are new every morning," murmured Mrs. Willoughby, much touched to think that the one whom the wayward girl had so deeply wronged should be the one to lead her at the last to Him who alone could give her peace and pardon; while to Stephen it was inexpressibly soothing to have been granted the opportunity of doing so, and it served as balm to heal his wound.

CHAPTER IX

LONGINGS FOR HOME

"Behold a Stranger at the door!
   He gently knocks, has knocked before;
Has waited long; is waiting still;
   You use no other friend so ill."—J. GRIGG

MEANTIME the monotony of her existence was becoming more and more intolerable to Dorothy. They were sad and terrible times for everybody, but for one who as yet knew nothing of the joy of serving others, or the peace that comes from bowing to God's will and seeing His hand in everything, it was far worse than for those who by ministering to others were earning blessings from them, and winning the approving smile of their Heavenly Master.

All this time no news or tidings whatever had come of Sir Richard. During the first few weeks that had elapsed after Lady Elizabeth's death Dorothy had anxiously and eagerly looked for his return as that which would release her from her enforced sojourn under Mrs. Willoughby's roof. But as the time went by, and week after week passed in unbroken silence so far as he was concerned, hope began to turn to despondency.

"What can have become of him?" was the constant cry of her heart. "Oh, why doesn't he come and take me home? If he doesn't come soon I shall die, I know, or do something desperate."

And like a bird beating its wings against the bars of its cage, so she chafed and fretted. Instead of making herself agreeable to Mrs. Willoughby, she tried her patience more and more; while the girl on her part was not slow to perceive that she was regarded with scant favor by her hostess.

"I know she would gladly be rid of me," she would say to herself; "and she can't long for me to be gone more than I long to go. Oh, that father would come and take me home!"

And now Hurstwood, the place she had once thought dull, and which she had been so ready to quit that she might taste of the pleasures of London life, seemed to her like a very paradise. Visions of the bright skies and sunny meadows—of the freedom with which she had been able to roam over the breezy downs or the flowery pasture lands, floated before her eyes, and presented such a contrast to the narrow streets and close atmosphere, the signs of woe and the mournful silence of the once gay city, that she longed, and not unnaturally, with an inexpressible longing to escape from the doomed place, and flee back to the happy home of her childhood and girlhood.

The yearning increased upon her from day to day, until she became utterly home-sick. Her cheek began to grow pale, her appetite to fail. Mrs. Willoughby, as she watched her, grew uneasy, and wished scarcely less earnestly than the girl herself, that Sir Richard would appear upon the scene. Often had she and her son discussed the matter together, and tried to conjecture every possible cause that could account for his silence, or, as they began to call it, his mysterious disappearance; but they could arrive at no satisfactory solution of the question.

In September the number of deaths from the plague first showed a decrease; then came a slight increase, then again towards the end of the month a decrease. October brought a further decrease, and by the end of the month many began to return to London, though the streets were still very empty and most of the shops shut. But people began to move about more freely, and to shut themselves up less indoors.

Dorothy, grown either more fearless or more reckless, would no longer allow herself to be kept a close prisoner, as she called it; and if neither Mrs. Willoughby nor Tabitha could accompany her would sometimes willfully insist on going out alone. Not that she derived much pleasure, poor girl, from her wanderings, for everything still bore a melancholy, neglected aspect.

One morning she had been standing by the river's side watching the boats moving up and down on the water, when on turning to depart she found herself suddenly face to face with a gay young cavalier in silken doublet and lace and plumes.

"Robert!" she exclaimed in tones of joyful surprise, scarcely able to believe that she saw aright, so long was it since she had looked upon an old familiar face. "Is it really you? Where did you spring from?"

"Is it Dorothy Devereux?" cried the young man almost at the same moment, and involuntarily recoiling a step or two, for in those days people feared coming into close contact with any one until they knew they were free from infection. "Can it be you, Dorothy, looking so pale and altered, I scarcely knew you?"

"I have not had the plague, so you needn't be afraid to come near me," said Dorothy, a little scornfully. "But what brings you here?"

"I have been obliged to come on business for my father. But I shall stay no longer than I can help in this dismal place. Why, it is almost like a city of the dead; grass growing in the streets, scarcely anybody going about, and those who do looking many of them most miserable objects. It's enough to give a fellow the blues."

"Then judge what it must have been to have had to stay here through it all."

"You don't mean to say you have been here ever since I took leave of you in Aldersgate Street?"

"I have never been out of London the whole time. I have been shut up as in a prison."

"How horrible! But why have you stopped on? Could you not all have gone home? Is Lady Elizabeth here too?"

The hot tears rushed into Dorothy's eyes, and she turned away to hide them.

"You don't mean to say—" began Robert, and then stopped short.

Dorothy nodded, as she tried to choke down her tears and the lump in her throat.

"What, dead!" he cried aghast, too startled and shocked to soften his expressions. "Dead of the plague?"

"Yes; and Cicely too," was the low answer in a husky voice.

The thoughtless, good-natured face of the young man was grave now, and wore an awestruck look.

"Oh, Dorothy, how dreadful! But where is Sir Richard?" He asked the question as if almost afraid to put it.

"I don't know," returned Dorothy, in despairing tones. "No word has come from him for months, and we cannot glean any tidings. Dr. Willoughby has done all he possibly could to get news of him, but all in vain. He seems to have quite disappeared. What can have happened to him or where he is, I know not. Oh, if he would but come! I have been waiting for him all this time."

"But who are you living with meanwhile?"

"I am with Dr. and Mrs. Willoughby."

"What, that Puritan fellow?"

"Yes, they are Puritans both of them, and the servant is a Puritan, and everything they have, even the very furniture is Puritan, and the clothes they wear and the way they live. It is all so ugly and plain and stiff and dull that I think I shall go out of my mind if I have to endure it much longer!" said the girl impetuously, making the most of this the first opportunity she had had of freely giving vent to her feelings to a sympathetic hearer.

"Poor Dorothy! What an awful time you must have had of it! But how came you to be there?"

"Mother had no one else to leave me with. Other people she knew had gone out of town; and she was expecting father back from day to day, so she thought it would only be for a little while that I should have to be with them. But it has gone on for nearly two months."

"Poor Dorothy!" said Robert again; his good-natured heart touched and his sympathies aroused by the picture she had drawn. "And you don't know how much longer it may go on?"

"No; if it depends on father's return. But I *must* get away! Only I don't know how to manage it. Robert, can't you help me?" cried the girl with eager looks, as the thought flashed upon her that through him she might find an opportunity for escape from her irksome surroundings. As her eye kindled and her cheek flushed with the new hope she looked more like the handsome, spirited Dorothy of old, and Robert Hay was not the man to withstand such an appeal.

"I am sure I am ready to do anything I can in the service of my fair cousin. In what way can I help you?"

"I scarcely know. I mean I hadn't formed any plan. Couldn't you take me home?" she cried, as with a sudden inspiration. "I long to go. It is no good waiting on for father. If he comes and finds me gone, he will follow me to Hurstwood; and he can't blame me, for I am sure I have waited long enough. Oh, take me home, Robert!"

"I am quite willing; but do you think they would trust you to my care?" he asked a little doubtfully, glancing, strangely enough for him, at the propriety of the step.

"If they won't give consent I will go without it," she returned impatiently.

He looked a little surprised.

"Mrs. Willoughby is not my mother," she said in answer to his look; for the thoughts of both had gone back to that day when his suggestion that she should go to the masquerade at Whitehall without her mother's consent, if she could not go with it, had met with an indignant refusal to do anything so underhand. "I don't see why she should control my actions; or why I should not do as I choose in this matter. Are you going straight back to Burnham Castle?"

"Yes, for a day or two, and then I rejoin the king. My father being unwell, I was bound to do his business for him; but I came very unwillingly, not knowing," he went on, with his old air of gallantry, "that I was to have the pleasure of meeting my fair cousin, for whose society I have been pining all this time."

"Don't stop to talk nonsense," returned Dorothy impatiently, "but just think how this thing can be managed. Should you mind going round by way of Hurstwood?"

"I am altogether at your service."

"And how could we travel?"

"I came here on horseback. Should you dislike riding on a pillion behind me? I have a serving-man with me on another horse; he would be a further protection and escort for you."

"That would do very well. And when do you go?" she asked hurriedly, in her excitement.

"Tomorrow, if possible. But," added Robert hesitatingly, as a vision rose before him of the gentle Lady Elizabeth and her watchful care over her young daughter, "I don't know whether people would say it was quite the thing for Mistress Dorothy Devereux to travel thus."

"Never mind what people may say; I don't care a straw. All I care for is to get away from this place and back to Hurstwood. If you aren't willing to help me, say so outright."

Whereupon Robert afresh declared himself her devoted servant, and made such voluble protestations of his readiness to carry out any commands she might lay upon him, that Dorothy in her impatience cut him short by asking, "When shall we start? And where shall we meet?"

"That is for you to settle. I place myself at your disposal.

Shall we meet here? It is a quiet place enough, and I and Thomas could be in waiting with the horses."

"Yes, perhaps that would do," said Dorothy after a pause. "Not that I intend to steal away secretly. I shall let them know what I am doing; but perhaps it would outrage their feelings too much if I started from their very door, in a manner of which perhaps they may not approve," she added, with a little mischievous laugh, as she pictured to herself Mrs. Willoughby's scandalized looks.

"Well, then, I will be here tomorrow about ten. We had better start as early as we can, in order to have as much daylight as possible for our journey; but I do not expect my business will be done before that hour."

Dorothy waited until dinner was over, and Dr. Willoughby had retired to his study, before she broached the subject of which her mind was so full, but which she felt would be a startling one to Mrs. Willoughby. She went straight to the point at once, not condescending to beat about the bush.

"I met my cousin, Lord Hay, this morning when I was out. He is returning tomorrow to Burnham Castle, which is not so very far from Hurstwood, and he is willing to go round that way to take me home. So by your leave I will accompany him."

Mrs. Willoughby looked up from her work with a face on which mingled feelings were depicted, of which, however, the prevailing element was blank astonishment. She could almost have thought that her companion must be talking in her sleep, or that she herself was dreaming. For a young maiden to take matters into her own hands like this, and settle things without any reference to her elders, was enough to take away her breath, and then to announce it in such a cool, determined manner, as if it was already arranged beyond dispute, and there was no need to obtain the sanction of her guardians—for in that light she and her son stood for the time being—was certainly, to say the least, not treating them with any respect or deference.

"What was it you said? I don't think I could have heard aright," she returned, casting a searching glance at the other, as if to reassure herself respecting her sanity.

Dorothy repeated her remark, but this time in a slightly defiant tone, as if preparing to do battle.

"This is very sudden, Mistress Dorothy," said the elder lady quietly, but with dignity. "And how about your father?"

"It is no good apparently to wait longer for him. I am sure I have waited quite long enough."

"But who is there at Hurstwood to receive you? Young gentlewomen cannot altogether dispense with protectors of some sort."

"There is Owen. She has lived with us all my life, and longer, and was my mother's trusted companion, and head of all the household. She has charge of everything, and sees to everything. It was all left in her hands when we came away. She will be there, and that is quite enough till father comes."

"And who is it you propose to travel with?"

"My cousin."

"I did not quite catch the name."

"Robert Hay."

"A son of the Earl of Burnham?"

"Yes, the only son."

"But this Lord Hay—I know nothing of him. Will he be a suitable protector? Is he a married man?"

Dorothy tried to repress a smile. "No, he is not married; but he is my cousin. And he has an old serving-man with him, so we shall do very well."

"And you propose to travel thus, without any female companion or attendant?" cried Mrs. Willoughby aghast.

"Why not?" said Dorothy. "I am not afraid."

"But appearances! Have you no regard for them?"

Apparently Dorothy had not, for she showed plainly that she was not disposed to let them stand in the way of her embracing this unexpected opportunity for returning home. Moreover she regarded Mrs. Willoughby's scruples as a part of her Puritanism.

All remonstrances proved vain, so far as shaking Dorothy's firm determination was concerned; and Mrs. Willoughby, having exhausted her powers of argument and persuasion, at length felt she could say no more. The headstrong maiden must have her way, and she would wash her hands of her. She had tried to fulfill Lady Elizabeth's dying request to the best of her power, and now she could no longer keep her guest against her will. She was shocked at such willfulness, while her notions of rigid propriety were scandalized by the whole proceeding; but it seemed to her that all that was left for her to do was to hope that no harm would come of it. Moreover Dorothy's pale and altered looks showed how she was pining for country air and the freedom to which she had always been accustomed, so perhaps for health's sake it would be better she should go.

"I thank you for having given me shelter for so long," Dorothy had the grace to say; but she could not bring her lips to frame anything warmer or more hearty. Whatever her faults might be, insincerity was not amongst them.

CHAPTER X

AT HURSTWOOD AGAIN

"Thou knowest what we feel,
Thou smitest, and Thou bindest up.
We look to Thee to heal!"—DORA GREENWELL

IT was a brilliant October day. The air was fresh and crisp, the sky blue and cloudless, the tints on tree and hedgerow of every shade of loveliness. To Dorothy, who had not looked for so long upon country sights, everything that met her gaze seemed to have acquired a new beauty.

Most exhilarating was it, after her long and close confinement, to find herself riding over the open country on a swift steed, every mile taking her farther from London and bringing her nearer to Hurstwood and freedom. Her spirits rose; her pale cheeks began to glow with something of their old richness of coloring; and occasionally a girlish laugh broke from her, provoked by Robert's sallies, or due merely to her sense of exultation in escaping from the restraints which had been so irksome to her.

Robert was on his best behavior. Though he had for some time now imbibed the atmosphere of Whitehall, yet he had not quite lost all sense of manliness, and felt put on his honor as it were by Dorothy's very trustfulness. He knew it arose from her ignorance of evil, from which she had been so shielded; and she should not, he said to himself, learn any from him. So he took no advantage of his position; he even refrained from his usual gallantries, and was simply friendly and good-natured, ready to fall in with Dorothy's wishes and to promote her enjoyment by every means in his power.

The two chatted merrily together as they rode along, the grave old serving-man following at a little distance behind, keeping eye and ear open, and ever on the alert to guard against any surprise or attack from highwaymen. But happily they escaped all perils by the way.

The October afternoon had closed in when they were still a good hour's ride from Hurstwood; but Dorothy wished to press on, and put aside Robert's proposal to stop for the night at an hostel in a little town through which they passed.

"We are so nearly there, let us hasten our speed, and we shall soon accomplish the distance that yet remains," she said in her impatience.

"But we have to consider our steeds," said Robert, patting his horse's neck. "However, I think Sultan can do it with a little coaxing, and since you wish it we will try."

Consequently when they reached the house and summoned the inmates to open to them, the latter were much startled by such sounds at such an unwonted hour. But when at length the door, the hinges of which seemed to have grown rusty, had been cautiously opened, and the old butler, holding a lamp in his hand and closely followed by Owen, peered out into the darkness, astonishment was not lessened on perceiving that it was a gay young cavalier with a maiden behind him on a pillion, who was demanding admittance.

"I don't know your voice, sir," said the man in doubtful tones.

"Lord Hay," shouted the young man, thinking the other was deaf, "and I have brought Mistress Dorothy Devereux home."

Dorothy at the same moment exclaimed with a laugh, "Why, Owen, don't you know me? You needn't look at me as if I were a ghost. Come, help me down, William, and then you will both see it is really myself."

"Mistress Dorothy! who would ever have thought of seeing you coming like this—after dark, and with no word beforehand to tell us to expect you; and when we haven't had tidings of you for months. But I'm sure I give you a hearty welcome, and I'm right glad to see you, my dear," said faithful Owen, as Dorothy, having dismounted, rushed to her and threw her arms about her. And then, overcome by emotion and the sense of desolation which came suddenly upon her in this sad home-coming, she laid her head down on Owen's shoulder with a smothered sob.

"My poor lamb!" murmured the latter, her own eyes moist with tears. "My poor dear!" and she folded the girl in a warm motherly embrace. She had known her all her life, had been a

"I HAVE BROUGHT MISTRESS DOROTHY DEVEREUX HOME."

sort of second mother to her from her birth, and the familiar endearments of childhood had never been dropped on either side.

"Farewell, Dorothy, I must be off," said Robert, who had also dismounted. "I congratulate you on having safely accomplished your escape, and now I must bid you adieu."

"Thank you very much for your help. It was very good-natured of you, and but for you I don't know how I should have got here. I am very much obliged to you," she said frankly and heartily.

"I am always at your service—your faithful servant," he returned in a low tone meant for her ear alone.

Then, after refusing Owen's hospitable offer of a bed for the night, and taking another farewell of Dorothy, he remounted his horse and rode away.

"Come to my room, Mistress Dorothy," said Owen. "You must be tired and cold after your long ride, and I have a nice fire there, but naturally there is none in the larger rooms, which have been shut up so long."

"So much the better. I always liked your snug little parlor."

And there, seated beside the fire on a low stool, leaning against Owen's knee, and from time to time feeling the soft touch of her hand stroking her hair with a sympathetic gesture, Dorothy related something of the sad events of the last few months.

It was painful to tell of all she had gone through, and yet it was soothing to find how deep had been Owen's attachment to her beloved mistress, as well as to her sweet young daughter; and eagerly did she listen to every detail Dorothy could bring herself to give. Letters were for the most part rare things in those days, and news travelled slowly into the country, so that beyond the bare rumor of the death of Lady Elizabeth and her younger daughter of the plague, Owen knew nothing.

"What a comfort Dr. Willoughby must have been to my dear mistress in her hour of dire need!" remarked Owen with moistened eyes, as she listened to Dorothy's recital. "But for him there would have been nobody with her. How his presence must have soothed and helped her. I know how much she valued him. She told me more than once how helpful she had found his preaching during that first visit to London, and how she looked forward to hearing him again. Oh, I feel as if I must bless him all my life for his goodness to my beloved Lady Elizabeth!" said the warm-hearted faithful creature, as she wiped away the tears that could not be kept back.

Dorothy's conscience smote her. How ungrateful she had been! She had never once thought of thanking Dr. Willoughby for all he had done for her mother; but Owen's words seemed to place it all in a new light.

"And how good it was of them, Mistress Dorothy, to take you to their home straight away from a plague-stricken house! It is not many who would have done so. And if they had not had compassion on you, what would have become of you? You would have been desolate indeed."

Again Dorothy's conscience smote her. Instead of being thankful to them, she had been proud and rebellious and discontented, and most ungrateful. She saw it now as if revealed by a flash of lightning, and the pang of shame it caused was most unpleasant to experience.

The next morning when Dorothy was able by daylight to gaze upon the old familiar scenes, it was with mingled feelings. She knew now how much she loved the old place, the home of her childhood; and never had it looked so beautiful to her as on this bright October morning, as she stepped forth into the open air, and saw the sunbeams glancing on the varied foliage of the stately oaks and elms, the beeches and the chestnuts, on the dark green of the tall straight firs, or the dull red of the many-gabled old house. She feasted her eyes upon it all, enjoying at the same time the pure fresh breeze which played upon her cheeks, and brought with it a delicious sense of health instead of the fear of infection.

She hurried from one spot to another, feeling as if each inanimate object were a friend from whom she had long been parted, and who now met her with a welcome. Had it been possible, she felt she could have taken each in her arms in a warm embrace.

But after a time she found herself pacing along the terrace walk, when suddenly back came the memory of that sunny morning when in the company of her mother and Cicely she had walked up and down discussing the wonderful news that had just been imparted to her of the projected visit to London. Oh! how happy she had been that day; how high her heart had beat with anticipation of all the pleasure in store for her!

And now how changed was everything; those dear ones gone never to return, and she left alone and desolate. How could the place be henceforth anything to her without them? It was the mother, with her heart full of unfailing love and tenderness, that had made it "home," and not the mere walls. They were left, but were now only like the bare skeleton which has been forsaken by the living spirit which once inhabited it.

She sank down on a bench in a side alley where she was concealed from view, and gave way to a perfect passion of weeping, as wave after wave of mournful tender recollections swept over her, until she felt as if her heart would break. Everything on which her eye fell called up some painful reminiscence; each sweet country sound seemed to recall the voices that now were silenced for ever; every plant and tree and flower around showing signs of vigorous life while their life had gone out, seemed an offence in this altered mood. For the dear hands which had trained so many of them were now still in the grave; the dear eyes which had rejoiced in their beauty would look on them no more. All appeared cold and silent and unmindful of her in her woe; no voice from them could reach her in her agony; alone she must suffer, and comfortless too, for there was none by to comfort.

Ah, but Dr. Willoughby had told her there was One. "As one whom his mother comforteth so will I comfort you," seemed wafted to her on the breeze. She remembered in what gentle sympathetic tones the voice of the young Puritan divine had spoken the words, and how he had sought to comfort her, or rather to point her to the true source of comfort.

But she had given no heed, or next to none. She had been then in a proud, hard, rebellious mood. Now softer feelings had been aroused. She was beginning to look upon her conduct and that of her late host and hostess in a very different light, and the more ashamed she felt of her own behavior, the more noble and generous and forbearing did theirs appear. She even found herself wishing, in the sense of utter loneliness that had come upon her, that she could again listen to Dr. Willoughby's words, and learn to act upon them; that she might find the peace and happiness which he seemed to enjoy, and which he said might be her portion too if she would seek it.

After a time Owen came in search of her, feeling the "poor child," as she mentally called her, ought not to be left too much to herself and her own sad musings. She proposed a walk down the avenue, to which Dorothy gladly assented.

"Let us go into the woods too; they must be looking so glorious in their autumn dress, and it was too dark last evening for me to see them in their beauty.

"Has Eugene been home all this time?" asked Dorothy, as they sauntered along paths carpeted with russet and gold.

"No; we have neither seen nor heard anything of him. But he was not likely to come. What should bring him?"

"What indeed? If he scarcely cared to come even when mother was here, it is not likely he would wish it now. I have not seen him since he went off with the court, months ago."

As they emerged from the woods and came upon the highway a stranger on horseback crossed their path. He wore the low-crowned, broad-brimmed hat of the Cavaliers ornamented with a mass of feathers, beneath which was an enormous periwig, according to the fashion of the times. His doublet and cloak were trimmed with rich gold lace; in fact, everything about him showed that he spared no expense over his dress. He started, and then lifted his hat to Dorothy with a prolonged stare, as if to proclaim himself so astonished at coming thus unexpectedly upon such rare beauty in these secluded parts as to lose his presence of mind.

"Who is that horrid man?" asked Dorothy as soon as he was out of hearing. "How rudely he stared! did you notice it?"

"Yes, I did. It isn't the way a gentleman ought to behave. And there he is looking back. Let us turn, Mistress Dorothy, and go another way."

"Do you know who he is?"

"Yes. It is Mr. Crawford of Wharton Park."

"I thought Mr. Crawford was quite an old man."

"The old gentleman was his father, and he died a few months ago, when this one came back from abroad, where he had always lived, to take possession. They say he had always been a bad son, and the father meant to disinherit him, but he died suddenly, and the son has succeeded to the property. And a very fine one it is. They say Mr. Crawford is one of the richest landowners about here."

"However that may be, he is a very horrid man, I am sure. He has such a low, dissipated look."

"You are quite right. He is no gain to the neighborhood, but quite the reverse. I am glad he lives no nearer than he does."

"How far off is Wharton Park?"

"It is about ten or twelve miles from here, I believe."

"Ah, well, then, he won't trouble us much," remarked Dorothy lightly, dismissing the subject from her mind, not how this stranger was destined to cross her path again.

"Shall we go into the village, Owen, and have a look at some of the people?" said Dorothy abruptly after a pause.

"I think you had better not, Mistress Dorothy, dear; at least not just for the present, until they have got accustomed to the idea," returned Owen hesitatingly.

"What idea?" asked the girl, looking surprised.

"Well, you see, the people about here are dreadfully afraid of any one coming from London; and no wonder, when you think of it, as the plague has been carried in that way into the country in more than one instance."

This was a new idea to Dorothy, and by no means an agreeable one. It is not pleasant to feel oneself shunned by others. She gave a little toss of her head, and her color rose as she said, "Oh, if that is the case, I will not trouble them with my presence. And perhaps," she added hotly, as she started away from Owen's side, "you are afraid of me yourself, and would rather I did not come near you."

"No," returned Owen quietly, "I am not afraid. My dear mistress taught me that we are all in God's hands, and He directs these things. All we have to see to is to do the duty He sets us, and leave the rest to Him. And my part is to welcome back, my dear lady's motherless daughter, which I do with all my heart, my dear Mistress Dorothy. Right glad I am to have you here again."

Mollified by these words, Dorothy gradually lessened the distance she had placed between herself and her companion, remarking, "Dr. and Mrs. Willoughby were not afraid to take me straight from the very house in which the plague was, and when it was raging at its height. Whereas now I have not come in contact with any infected person all this time, for no one in Mrs. Willoughby's house took it."

"Yes, my dear, I know; but you mustn't be angry with the people, even if their fears are foolish. In a few days, when they see no harm has come of it, they will be accustomed to the idea, and forget all about it; but just at present it is as well perhaps to keep away from them."

"Very stupid of them!" said Dorothy a little wrathfully, con-
trasting in her mind the conduct of Dr. and Mrs. Willoughby,
very much to the advantage of the latter.

CHAPTER XI

SILENT WORK

"Lord, dwell within my heart, and fill
   Its emptiness;
Set Thou its hope above the reach
   Of earthliness;
Baptise its love, through suffering,
   Into Thine own,
And work in me a faith that rests
   On Christ alone."—MARY STONE

DOROTHY'S life for the next two months was quiet and un-
eventful. Owen was her chief companion, and under her
guidance she was beginning to try to imitate her mother in
ministering to and caring for the poor around. More and more
was the desire growing upon her to follow in that sweet mother's footsteps, and to take for hers the God she had served and
loved.

She had plenty of time for quiet musings, either as she
paced up and down the terrace walk, which was hallowed by
memories of many a talk she and that dear mother had had
there together in the days gone by,—or as she sat in her chamber by the oriel window gazing at the extensive prospect it
commanded of hill and dale; the foreground beautified with
stately woods which clothed the slope of the valley on one side,
while on the other were the billowy downs with their rounded
outlines, and again farther off the soft misty distance with its
lovely purple tints and endless suggestions of beauty to the
imaginative mind.

She was very fond of sitting there on a bright sunny day,
letting her eyes roam over the landscape, which, familiar as
it was, yet showed constant variety and changes, according to
the lights and shadows thrown upon it. On dull rainy days,

however, she preferred the fireside and Owen's company; but on the fine ones she liked to ensconce herself in a low seat near her favorite window, where she knew she would be undisturbed; and on such occasions a little Bible might often have been seen lying open on her lap.

She was learning many a lesson in the peaceful quiet of her present life. The enforced solitude was good for her, now that her thoughts and longings were beginning to turn into fresh channels; and as she sat alone many a long-forgotten word of her mother's—which when spoken by the dear voice now for ever silent had been allowed to pass unheeded—came back to her as a precious legacy, to be stored in her memory and pondered over; while often there rose before her mind's eye the picture of Cicely lifting up her joyous face from her book as she told of the happiness that loving God brought with it.

And now Dorothy was seeking to know the same Divine Friend, was slowly but surely yielding herself to the same Divine Master, asking Him to make and keep her His. The proud heart was being subdued; the coldness was melting away, like snow under the sun's rays, as she read and pondered over the love of Him who had laid down His life for her, but whom she had hitherto despised and rejected.

The honesty and truthfulness of her nature prevented her from trying to gloss over even to herself the transgressions and willful wrong-doing of the past; she called it all by its right name, she saw and confessed how she had hardened herself against the good, and had deliberately turned to the world and its pleasures, seeking her portion there. But all that time—and it touched her heart to think of it—He whom she was rejecting had been patiently standing beside her, calling to her again and again, though she had still refused to listen. And so He had sent her that crushing sorrow, because He had seen that nothing less—nothing short of that bitter feeling of utter loneliness and emptiness—would avail to bring her back to Him.

She had been like one wandering in the far country, trying to satisfy herself with the husks that could not possibly stay the cravings of her soul-hunger; and weary and bitter had the struggle been. Whereas she might all that time have been feasting in the King's palace upon the bread provided for the King's children, if she had not been so foolish, so willful, so blinded. She had indeed been as a sheep going astray; but now—now at length after all her wanderings, she was seeking to find her way back to the fold. Would the Good Shepherd receive her and open to her—who had gone so very far astray—the door of the sheepfold? Ah, yes; why should she doubt it? She turned over the leaves of her Bible until she came to the verse, "Him that cometh to me I will in no wise cast out;" and she took the words in simple trust as spoken to herself, and rested herself upon them.

Her nature was too reserved to allow of her pouring out what was in her heart to Owen, but the latter was observant, and perceived the change that was stealing over her the growing gentleness and thoughtfulness, the expression of rest which was beginning to replace the look of restless misery which had so often dwelt on her face when she first returned. Her quick sight often told her that the dark eyes had been shedding tears, but she could see they were tears that were bringing relief and healing to the overburdened heart, and with wisdom and tact the good Owen, without seeking to force the confidence of the other, would often try to turn the conversation into channels which she hoped might be helpful and comforting.

And so in silence and quiet the work in Dorothy's heart went forward and deepened. Those were blessed days for her. It was as if she had been all this time a weary traveler in a barren desert, parched with thirst and like to die, without a drop of water within reach; and now a boundless, inexhaustible river had opened at her feet, at which she could quench her thirst, and of which she was free to drink again and again deeper and yet deeper draughts from its life-giving streams. Very sweet were the waters to her taste; sweeter than anything of which she could have conceived. And yet they had been there all the time, only she had shut her eyes to them, and so had been forced to endure that terrible thirst. How foolish she had been!

But now she had found that which could satisfy. And now, in her longing to do something for the Friend and Master whom she had hitherto slighted, she delighted in trying, under Owen's guidance, to make herself of some use to those around, and would go to read to one or make a warm garment for another; it mattered not much what it was, she thought, so long as it was some little act of service which He could accept.

CHAPTER XII

UNWELCOME GUESTS

"The tempter hath his legions; earth is trod
By their hard feet imprinting sin and care."
—E. Brine

THIS peaceful state of things was interrupted when Christmas came, bringing with it most unexpectedly Eugene and a party of his friends. Seeking for some novelty in their round of pleasure and dissipation, the whim had seized them to try what country life could produce in the way of attractions.

They were a riotous, noisy set, and filled the old Hall with strangely unwonted sounds. Much to Dorothy's disgust, she found that Mr. Crawford made one of the guests. The dislike she had conceived for him on the occasion of their first meeting only increased upon further acquaintance. She felt a sort of loathing towards the man, an unaccountable shrinking from him; and involuntarily contrasted his bold looks and dissipated aspect with the purity and nobleness of a certain face which not unfrequently arose unbidden before her mind's eye.

Mr. Crawford on his side, in spite of all absence of encouragement, seemed determined to prosecute the acquaintance, and pursued her with attentions which were anything but welcome. He would take no repulse, would not even see that one was meant; either because he was too obtuse, or that the good opinion he entertained of his own charms and advantages was too profound to allow him to perceive that others did not always estimate him at his own valuation.

Annoyed by his persistence, Dorothy tried more and more to withdraw from the company of her brother's friends, and take refuge in Owen's room, where she could at least enjoy peace and quiet. But this did not meet with Eugene's approval, and he took her to task for it, insisting that she should grace his table with her presence, and perform the part of lady of the house, winding up by saying, in an irritated tone, "I will not have you put a slight upon my guests by absenting yourself as you do."

"If you wish for my company, you should choose guests who would behave as gentlemen, and not try to take liberties—like Mr. Crawford, for instance. When he is gone, I shall not mind so much."

"He is not going; and look here, Dorothy, I will not have you uncivil to him," said Eugene, in an angry, almost a threatening tone. "I have noticed your treatment of him, keeping yourself aloof, just as if he was not fit to be spoken to; but let me tell you he is one of the richest men about here, and a catch for any girl."

These last words sent the hot color into Dorothy's cheeks and an indignant light into her eyes.

"I don't want to 'catch' anybody; and I care not whether he is rich or poor. He is a bold, bad man, and I do not wish to have anything to do with him."

"Now, Dorothy, I am not going to stand any nonsense of this sort. He has it in his power to be very useful to me. And any other girl would feel flattered that a man like that should pay her any attention."

"Oh, Eugene," burst from Dorothy, "what would our mother have felt had she heard you talking so! What a change must have come over you in these last few years, if you can be content to associate with men like that, and can even bring them to the house which has been hallowed by her sweet presence! It seems to me a sort of profanation of the place which was her home to have all this noise and rioting going on."

"What a change must have come over you," retorted Eugene, "that you should be so prudish! Have you turned into a Puritan outright?"

"No," calmly returned Dorothy; "but I do not forget our mother, and I want to do and be what she would have had me, had she been here. Oh, Eugene, are you forgetting her quite?" pleaded the girl, tears filling her large dark eyes as she realized, in a manner she had never done till that moment, how very far her brother had drifted from the high standard of honor and purity that had ever been set before them by Lady Elizabeth. How much lower would he sink? Oh, was there nothing she could do to stop him in his downward course?

But he turned away impatiently, refusing to be softened.

"I can't think," remarked Dorothy, after retailing this conversation to Owen, "why Eugene makes such a point of my being civil to Mr. Crawford, of all people,—the very man I dislike most of all. He said nothing about any of his other guests."

Owen had her suspicions, but thought it best to keep them to herself, at any rate for the present.

"I shall be heartily glad when they are all gone," she said. "I suppose they learn those free manners at court, where, I have heard, all kind of evil goes on; but they don't seem to me fit company for you, Mistress Dorothy, and I would fain keep you out of their way altogether if I could. I don't know what my dear mistress would have said to these goings-on; and oh, how sad it would have made her to see the young master so altered for the worse! It is very grievous."

"And I am sure he is not happy," rejoined Dorothy, "I have never known him so irritable and easily put out of temper. He used to be good-natured enough, and kind, and brotherly. But now—oh, he is so different!" she added sadly. "I quite feel like you—I shall be glad when they are gone."

The next morning, under the impression that the whole party had set off to join the hunt, and with a sense of relief that for the present they were well out of the way, Dorothy felt free to roam out of doors, to enjoy the bright sunshine with which they were favored that day. There had been a white frost the night before, and the sparkling crystals still lay scattered thickly in the shade, decorating with their delicate tracery leaf and stem and blade of grass, imparting to them a new and exquisite beauty.

Owen was to join her in a short time, when they were to visit the village in company. While awaiting her Dorothy sauntered from one favorite haunt to another, not, however, going very far from the house.

She had just turned into the lime-tree walk, when she became aware of footsteps behind her, and looking round to see if it were Owen, she perceived Mr. Crawford following her. Startled and annoyed, she tried to quicken her footsteps, in hopes of escaping from him, but a few of his hasty strides soon enabled him to overtake her.

"Whither away in such haste, Mistress Dorothy? Stay a moment, I pray you."

"I want to go indoors to rejoin Owen; she will be waiting for me."

"Then let her wait, I have something to say to you."

But Dorothy, taking no notice of his request, only walked the faster.

"Nay, Mistress Dorothy, you shall stay and give me a hearing," said her unwelcome companion, laying a detaining hand upon her arm.

Dorothy indignantly tried to shake it off. "Leave me, sir, and suffer me to go my own way," she said haughtily.

"Not until you have listened to me," he returned, again laying his hand on her arm. "You do not know what it is I have to say to you."

"Whatever it is, it can wait for some other time. I am in a hurry now, let me go."

"I will not," he said, angry at being thus treated by the girl whom he was about so to honor as to make her the offer of his hand.

"Then make haste and say what you have to say, and let me go."

Any other man might have felt this an awkward commencement, but Mr. Crawford, nothing discomposed, went on to explain his views, only, however, to meet with a decided refusal from Dorothy, couched too in somewhat unflattering terms.

Too much amazed to believe her in earnest,—for was it possible that any girl in her sober senses could refuse him, Mr. Crawford of Wharton Park?—he continued to urge his suit, but only with the effect of exasperating Dorothy more and more, as she struggled to free herself from him: for he had planted himself right in front of her, and had taken hold of both her wrists, which he held firmly, fixing meanwhile his bold admiring gaze upon the handsome face, which looked handsomer than ever with its flashing eyes and flushed cheeks. But there was that in her which held him at bay in spite of all.

"If you do not let me go this instant I will call for help!"

"There is no one to hear you. The men are working in a distant part of the grounds."

Her heart sank with the sense of her helplessness, and she could only devoutly hope that Owen, finding she did not return, might come in search of her.

"I will not take your refusal," he went on impetuously.

"Young maidens don't know their own minds. I am not accustomed to be thwarted in anything, and I generally accomplish my purpose. Moreover, your brother has agreed to my proposals."

It was a strange way of wooing, and not likely to be very successful with a girl of Dorothy's spirit.

"Eugene has nothing whatever to do with the matter!" she returned with a touch of scorn. "I certainly should not ask his permission, or allow him to choose for me. Ah, there is Owen calling," she exclaimed joyfully. "Let me go, sir, and I beg you will consider my answer a final one."

Perceiving Owen at a little distance bearing down upon them, Mr. Crawford thought fit to release Dorothy, and turned away with a muttered oath and an ominous scowl upon his face.

Thus freed, Dorothy flew to Owen's side, and passing her arm through hers almost dragged her towards the house, half sobbing in an undertone in explanation of her conduct, "Wait till we get indoors, and I will tell you all. Come quickly, oh, do make haste!"

Having reached the shelter of Owen's room, Dorothy sank down on a low seat trembling with excitement, and with two bright spots of red in her cheeks.

"That horrid man has actually been asking me to marry him! He quite frightens me; he looks so fierce and so determined to have his own way. But he can't make me do it against my will, can he? Oh, Owen, you must save me from him!"

"You had better keep with me, Mistress Dorothy, dear, and not go out alone even in the grounds as long as he is here. Happily, this is the last day, as they are all to depart tomorrow," said Owen soothingly.

For the rest of the day Dorothy stoutly refused to leave Owen's side, and firmly declined to join the party at supper time, even though Eugene came to fetch her, and showed much vexation at her persistency, which he called obstinacy.

CHAPTER XIII

THE SECRET CHAMBER

"Too high to mate with an unequal soul."

Epic of Hades

THAT night, some little time after Dorothy had gone to bed, and when she was just on the point of falling asleep, Owen quietly entered her room, deliberately closing the door behind her.

Dorothy started up. "What is the matter, Owen? What makes you come at such an hour, and with such a grave face too?"

"Lie down, Mistress Dorothy, dear; and I pray you speak softly. I would not that any one should overhear us talking."

"Who is there to overhear us? We have this corridor to ourselves."

"Yes; but one never knows who may be about," returned the other, coming to the bedside and standing over Dorothy.

"What have you to tell me?" asked the latter.

"Well," said Owen hesitatingly, "I am afraid there is a little plot against you. After I thought every one had gone to bed, I went into the withdrawing-room to bolt and make secure a window that Marjory had omitted to fasten. I went in by the door from the south parlor, and through the other door, which leads into the hall, and which stood a little ajar, I heard voices in conversation, showing that some of the gentlemen were still sitting there over their wine. I should have taken no notice, but that I suddenly heard your name, and found that the young master and Mr. Crawford were talking about you. The latter was telling how you had rejected his proposals, whereupon your brother seemed much vexed, and vowed he would make you behave very differently."

"How shameful of him!" exclaimed Dorothy indignantly.

"He who ought to be my protector. What can have come over him?"

"I fancy from what they were saying that Mr. Eugene has been getting deep into debt through gambling and in other ways, and is in some great difficulty which he cannot get out of without a large sum of money, and Mr. Crawford has promised to give him the needed help and free him from his dilemma provided he carries off you as his prize. He seemed to be stipulating that on that condition alone would he give any help."

"Then that accounts for Eugene's wishing me to have the man. I could not understand why he should."

"It is a disgraceful affair, Mistress Dorothy, and I would not let you know anything about it, but that we must take some steps to hinder it."

"Hinder it! You don't think I am going to consent?"

"No, not willingly, but they were talking of using force," returned Owen reluctantly.

Dorothy's cheek grew pale. "So Eugene wants to sell his sister, that he may save himself from disgrace! One would think he must be mad to be willing to consent to anything so base and mean! Who could have believed it of him?"

"I felt bound for your sake," pursued Owen, "to hear all I could, so I remained where I was, concealed behind the door, which of course they imagined was shut. And no doubt they thought every one was gone to bed, or they would have been yet more cautious in their tones. Still, they spoke low, but I have quick ears."

"And what did you hear?" asked Dorothy.

"The plan they were making is this. Tomorrow Master Eugene is to persuade you to take a little farewell walk with him down the avenue, and then he is to beguile you into one of the roads through the woods where you will be screened from observation. There a hackney coach driven by Mr. Crawford's own man is to be in waiting; you are to be placed inside and borne off to Wharton Hall, Mr. Crawford thinking that then there will be no further difficulty. And he is at once to send for a clergyman to come and marry you."

Dorothy's eyes dilated with horror as she listened.

"What a wicked plot! And to think that my own brother should be a party to it! Oh, that father were here to protect me! Owen, what can be done? Let me escape from the place this very night. But where can I go? Oh, that London were not so far of!"

At that moment Dr. and Mrs. Willoughby's peaceful abode seemed like a very haven of rest, where safety and shelter were to be found.

"I have a plan, Mistress Dorothy," said Owen, bending over the girl, and speaking in a whisper. "You have never heard of there being a secret chamber in the house, have you?"

"No, never!" cried Dorothy eagerly. "Is there really one?"

"Yes; but only Lady Elizabeth and I knew of it beside Sir Richard. The secret has always been most carefully guarded; but during the Commonwealth, when the Parliament turned so many of the clergy out of their livings, my lady sheltered one of them there for some time; a godly man he was. But I must not stay to speak of him. Mistress Dorothy, I can trust you with the secret, can I not?"

"Of course you can."

"You promise to keep it faithfully, and not let the fact become known through carelessness?"

"I promise," said Dorothy, shortly and decisively.

"Well, I thought that in the morning early, before any one is about, I would take you there; and there you could remain until they are all safely away from the place. They will never find you, search as they may, and it seems an easy way of getting out of the difficulty."

"Capital!" cried Dorothy. "How completely we shall frustrate their scheme! And how clever of you to have found it out, and to have thought of this plan!"

"I will go now and make a few preparations. I will put some meat and milk and bread there, so that if I am unable to come to you, you will not be quite without food. For one does not know how the matter will go," added Owen to herself.

Dorothy looked as if she found the affair exciting.

"Let me come with you and see my hiding-place," she said, springing up.

"No; remain where you are, and get some sleep if you can—you may rely upon my coming for you in plenty of time. And when they fail to find you I trust they will simply go off, and there will be an end of the matter. I do not imagine your imprisonment need last more than the day, or even a few hours."

"But, Owen, what shall you say to Eugene? He will suspect

you of having a hand in the matter, and I am afraid his vexation will fall on you."

"If so, I dare say I shall be able to bear it. I shall merely say I have sent you out of the way, not thinking the present company good for you."

"And if they insist on knowing where you have sent me?"

"That I shall refuse to tell them."

True to her word, Owen reappeared, long before the revelers of the previous night had left their couches, and after assisting Dorothy to make a hasty toilet, conducted her to her place of concealment.

The latter's indignation at the conduct of her brother and his friend alternated with amusement at the novel position in which she found herself. The revelation of the fact that there was a secret chamber in the house, of which she had hitherto known nothing, interested her greatly, and she was all impatience to see for herself where it could be situated, and how it could have been so cleverly contrived as always to have escaped observation.

Owen, cautioning her to be silent and to move noiselessly, led her along the corridor, down the stairs, and through one or two narrow passages until they had come to the older and almost disused portion of the building. Then they ascended a steep stairway which led, as Dorothy had always supposed, simply to some lumber rooms, where as children they had sometimes played at hide-and-seek, or had woven romances as to what in the days gone by might have taken place within those walls, which, long ago, before the restoration of the house and the addition of the new wing and front, had formed the principal portion of the dwelling.

In some of the rooms old and faded tapestry still hung on the walls, which were of unusual thickness, as the deep embrasures of the windows proved. The flooring showed signs of being worm-eaten, and in places was almost crumbling with age. Antique pieces of furniture stood in some of the rooms, while others had been cleared out and appropriated as a place for storing apples and other winter fruits.

In the largest apartment, which had once been the principal bed-chamber, Owen, putting aside the tapestry in a corner near the ponderous old four-post bedstead which still stood there, pressed her finger upon a certain spot in a panel of the wainscoting, which immediately sprang back. Stooping down they passed through the aperture, when the panel was carefully replaced.

Dorothy found herself in a short dark passage or landing. A few steps farther on Owen unlocked the door of the place of concealment. It was a small closet or room taken in a great measure out of the thickness of the walls, and lighted only by small narrow slits in the outer walls, something like loopholes, for a window might have betrayed its existence; a little table stood there, two or three chairs, a small couch, and one or two other trifling articles of furniture.

"Why, it is quite cozy," exclaimed Dorothy. "Anyone might be comfortable enough here. But there is another door."

Owen opened it, and Dorothy passing through found herself standing at the head of a narrow secret staircase.

"And where does this lead?" she asked eagerly.

"To an underground passage, which comes up by a sort of trap door in the woods near the old well, which you know was stopped up long ago. You remember how thick the trees and bushes are there? They have been planted so purposely, to form a screen. It certainly is a very secure hiding-place. It was contrived, so my lady said, at the time of the Wars of the Roses, or at any rate it was made good use of then by the master of the house; and again in the time of Queen Mary, when some of the family had embraced the true faith, and were in danger of being led to the stake, they escaped by concealing themselves here for some length of time."

"They little thought that one day a forlorn damsel would come to take refuge here from the pursuit of a lover," said Dorothy laughing; "not that that is the right term to apply to him, for it is impossible that he can care a straw about me. It is just some passing whim, and because he is thwarted, to which he says he has never been accustomed, he is the more determined to have his own way."

Owen, as she looked at the bright face before her in all its frank youthful beauty and freshness, felt it not so very wonderful that even a man like Mr. Crawford should wish to call her his own.

"I hope you will come and keep me company as much as you can during my imprisonment; and I want to hear more stories about the people who have been concealed here," said Dorothy.

"I must not be here too much, lest I should be missed, and have all the household searching after me. No; I had better be on the spot to throw them off the scent. You will remain here patiently till I come for you, won't you, Mistress Dorothy, dear? And see, I have put your embroidery frame here, so that you can amuse yourself with that; and there is also a book or two."

Some hours passed, and Dorothy began to get tired of her confinement. She wondered much what was going forward below, and strained her ears to catch any sounds. But few could penetrate her retreat, and those only from without.

At last she fancied she heard faintly in the distance the trampling of horses' hoofs, and hoped that it meant that the party, having given up the search as useless, were all departing. Not yet, however, did Owen appear. There was another spell of tedious, impatient expectation on Dorothy's part, before the door at length opened to admit Owen.

"I had to wait until I could steal up unperceived," she remarked. "I dare say the time has seemed long to you."

"Yes, it has appeared an age. But are they gone now, and safely out of the way?" asked Dorothy eagerly.

"I hope so. They have departed, at any rate, and I trust they will not return."

"Eugene cannot, for he received a summons back to court yesterday, so he is bound to present himself, and the same with his other two friends. I thought Mr. Crawford too had to be there."

"I think he said he should follow them, as he had a day or two longer at his disposal."

"And what did they say, Owen? Do you think they really did intend doing what you thought?"

"Yes, I quite believe they would have done it had we not circumvented them."

"Was Eugene very vexed about it?—at not being able to carry out his purpose, I mean?"

"Yes; he was dreadfully angry when you could nowhere be found. But I don't know which of the two appeared the more put out. However, I got rid of them at last, and much I trust it is for good."

"So do I. And I hope I shall never come across that man again. Once I was so foolish as to like the flattery I got from the young gallants in London," said Dorothy, a little flush of shame mounting into her cheek as she made the confession; "and I remember saying one might as well be as ugly as a scarecrow if one never went beyond Hurstwood, as there was nobody here to notice whether one was good-looking or not. But I shouldn't talk like that now. I know better. Mr. Crawford has cured me of any nonsense of that sort. Much better to be as ugly as a scarecrow," she added laughing, "than to be persecuted and annoyed by unwelcome attentions."

"Yes, my dear, good looks are not always a safe possession, or one to be coveted. People are often happier without, and are saved a good many temptations. But I must acquit you of any blame in this matter. If you had encouraged or trifled with him, I should have felt that you had brought all this upon yourself, but you have behaved as a discreet young gentlewoman should do."

"Well, now I hope all is over, and we shall go back to our former peaceful life."

"Only for a time you had better not go out of doors alone— until we hear for certain that Mr. Crawford is safely out of the neighborhood."

CHAPTER XIV

ANXIOUS VIGILS

"One by one thy duties wait thee;
Let thy whole strength go to each."

ADELAIDE PROCTOR

WHERE is Mistress Owen?" asked Dorothy of a serving-maid a day or two later, when on descending from her chamber in the morning she failed to find the other waiting to greet her as usual.

"She is in bed. She finds herself too unwell to rise. But she bade me say she will doubtless be better soon, and she begs you not to trouble about her. She would rather you did not go to her."

"As if I should leave her all to herself," was Dorothy's response, as she at once turned to go up stairs to Owen's apartment.

"Nay, Mistress Dorothy, she prayed you not to visit her for the present," said the maid interposing. "She charged me to do all I could to hinder you from entering her chamber."

"But why should I not go? and why do you look at me so oddly, Betty? Is there anything particular the matter?"

"Oh, I don't know," returned the girl in a nervous manner, "I'm sure I hope it's not the plague or the small-pox, or any of those dreadful things."

"I hope so too," said Dorothy gravely, as after pausing for a moment she turned to pursue her way up stairs.

"You are never going nigh her surely, Mistress Dorothy!" exclaimed the maid, who thought the suggestions she had thrown out would have effectually deterred her young mistress from venturing near the room. "I should have thought you would have been scared at the idea of small-pox. I know I wouldn't go nigh her."

"I must go and see how she is, and what can be done for her," quietly answered Dorothy. "It would be very unkind to leave her all alone when she is ill. And you are a foolish maid, Betty, to take fright so easily. It may be only just a headache, or some other ailment that will pass off in a day or two. I saw she was not well yesterday."

Dorothy found Owen with flushed face and heavy looks; and to even her inexperienced eyes it appeared evident that this was more than a temporary indisposition.

"Mistress Dorothy, dear, I sent a message to pray you not to come near me," said Owen, evidently distressed by her presence.

"But why should I not come? I want to see how you are, and know what is the matter with you."

"I am afraid I am going to be ill, and I would rather you kept away, in case it should be anything infectious."

"But I am not afraid, so you mustn't say anything more against my being here."

"But I think I know what is the matter with me. I have nursed others in the same complaint, and can tell the symptoms, and I would not have you exposed to the risk of infection for the world."

"What do you think it is?" asked Dorothy. "Is it small-pox?"

"I fear me it is," answered Owen; "and so now, Mistress Dorothy, I pray you leave me."

"Nay, if it be that, there is the more reason I should stay with you, for I know how terrified many are of smallpox, and perhaps the maids may refuse to come near you. Then you will have to put up with me. Besides, have you not yourself taught me," added Dorothy with a smile, "that the only thing we need concern ourselves about is to do the duty God sets us, and leave the rest to Him? That was what you said when I came back from London, and you did not know but that I was bringing the plague with me. I am going to follow your example. I think this is my duty—to nurse one who has been so true and faithful a friend to me and mine. So it is no use your saying anything more about it; for my mind is made up, and it must be bad for you to talk too much. And now I shall send for the doctor, and hear what he says."

Owen gave a pathetic glance at the handsome face, which had never looked so beautiful as it did at that moment, with its expression of high resolve mingled with tenderness and self-devotion; but she did not give utterance to the pain it caused her to think of the possibility of that fair face being seamed and marked and marred by the ravages of the dread disease which small-pox was at that time.

The doctor when he came confirmed Owen's suspicions, and inwardly marveled much at the courage and fearlessness of the young gentlewoman who seemed to have installed herself as chief nurse.

"I'm sure I hope she won't take it," he said to himself as he pursued his homeward way. "It would be a thousand pities if such a face as that were spoiled. What a fine creature she is! and how noble of her to sacrifice herself for the waiting woman!"

As Dorothy had suspected, it no sooner became known that Owen was attacked by small-pox than some of the more timid among the servants actually fled in terror, while others refused to come near the sick room. In those days small-pox was a terrible scourge, and intensely dreaded; while people perhaps gave way the more to foolish fears from ignorance of the right methods of treatment, or of the use of disinfectants for hindering the spread of infection. Even Dorothy's example failed to inspire any with the like courage. Betty was the only one who could be prevailed upon to render any assistance; and she would not put her nose inside the sick room, but considered she did her part well by consenting to bring food and other necessaries to the door, outside of which she left them for Dorothy to take in.

It was no light task which the girl had thus bravely taken upon herself. Owen rapidly grew worse, and soon was past remonstrating against Dorothy's waiting upon her. Unflinchingly and devotedly the latter performed her part, astonishing Mr. Wood by the aptitude she showed for nursing, and the unwearied manner in which she kept at her post.

The good doctor tried to find some one to assist her, but was unsuccessful, so great was the horror that the village people had of the disease.

So Dorothy struggled on. At length, however, willing as she was, she began to see that there are limits to the powers of endurance of even the strongest. She felt she could not go on much longer under the present strain. If it were merely the loss of sleep which her many nights of watching had already entailed, it would have been enough to have broken her down. She had not had her clothes off for so long that she could scarcely remember exactly how long it was,—it seemed so far back in the dim distance.

At last matters were becoming so desperate—inasmuch as, in spite of all her efforts, she could scarcely keep herself awake during her solitary vigils by the sick bed—that she resolved upon making a bold attempt to obtain some assistance. In thinking over who would be the most likely person to whom to apply she recalled to mind an elderly woman, Dame Short, to whom Lady Elizabeth had shown great kindness, and who had always professed great attachment towards the Devereux family. She lived alone, being without kith or kin, and therefore, as there was no one who would be imperiled by her so doing, she might, Dorothy thought, be prevailed on to come and share her watch. She resolved at any rate to make the attempt, for the case was becoming urgent. If she herself were to fail altogether, what would become of Owen? And the faithful creature's life was very precious to the lonely girl.

She could not bear to own even to herself that she was uneasy about her; that it was a doubtful question which way the illness would end; that she who of late had seemed the only friend left to her was perhaps about to be snatched away. She could not face the thought; she felt it would unfit her for her duties even to glance at future possibilities; she could only try to leave all in God's hands, and go on from hour to hour doing as far as in her lay what was required, without seeking to look ahead.

Catching at the faint gleam of hope which the remembrance of Dame Short had brought with it, she seized a favorable moment when Owen had fallen into a heavy slumber, and leaving her for the first time since she had been taken ill, she hastily donned cloak and hood and sallied forth on her errand.

As she stepped out into the open air she felt its crisp freshness invigorating after her long confinement; while the brilliant sunshine seemed to make everything look brighter, and inspire her with the hope that her errand might be successful.

She had a good distance to go, as Dame Short lived away from the village on the farther edge of a stretch of common; and Dorothy had not reached the end of the avenue before there flashed across her mind Owen's caution about not going out alone and unattended, until they knew for certain that Mr. Crawford had left the neighborhood. Owen's sudden illness had entirely driven him out of her mind until the present moment, and it was almost with a start of dismay that she recollected him now. But then she remembered for her comfort that doubt-less the rumor of the presence of small-pox at the Hall had long since got abroad, and would be sure to have the desired effect of keeping him at a distance from the infected house. He was not a man to imperil himself needlessly, and perhaps no more effectual means of banishing him from the place could have been devised.

The thought was a reassuring one. In spite of being so sad at heart, and worn out both mentally and bodily, she almost smiled at the idea, and taking fresh heart pursued her way; for had she returned to the house, she reflected, there was no one to have accompanied her; old William, who might have served as escort, having been incapacitated by ague for the last week or more.

"As the mountains are round about Jerusalem, so the Lord is round about His people," were the words that ran in her mind as she walked on; and her inward response was, "I will lift up mine eyes to the hills, from whence cometh my help. My help cometh from the Lord, which made heaven and earth."

With a happy sense of the unseen protecting arm that was round about her she pursued her way, and at length reached Dame Short's cottage, only, however, to find, to her profound disappointment, that it was entirely shut up, the door locked and barred, and no signs of life about anywhere. The dame had evidently gone off somewhere for a time, perhaps on a visit to a friend, perhaps to nurse some sick person, for her services were occasionally sought in that way.

Sadly Dorothy turned away with the sense of weariness so increasing upon her that it almost seemed as if she would nev-er be able to make her way home again. The hope which had sustained her having been quenched, she felt doubly despond-ing, and with slow, uncertain steps she prepared to retrace the way by which she had come across the common. She could not think of any one else to whom it would be the slightest use to apply. It seemed to her there was nothing to be done but to go back, and trust that strength according to her need would be supplied, as it had been up to that hour.

The common was a level stretch of ground intersected by two or three roads or bridle paths. It was beautiful in summer, when masses of golden gorse or patches of purple heather adorned it, and the fresh cool breeze swept over it, and the hills which formed a background stood out against a clear blue sky. But now it all looked bare and bleak.

The absence of tree or hedge allowed of an extended view, and after a while Dorothy, lifting her drooping eyes, which had been fixed upon the ground, perceived the figure of a woman in the distance coming towards her on the same road which she herself was treading.

Could it be Dame Short? Her heart bounded at the thought. Perhaps after all she might be able to obtain her help. But as the distance between them gradually lessened she saw plainly enough that the tall upright figure before her was very different from the bent form of the old woman.

Much dejected at this second disappointment, Dorothy listlessly pursued her way, ceasing to feel any interest in the advancing stranger, who, she noticed, was attired in the Puritan costume. As they drew near one another, however, and were about to pass each other, she mechanically raised her eyes, and then uttered an exclamation of surprise.

"Mrs. Willoughby!" she cried in utter astonishment, "is it possible? Can it really be you? Oh, I am so glad!" and Dorothy advanced with outstretched hand.

Mrs. Willoughby, though a little surprised by the warmth of the greeting, yet returned it cordially.

"You are the last person I expected to meet," pursued Dorothy; "but I am heartily glad to see you, for the sight of a friend's face is pleasant. And I have come to feel how truly you acted the part of a friend by me, and how little gratitude I showed while with you. I fear I behaved like a spoilt child," she added candidly, with a smile of such sweetness it was enough to have disarmed the wrath of the most implacable; while the frank confession and ingenuous manner, so different from the former proud, almost haughty bearing, quite vanquished Mrs. Willoughby.

"It was a trying time for you, my dear," she answered kindly. "The Lord was bringing you through deep waters; and you seemed to be refusing to grasp the hand which He was stretching out to you to uphold you."

"Yes; but I hope it is not so now," said Dorothy, half shyly. "I have come to know Him better than I did once; and now I wonder how I could so long reject and turn from Him."

"Thank God!" responded Mrs. Willoughby, with a wonderfully softened expression of face. "I rejoice to hear you speak like this."

"But you are looking pale and worn," she remarked, scanning the girl's face. "Are you not well?"

Dorothy explained about Owen's illness and how matters stood, adding, "I ought now to hasten back to her, in case she may awake and want me. It was only dire necessity that made me leave her thus."

"I will not hinder you. I will turn and walk with you part of the way. But, my dear, this is a very serious task for one so young. You will not be able to go on much longer, I can see, and the wonder is you have been enabled to do what you have done," said Mrs. Willoughby, refraining from expressing her admiration for Dorothy's heroism and self-devotion, though something of it showed itself in the look with which she regarded the brave girl beside her, who in the simplicity of her character was evidently far from thinking of any praise or admiration being due to her. How could she have acted differently? she herself would have said.

"And so you cannot find any one to help you?" pursued Mrs. Willoughby.

Dorothy shook her head sadly.

"Then I think I must come myself; that is, if you would like to have me. I am accustomed to illness, and flatter myself I am a good nurse."

"Oh, how very kind of you!" cried Dorothy, with brightening looks. "Do you really mean it? That would indeed be good of you, and I cannot tell you the comfort it would be; so great that I don't know how to thank you," she added, the tears coming into her eyes, for the sense of relief was great after the intensity of the long strain. "But ought I to let you do it?"

"Yes, you may do it with an easy conscience, for it will be pleasant to me to feel of use to some one, and my son does not need me at present."

"And now will you not tell me something about yourself?" said Dorothy, as they pursued the road towards Hurstwood. "I never expected to meet you in this part of the world."

"No, you may well be surprised; but much has happened since you left us. My son is now in prison, and our little home in Knightrider Street is broken up."

Dorothy looked aghast at such tidings. "Dr. Willoughby in prison!" she exclaimed, in almost incredulous tones.

"Yes, it is even so."

"But how could they put him there?"

"You know how, after his eviction, when the plague came, and St. Benedict's pulpit was left empty through the flight of the vicar from the infected city, my son, in common with some other Nonconformists, felt the times were so solemn and the need so urgent that all minor considerations should be waived, and so he again ascended his former pulpit, and preached to the people. He was left unmolested until the distemper began to abate, and then the persecuting spirit of those in power revived, and the Conventicle Act was renewed. It forbids them to preach to more than five persons besides their own families at a time. My son, feeling it not right to be silent altogether, was preaching to a few who had gathered quietly at our house, when the constables suddenly entered and carried him off to Newgate."

"What a shame of them!" exclaimed Dorothy indignantly; "and how dreadful for Dr. Willoughby! How long will he have to be there?"

"Three months altogether; the time will be up in March."

"And did you leave London at once?"

"Very soon after; for a fresh Act had been passed, which they call the Five Mile Act, forbidding any Nonconformist minister to come within five miles of any town where they have been preaching, unless they will take the Oxford Oath, swearing never to seek to make any alteration in the government either in Church or State; and this my son feels he cannot do. The penalty is a fine of forty pounds."

"What dreadful persecution!" cried Dorothy.

"Before he was taken," continued Mrs. Willoughby, "we had come to the conclusion that we must leave London, and had determined to sell our household goods, for the purpose of raising a little money with which to start on some fresh mode of life. After they had carried him off to gaol I had no means of support left—for we have been dependent upon his earnings in the way of teaching since he left St. Benedict's. So I felt I had better break up the home at once."

"And what has become of Tabitha?"

"My faithful Tabitha would even then have preferred to cast in her lot with ours, but that just at that very time she was summoned to her mother, who, they feared, had been seized with her last illness, and had no other daughter to nurse her. Her duty was plain, so we were forced to part, though it cost me much to let her go. Thus I came forth stripped, so to speak, of well-nigh all, and scarcely knowing whither to go."

"How very sad for you!" said Dorothy with genuine sympathy, "and so you came here?"

"Yes, I could think of nothing better. We have no relatives left to befriend us, and no property save a cottage in this neighborhood, which alone remains to us of several houses and some land which was once my husband's, but which in a time of difficulty he was forced to sell. The tenant had lately given it up, and we had not found another, so I felt it would at least serve as a roof over our heads, and I must manage as I can until my son comes out of gaol, and succeeds in getting employment of some sort."

"How hard it all seems for you!" remarked Dorothy, as she noticed how many fresh lines all this care and trouble had marked on the face of her companion since she had seen her last.

"Nay, my dear, say not so. Nothing can be 'hard' which is the will of the Lord, for oh! He is not hard, but full of tender pity and loving-kindness. He doth not willingly afflict; but He hath purposed for us a noble destiny, and He has to train and fit us for it. And though the pruning is not pleasant, and the knife is sharp, yet when we remember that it is His hand which holds it, we may well be content. I would wish to praise Him for all His faithfulness, even if at times my heart may fail me for the moment."

There was a short pause, and then Dorothy asked, "Have you taken possession of your cottage?"

"Yes, I came two days ago, bringing with me a few necessary articles."

"How lonely it must have felt all by yourself!"

"It will be pleasant to have my son with me again, when his term of imprisonment is over, and I hope he will find some means of support. Another reason for coming into this neighborhood was that a wealthy squire of these parts was a great friend of my husband's, to whom, indeed, he was much indebted for services rendered in past days, and for which he always said he should be glad to make some return. I thought perhaps he might procure some teaching for my son, or recommend him for employment of some sort."

"Does he live near here?"

"I do not quite know how far off, but I think no very great distance. It is Mr. Crawford of Wharton Park."

"Mr. Crawford!" echoed Dorothy, in tones of astonishment and consternation.

"Yes, do you know him? He must be quite an old man by this time."

"Ah, I see, you mean the father. He is dead, and his son has come into the property."

"Dead! Alas, alas! this is another blow. I had counted on his friendship for Stephen for his father's sake. And what is the son like?"

"He is a bold bad man," returned Dorothy with flashing eyes; "the worst man I ever came across, a regular scoundrel!"

"My dear Mistress Dorothy, you use strong expressions," said Mrs. Willoughby, looking a little astonished at such an outburst.

"But not one whit too strong," maintained the girl stoutly.

"Have you seen much of him?"

"Far too much, and I hope I may never come across him again."

"What has he done so to excite your anger and dislike?"

A blush overspread Dorothy's open face, as in a few words she briefly told something of Mr. Crawford's misdemeanors.

"Do you not think I have cause to feel annoyed?"

"Yes, my dear, indeed you have; and I am sorry to hear you have been exposed to anything of the sort. The son must be very different from what the father was."

"Yes; they say old Mr. Crawford meant to disinherit him, but I suppose he died without a will, for the son is now in possession of the place."

"I wish you had your father's protection. Have you heard nothing of Sir Richard all this time?"

"Nothing," said Dorothy sadly. "I sometimes think we shall have to give up all hopes of ever seeing him again. Poor father! if I could but have him back! What do you think can have happened to him? Have you heard anything of him?" she asked with sudden eagerness, as the thought flashed across her that perhaps Mrs. Willoughby knew something, and was preparing to tell her.

"Nay; we have had no tidings whatever. It is all very strange."

"And if he never comes back then Eugene will be master here," remarked Dorothy in desponding tones. "How dreadful that will be, if he continues what he was during this last visit! He was so altered that I felt ashamed of my brother."

"We must hope Sir Richard may return; for from what you tell me your brother would be no protector for you, but worse than none. This would then be no fit home for you."

"But I have no other; so I earnestly hope that until Eugene has changed, and grown more like he used to be, he may not become master."

"I was thinking," said Mrs. Willoughby, after a pause, "that I would return to the cottage to fetch a thing or two, and then join you later on, and relieve you of your watch. But after what you have told me I do not like you to be walking alone; and I can easily go for what I want tomorrow. Besides, the short winter's afternoon will soon close in; so I think I had better go straight back with you."

"Thank you very much. It is indeed kind of you," returned Dorothy gratefully. "How fortunate for me that I met you!"

CHAPTER XV

OUT OF PRISON

"That is not losing much of life
Which is not losing Thee,
Who art as present in the strife
As in the victory."
Translated by GEORGE MACDONALD

AS they entered the park gates and walked up the avenue of grand old beeches, at the end of which appeared the west front of the picturesque old house, the great oriel windows of which were reflecting the bright beams of the already sinking sun, Mrs. Willoughby exclaimed, "You have indeed a beautiful home, Mistress Dorothy. So this is where your sainted mother, whom I truly loved, spent so much of her life? It is a sweet spot, and it must be a hallowed one to you."

"It is; no other could ever be like it. But oh! I miss her at every turn."

Mrs. Willoughby, seeing how utterly worn out Dorothy was, very soon dismissed her from Owen's room, insisting that she should leave the patient in her hands, and go herself to get a good night's rest.

Dorothy, knowing that Mrs. Willoughby quite understood the art of nursing, thankfully availed herself of the opportunity for obtaining the much needed repose.

It was restful to both mind and body to have the presence in the house of such a person as Mrs. Willoughby,—energetic, capable, and entirely free from nervousness, while her strong faith and cheerful manner were inspiriting, at the same time that her true kindness of heart and sympathy were soothing. These altered circumstances had made her appear in quite a new light, so Dorothy thought; but perhaps the alteration was more in herself.

She lay down to rest with a heart full of thankfulness at
God's goodness in sending her such a friend in her hour of sore
need; and then her thoughts wandered to Newgate, and she
began wondering what sort of place it was, and what hardships
and miseries Dr. Willoughby might even then be enduring. She
pictured his calm, pale face, which doubtless was even then
looking unruffled, and reflecting heaven's own peace; and then
her indignation arose that such a man as that, so gentle, so
good, should be subjected to such an indignity as that which
a sojourn in Newgate appeared to her. And all this was borne
for conscience' sake! She was beginning to look upon him as
a martyr. Certainly he was one of those who, had he lived in
Queen Mary's days, would have gone to the stake without a
moment's hesitation, rather than deny his Lord or be false to
his convictions.

After a time she fell asleep, to dream of prison cells peopled
by crowds of evil-doers and abandoned wretches, surging and
clamoring around one whose countenance was as that of an
angel contrasted with the coarse brutal ones that scowled upon
him, one whose very look seemed to quell their angry passions
and silence their insults.

For some days longer Owen's life hung in the balance, and
it was a hard fight between life and death. Unwearied was the
devotion Dorothy showed; and Mrs. Willoughby, as she watched
the tall, graceful figure bending over the prostrate form of the
invalid, nothing daunted by the loathsome nature of the disease, and in her self-forgetfulness utterly regardless of any
possible consequences to herself, wearing meanwhile upon her
face a look of tender concern which imparted the gentleness
and softness it had once lacked, felt she must formerly have
grievously misjudged the girl, or else that a wonderful change
had been wrought in her. It had always been a strong character, and now this new element of mingled tenderness and
sweetness made it very attractive and winsome. The Refiner's
fire had been hot, but it seemed already to have purged away
much of the dross, and to be doing its work in purifying the
gold.

After a time of prolonged anxiety the patient showed symptoms of improvement, and then came the long slow process of
gradual recovery and convalescence.

It had come to be regarded as a settled thing that Mrs.

Willoughby should remain at Hurstwood until her son should be again at liberty to rejoin her, and great was the comfort her presence afforded to both Dorothy and Owen.

The gratitude of the latter to both her kind nurses, more especially towards Dorothy, who had so bravely borne the chief brunt of it alone and unaided, was unbounded; and they on their part, but naturally Dorothy most of all, were full of thankfulness for her restoration. They had moreover the satisfaction of finding that, partly owing to the care that had been taken of her, the traces left of the disease would not after all be so very marked.

By the end of February she was pretty well again. But just as March set in, with its bleak east winds and ungenial weather, Mrs. Willoughby got a chill, and was laid up with a sharp attack of rheumatism and fever, which made it impossible for her to rise from her bed.

"It is the more unfortunate," she remarked, "as my son's term of imprisonment is nearly up, and I wanted to be at the cottage to make all ready and to give him a welcome; for I expect he will come to join me at once, though of course something or other may detain him for a while. So I cannot be sure as to the day he will arrive."

But, however anxious she might be to be up and about, she had no choice allowed her but to resign herself to helplessness and inactivity until the attack should pass off. It was a new thing to her, who had always been strong and active, and the one to wait upon others, to be thus laid aside, and she found she had need to seek for help to enable her to bear it patiently, even while satisfied in her own mind that it was all for some wise purpose.

Dorothy, now happy in Owen's restoration, and grateful to Mrs. Willoughby for all her kind services, gladly and cheerfully gave herself up to waiting upon her; and Owen herself was now able to give some assistance, though her strength had not yet fully returned. Moreover this was a case in which the servants' aid could also be given, as it was nothing infectious, and they had by this time recovered from the scare caused by the presence of small-pox in the house.

March had set in cold and blustering, with bitter east winds; but after about ten days of such weather there was a sudden change. The wind shifted to the south, and became soft and balmy; a few gentle showers laid the dust, after which the sun shone out brightly, and all was for the time spring-like and delightful.

Dorothy, who dearly loved fresh air and exercise, sallied forth on one of these beautiful afternoons for the purpose of picking some early spring flowers with which to brighten Mrs. Willoughby's room. It was exhilarating to feel that winter was well nigh over, and that now still warmer sunshine and softer breezes and longer days might be anticipated.

Though she had gathered almost as many flowers as her hands would hold, she still lingered in the open air, unwilling just yet to return to the house. She had wandered into the avenue, where, attracted by the cawing of the busy rooks overhead, she stood still for a few minutes watching their rapid movements.

On withdrawing her gaze she perceived a figure before her coming up the avenue. It was the figure of a man; and her first impulse was to turn and flee. But a second glance showed her that this was no dreaded Cavalier in satin doublet and plumed hat, but a sober divine in Puritan costume. Who could it be? The next moment, with a sudden quickening of all her pulses which made her heart beat rapidly, and sent a rosy glow into her cheeks, she recognized Dr. Willoughby.

Yes, it was he himself, but looking worn and weary, she noticed, as he drew nearer. She stood where she was awaiting him. No need to flee from him. Rather he would be one to flee to in any difficulty or danger. How different a man from Mr. Crawford! she was thinking. Were they not sundered as far as the poles? as distinct as light from darkness?

And so she quietly awaited him;—quietly but for that tumultuous beating of her heart, which she could not understand; it was such a novel sensation.

His eyes were fixed meditatively upon the ground, and consequently he did not notice her until he was within a few paces of her. Then, looking up, he perceived a tall and somewhat stately maiden, with hands full of spring flowers, and hood slightly thrown back, from underneath which some glossy brown tresses were escaping, while the rosy lips were wreathed in a smile of recognition; the whole making a pretty picture against the background of tree and sky. The half shy, half pleased expression on her face was so different from the cold proud look it had so often worn, that for the moment he did not feel quite sure whether this could indeed be the wayward damsel whom they had sheltered in Knightrider Street.

"Do I see Mistress Dorothy Devereux?" he began, lifting his hat courteously.

"Yes," she replied with a smile. "And you are coming. I suppose, to see your mother?"

"I am in search of her. I expected to find her in the cottage she spoke of; but I do not know these parts, and on inquiring my way thither I was told that she was at the Hall, and I was directed here. Can you enlighten me further?"

"Yes, it is quite true that she is here; and very sorry she is herself, as she had hoped to have been at the cottage ready to welcome you on your return; but she is laid up with an attack of rheumatism, and cannot leave her bed. However, we hope in a few days she will be better and about again. Meantime you must come and see her," said Dorothy, turning towards the house.

Dr. Willoughby looked much astonished at finding his mother thus installed at Hurstwood Hall.

"But how has it come about that she is here?" he asked.

Dorothy explained as they walked along, adding, "I cannot tell you how grateful I feel to her for all her kindness and help at such a time. It was indeed good of her, and I do not know what I should have done without her."

"I am sure she must have been very glad to give any assistance in her power. It is a great pleasure to be able to be of use to others, especially those in need. Besides, we are bound to follow the command of our Divine Master, who tells us to weep with those who weep. And how many there are in this sad world of ours who are in sorrow or trouble of some sort!"

"My troubles seem to have blown over for the present," remarked Dorothy gaily, feeling at the moment wonderfully lighthearted; and it was long indeed since she had experienced such a feeling. But now a sudden sense of rest and protection had come to her; the burdens which had been weighing upon her appeared to have rolled off and the clouds to have dispersed. She did not stay to question whether this would last; she only felt conscious that the general aspect of things was brighter than it had been for a long while.

"And could you bear to have the clouds return?" asked

Stephen Willoughby, looking at her attentively and almost compassionately as he awaited her answer.

"Oh, do not speak of it," she answered quickly. "I have gone through so much, and the sunshine is so pleasant."

"But for maturing the fruit cloudy and even rainy days are needed as well as the sunshiny ones."

"You have had many of the rainy ones of late," she remarked, somewhat abruptly, her thoughts turning from herself to him, as she marked how pale and worn he looked; and there was sympathy in the glance of the honest eyes, which always told so truly what was in the mind of their owner.

"Yes; but there has been an intermingling of brightness too. He whom I serve does not leave His followers to suffer alone. He cheers them from time to time with His presence, and that is worth more than anything that earth can give. He was with me in prison, as He was with Joseph of old, for He changes not."

"I suppose Newgate is a very dreadful place?"

"It is not a place one would choose for a residence, if choice were allowed," he replied with a smile.

"Were you in a horrid dungeon?"

"Not one of the very worst, but it was damp and unwholesome and over-crowded. That was about the worst part of it to me; I should much have preferred solitude and quiet. And yet good came out of it, for I was able to tell them of a Savior for the lost and perishing, of a Friend for the outcast and lonely. There were men of all types and classes there; and some needed one message, some another; but I felt more than ever how great was the fullness and sufficiency of Christ to meet every need, however varied. And it was blessed work to deliver this message,—to tell of One who, having borne their penalty for them, had now set wide open the prison door, so that they had but to avail themselves of the freedom offered them and shake off Satan's yoke."

"And did they listen?" asked Dorothy with interest.

"Not all; some gave heed, some shut their ears, some scoffed and mocked. Strange it seems," he went on musingly, "that any should prefer bondage to liberty, should choose slavery to Satan rather than deliverance from captivity; but so it is, and so it has ever been."

"But how dreadful it must have been to have to associate with all sorts of people like that—low wretches, as I suppose most of them were!" remarked Dorothy with a shudder.

"I also had the company of my Lord," returned the young divine. "And there were some who were there for the same cause as myself. I do not know whether we should come under the designation of 'low wretches,'" he added with a smile.

"No, but those who put you there deserve the term," said Dorothy in her hot indignation. "You deserve the title of 'hero,'" she added inwardly; for her quick perception did not fail to note how bravely he had borne it, although his face showed the traces of what he had suffered; how lightly he had passed over all the discomforts and miseries of his prison life, never uttering a word of complaint at what seemed to her his unjust detention; how entirely free from bitterness or malice of any sort was that noble heart, which was so filled with the desire to win souls that it had seemed to him matter of small moment whether he delivered his message to the prisoners in the noisome dungeons of Newgate, or from the pulpit of St. Benedict's, where a fashionable audience, numbering many among the great of the land, had been wont to hang admiringly upon his words. It struck a chord in Dorothy's generous nature, and kindled in her a boundless admiration. And as there flashed across her memory all that she had seen while under their roof of his unflinching devotion and self-sacrifice during the time of the plague, to the beauty of which prejudice had then blinded her, she wondered at her own dullness in having ever failed to see his true nobility.

She was sensible of it now, at any rate, after having experienced the contrast presented by the company into which she had been so recently thrown; where the only aim was to please self, to live for self, to gratify the passing fancy, to yield to each ruling passion.

As an inexperienced girl on her first visit to London, with her eyes dazzled by the glitter and glamour around her, she had indeed failed to detect the base metal beneath the outward show of gallantry and fine manners; but ages seemed to have elapsed since that time; she had grown older, and was no longer a child; such experiences as those through which she had passed rapidly develop the character, and now she was learning to prefer truth and honesty in however homely a garb to untruth and baseness, even if set off by every adornment that art could devise.

CHAPTER XVI

SAD TIDINGS

"What have I left?
   Of friend, aim, love, bereft;
Stripped bare of everything I counted dear.
   Lord, I have all,
And more beside, if only Thou art near."

ADELINE SERGEANT

BY this time they had reached the house. Dorothy first of all led her companion to Owen's parlor, that they might learn whether it would be a fitting moment for Dr. Willoughby to go to his mother's chamber, or whether, if she were slumbering, it would be better to wait a while.

"I have just come down, and she was awake then, and seems much better this afternoon, so I think Dr. Willoughby might go up at once," was Owen's reply; and accordingly he followed her up stairs.

Dorothy remained below to arrange in water the flowers she had gathered, handling them lovingly, as if they spoke to her of pleasant things.

After a time Owen rejoined her.

"Do you not think, Mistress Dorothy, we might send one of the maids to the cottage to light a fire and put things a little straight for Dr. Willoughby? It seems awkward for a man to find nothing prepared for him, and to have to shift entirely for himself. Some of them are poor helpless creatures in that way."

"Is he going to the cottage at once? Why does he not wait till his mother could go too?"

"That is what I thought; and I felt sure you would agree that he ought to be asked to remain here with her, for it was always Sir Richard's way to show open-handed hospitality; but both he and Mrs. Willoughby appear to prefer the other place.

I'm sure I don't know why, for it seems so comfortless. But they must know their own minds best. So the only thing to do is to help put things a little straight for him there."

"By all means let one of the maids go and do what she can."

"And I will send a few provisions ready cooked, that he may have something to eat," said Owen; "for he looks as if he had not fared over well in prison, his face is so thin and white. But oh, Mistress Dorothy, what a heavenly face it is! just as if he lived always in the very presence of his Lord and master, and reflected something of His brightness."

Dorothy smiled at the other's enthusiasm, not sarcastically, but as if well pleased at the tribute paid him.

"I am sure he is a wonderfully good man," pursued Owen. "I have heard so much about him from my dear lady; but I never thought I should see him for myself; so I am the more pleased. And he gave me such a pleasant look and smile, as he said he had heard Lady Elizabeth speak of Mistress Owen, whom she had left in charge. But now I must go and see about sending off Betty or Molly."

As, after spending an hour or two with his mother, Dr. Willoughby descended the stairs; he came upon Dorothy, who was crossing the hall.

"Can I have a few words with you, Mistress Dorothy? I have brought tidings which I wish to impart to you."

"Tidings!" echoed Dorothy, as, replacing the hood which she had been carrying in her hand, she turned to accompany him a little way down the avenue, feeling that there they would be undisturbed. "Are they tidings from abroad—from my father?" she asked eagerly, with scarcely repressed impatience; and then there quickly followed a sinking of heart, and a feeling of dread as to what she might be about to hear; for Dr. Willoughby's face, which she was attentively scanning, wore a grave look.

"It is about Sir Richard," he replied. "At length I have obtained news of him."

"Oh, is it good or bad? Do make haste and tell me. I would rather hear the worst than be kept in suspense."

"Are you prepared for the worst?" he asked, gently and gravely.

The color left her cheeks, and the light seemed to die out of the eyes which had been so bright a short time before.

"Is it indeed the worst that I must hear? Have you no good news for me?" she said, half pleadingly.

"Alas, no; I cannot bid you hope any longer."

"Is he dead?" she asked in a low voice, the words coming slowly, and a mournful look creeping over her face.

"Yes; it is even as I feared it must be. It was last summer out in Spain."

There was silence for a moment, and then with an effort at self-control Dorothy asked, "How was it? What was the cause?"

"That is the painful part of it. I had better perhaps tell the story from the beginning. But can you bear it?" asked Stephen Willoughby, looking at her compassionately; "or shall I defer it to another time?"

"Oh no; tell me all now. Of course I have feared it must be so, but I have clung to hope almost against hope."

"Which was very natural. But to proceed. It was in Newgate, of all places, that I gleaned these tidings."

Dorothy looked surprised, but did not speak to interrupt.

"There was a man among the crowd which filled the common ward, who seemed at first one of the most brutal and degraded of them all; appearing to scoff at all that was good, while it was dreadful to listen to the oaths that often fell from his lips. But by degrees a change came over the man; he seemed to grow softer and gentler, and would sometimes join the knot that used to gather to listen to the reading and expounding of God's Word. And, in short, the Word laid hold on him; it was in his case as a hammer breaking the rock in pieces; the heart of stone was taken way and the heart of flesh given to him. The change seemed almost as great as that in the demoniac of old.

"After a time there was an outbreak of fever in the gaol, and he was one of its victims. It went hardly with him from the first. I did what I could for him, and watched by him at night. At last the fever departed, but left him so weak that there was evidently no hope for him. In the quiet of the night he told me he had a secret weighing upon his conscience, and he longed to unburden himself of it, that he might hear whether I could assure him, after I knew all, that God would indeed be ready to pardon such a wretch as he felt himself to be. I bent over him, for his voice was low; but I was utterly unprepared for the revelation he made."

Stephen Willoughby paused.

"What was it?" asked Dorothy, in a tone of awe.

"He told me how he had been a sailor for many years, and the ship's company was a godless, lawless set. Last August they put into a small port on the Spanish coast for the purpose of trade or of obtaining provisions; I forget which, but that does not matter. He went on shore with leave of absence for a few days. To cut the matter short, he fell foul of Sir Richard in a lonely spot, having already learnt that he was travelling with a good deal of gold upon him. The temptation was too much for him, and he set upon him with the intention of plundering him. But Sir Richard resisted, and showed fight. Shall I go on, Mistress Dorothy?"

"Yes, yes," said the latter, who was listening intently, with a sort of dreadful fascination.

"The man with his powerful frame was more than a match for the other, and the result was that Sir Richard lay dead at his feet."

Dorothy seemed to catch her breath, while a look of horror overspread her face.

"Dragging him farther into the depths of the dense forest, where no one was likely to penetrate, he hastily buried the body, and made off with his booty. His vessel sailed the next day, and ever since the secret had been locked in his own breast. It was the conviction of sin and the near approach of death that made him seek to relieve his conscience by confessing the crime. He died the next day."

"But are you sure it was my father? Might it not possibly have been some one else?" said Dorothy, catching at any hope, however visionary.

"No; for he was familiar with the name, and even knew him by sight, as he had lived in his youth in this neighborhood. To make doubly sure, I have this, which he gave me, and which he said he had taken, thinking it might contain some valuables," continued Dr. Willoughby, producing from his pocket a well-worn little memorandum book.

Dorothy opening it recognized her father's initials, R. D., inscribed on the fly-leaf, and knew his handwriting in the entries made in it.

"I wondered at his keeping anything that might have proved strong evidence against him," remarked Stephen Willoughby; "but he seemed to feel he had done the deed so secretly and cleverly that there could be no chance of its ever coming to light, or of any suspicion attaching itself to him. Besides, he had ever been utterly reckless and thoughtless. This is a dreadful story for you to listen to, Mistress Dorothy, and I grieve much to have to impart to you such painful tidings."

The look of horror had deepened on Dorothy's face as she listened, but she had restrained herself from interrupting the narrative, and had exerted great self-control. Now that Dr. Willoughby paused, she said in a voice which she tried to steady, "Thank you for telling me all. I would rather know, of course. But it is dreadful. Oh, I had never thought of anything so dreadful! I don't seem able to take it all in yet. I shall understand it better presently. But oh!" she cried suddenly, in a tone of dismay, "it means that Eugene is now master at Hurstwood, and I have no other protector left, and he is worse than none."

"Nay, Mistress Dorothy; earthly friends may be removed, but God remains; and He is an Almighty Protector, ever round about His people as a wall of fire, to shield them from evil. No harm can come nigh them without His permission; for does He not keep them as the apple of an eye? And He is especially the God of the fatherless. You will be safe in His keeping if you place yourself there."

Though the tears were in her eyes Dorothy gave a smile, which thanked him for his words and the comfort they had brought with them.

"To know what it is to be hidden in the secret of His presence," pursued Dr. Willoughby, "to dwell under the very shadow of His wings, it is worth while to be brought into straits and difficulties and dangers. Then we learn what He is—how powerful to uphold, how mighty to help—in a way we never should do if the path were smooth and easy. May this be your experience."

"When did you hear this?" asked the girl suddenly.

"Only a short time ago. I should have written, but that I thought it would be better to tell you myself, and I knew I was soon to leave Newgate. Besides, letters are unsatisfactory, and often get lost. But I came here this afternoon as much for the purpose of bringing you the news as of seeing my mother."

Engrossed in the conversation, Dorothy had scarcely noticed that they had left the avenue, and had emerged upon the high road, but at a turn in it she noticed a figure approaching, and the next instant recognized Mr. Crawford. Much discomposed, she involuntarily drew closer to her companion.

The scowl which came into the bad face, and the significant look which the restless eyes darted at the young divine from underneath lowering brows, did not pass unperceived by her as he strode by, and added to the feeling of disquietude which the unexpected meeting of itself was enough to cause.

She held her breath, and kept silence until he was out of hearing, and then said hurriedly, "I must return now. I had only meant to come as far as the end of the avenue. I am glad I was not alone, but I hoped that dreadful man had left the neighborhood."

"You know him then?"

"Yes, it is Mr. Crawford of Wharton Park."

"Ah," was all Dr. Willoughby's response. And then he added, "You must suffer me to see you home."

"But that will be delaying you."

"Nay, I could not think of allowing you to return by yourself. These are not times for a young gentlewoman to wander about alone, when the evil example set at court spreads into the country and all over the land."

It was with a slow step and sad countenance that Dorothy entered Owen's parlor on her return. The latter was full of sympathy and commiseration on hearing the tidings which Dorothy had to impart. The fact of Sir Richard's death did not come to her with any surprise, as she had for a long time felt that the probability was that he had come to some untimely end. But it shocked her much to hear what the end had been.

"So now Eugene will be master," said the girl in a desponding tone.

"But perhaps it will not make a great deal of difference after all," said Owen, trying to be encouraging. "He is not likely to care to be here very long at a time, and so things may go on pretty much the same."

"Poor father!" sighed Dorothy, the tears filling her eyes.

"How little I thought when he bade us adieu that I should never see him again! But it is too dreadful to think of what the end was!" she added, with a shudder.

Owen silently stroked the glossy hair of the bowed head resting on her knee. What could she say? What words of hers could lessen the horror with which the young girl must shrink from the thought of her father meeting with such a death?

After a pause Dorothy said in a husky voice, "How dreadful it would have been for mother to have had such news brought her! But she was spared that. Oh, I am so glad! And now she is beyond the reach of anything that can harm or hurt or sadden."

"And that is a blessed thought, dear heart. She is at rest for evermore. And some day for you too the rough path will come to an end, and all will be peace and joy and blessedness."

They sat on for some time in the deepening twilight, the fire casting a ruddy glow all around; and Dorothy shed some silent tears, while many an anxious thought and foreboding passed through Owen's mind as she pondered over the possible changes that this might bring, and what would be the best course for her young mistress to pursue, should Hurstwood become an unfit home for her, or should the day come when her brother would no longer be willing for her to reside under his roof.

It seemed probable that further trials might be in store for the lonely girl, and her heart ached for her. But after a time came the comforting reflection that all was in the hands of her Heavenly Father, and He would never leave her nor forsake her. He had already "appointed the bounds of her habitation" and His purposes were all wisdom and love. She could trust her darling to Him; He would not suffer the way to be rougher than need be.

After a long silence Owen was the first to speak.

"You must let Master Eugene know of this, Mistress Dorothy, dear. Do you not think you ought to write at once?"

"Yes, I suppose I ought," admitted Dorothy, rather unwillingly. "I will do it presently. But I must go up and see Mrs. Willoughby first. How sorry I shall be when she has to leave us! but of course her son will be glad to have her."

Letter-writing did not come easy to Dorothy. She had scarcely written more than two or three in her life, for ladies in those days were not as a rule accomplished scribes; and often there was a difficulty in dispatching letters even when they were written. In some of the more distant parts of England they were only received once a week; in others on alternate days. Often there arose unexpected delay in their delivery, and there also existed a measure of uncertainty whether they would reach their destination at all. Thus the exchange of letters was a rare thing compared with what it is at the present day, more especially among people living in the country.

Dorothy sat down to apply herself to her task, but found it a difficult and an uncongenial one. More than one tear fell on her paper as she bent over it. They were painful details to write, and it was painful to feel with regard to an only brother that his absence was more to be desired than his presence; that instead of begging him to come to her that they might mingle their tears together, instead of looking to him for comfort, she dreaded another visit from him, lest it should be in any way a repetition of the last.

She did not expect an early reply from him, and therefore was not surprised that for some time none came. Meanwhile things went on as usual.

CHAPTER XVII

IN DANGER

"I was rapt
In faith, and a high courage, driving out
All doubt and discontent, and womanish fear."
Epic of Hades

"HOW much I wish I could hear Dr. Willoughby preach!" re-marked Owen one day, when she was sitting in Mrs. Willoughby's room. Dorothy too was there with her embroidery frame.

"He is always ready to do so when opportunity offers," said Mrs. Willoughby. "I am sure he would be very happy to come and expound the Scriptures to us sometimes."

"That would be a privilege indeed," said Owen, looking eagerly towards Dorothy, as if to ask what she thought of it.

The latter assented warmly. "Will you ask him about it?" she added, turning to Mrs. Willoughby.

"Yes, if you like. He promised to come to see me today, and then I can mention it."

The result was a little private service or Bible reading among themselves, which proved such a refreshment and help that after a few days both Owen and Dorothy felt it was not right to keep such a thing all to themselves, but that the privilege should be extended to others as well. So an invitation was given to any of the servants, either indoor or outdoor, to join if they pleased.

Some of the latter, after coming once or twice, begged leave to bring their wives or other relatives; and soon quite a little company of hungry souls gathered from time to time to listen to the young divine's earnest, helpful words.

"You must recollect, my dear, there is a certain amount of risk in this," Mrs. Willoughby remarked one evening, when there had been an increase in numbers.

"Wherein lies the risk?" asked Dorothy, to whom the words had been addressed.

"The Conventicle Act makes it unlawful for any one above sixteen to attend any religious exercise, not according to the Church of England, if there be five persons present besides the members of the family; and it is also made unlawful for any one to hold such a service. The penalty, as my son has found, is three months' imprisonment, or a fine of five pounds for the first offence. For the second offence the penalty is doubled."

Dorothy looked grave. "So it is involving him in possible trouble! Then we must cease these meetings," she added in a tone of regret.

"Nay, not in so far as I am concerned," interposed Dr. Willoughby, who had remained behind after the little company had dispersed. "If God calls me to this work for Him, far be it from me to shrink from it on the score of danger. The exercise of my ministry is, next to Christ, dearer to me than anything in the world. It is my heaven while here below to spend this life in gathering souls to Him. To be laid aside from it would be a sore trial; and speak for Him I must until He bids me be dumb and silent.

"But the question is about yourselves," he went on; "for by the Act those who listen are involved in much the same trouble as those who preach, though I do not say it has so often been put in force against them. It is generally the preacher who excites their wrath," he added with a smile.

Dorothy still wore a grave, pondering look.

"Then if you are willing still to preach, let every one be warned of the risk they run in coming, and then let them take their choice," she said, after a moment's pause, with a look of courage and steadfastness in her eyes. "I for my part shall hope to be present, and so I expect will Owen."

The latter without any hesitation signified her assent.

"But after all," went on Dorothy, "I can't fancy there can be any danger in this quiet, out-of-the-way place. It may be very different in the towns, but who is there here except ourselves to know what is going on, or to inform against us?"

"That may be so; but still you had better caution all who come to be wary, and keep the matter a secret from those who might regard it with unfriendly feelings."

The next day Dorothy and Owen were returning from a

walk when on reaching a cottage not far from the park gates Dorothy stopped, saying she would go in and pay a visit to a sick child in whom she was much interested; and as she intended to remain awhile to amuse her and sing to her, Owen, who had things to attend to at home, left her and proceeded on her way, the mother of the child promising to accompany the young gentlewoman home.

However, when the time came, Dorothy, quite forgetting for the moment what she was inclined to consider a tiresome precaution—for she dearly loved to be free to roam at her own sweet will—started off without summoning her attendant.

She had gone some little way when a rustling in the trees and bushes which skirted the road attracted her attention, and with a start of dismay she perceived Mr. Crawford emerging from their shelter right in front of her.

Her first impulse was to turn and flee, but he was too quick for her, and placing his hand on her shoulder he forced her to remain where she was.

"Why do you seek to flee from me thus?" he asked, in tones which he tried to make soft and persuasive. "Why does the queen of my heart treat in this manner one who is her devoted slave? Nay, it is useless to struggle thus. I have been waiting for an opportunity of again pleading my cause, and now I have found it, I will make the most of it. Give me the promise I seek; that is all I require."

Dorothy shook her head. "What I said before I say now," she replied firmly, refusing to be intimidated, though her heart was beating fast. "I can never give you any other answer; and if you were an honorable man you would not force your company upon me, knowing that it is unwelcome."

His brow darkened, and a muttered oath escaped his lips. Dorothy, recollecting that ever-present Protector of whom Dr. Willoughby had spoken, found her courage rising with the occasion, and showed an undaunted front. Before her indignant glance and almost queenly bearing the man of the world faltered for the instant, and felt kept at bay. Never till he met Dorothy had he been brought in contact with the higher type of woman, and perhaps it showed that there was still, debased though he was, some latent spark of good in him, that he had been thus captivated not only by her beauty, but by the freshness and purity and simplicity of her nature, and his feelings towards her were different from those he had ever conceived for any other woman. For, after the manner of the times, he had regarded them lightly, and thought slightingly of their virtue.

The very fact that Dorothy was so hard to win made him the more set on winning her; while at the same time her obstinacy, as he termed it, and undisguised contempt for himself angered him.

"And now let me go," said Dorothy, making a sudden effort to free herself from his grasp.

"I will not," he muttered, "until you have yielded;" at the same time so tightening his hold upon her that Dorothy gave an involuntary cry.

It had scarcely escaped her when a voice from behind said, in indignant authoritative tones, "Let that young gentlewoman alone. What do you mean by assaulting her like this?"

To her intense relief Dorothy recognized Dr. Willoughby's voice even before she could turn to see who it was.

In supercilious tones Mr. Crawford retorted, "And pray who are you to talk thus? Interfere in matters that concern you; go and look after your conventicles and your canting Puritan fellows, and leave gentlemen to settle their own affairs."

The insulting words brought a momentary flash into Stephen Willoughby's eyes, but in a calm voice he replied, "This is the affair of every honest man; and again I say, loose your hold of that young gentlewoman immediately, or I shall have to force you to do so." The manner in which the words were spoken was quiet and dignified, but very decided.

Mr. Crawford glared at the speaker, his face crimsoning with rage, as with a mocking laugh he hissed out the words, "I am not going to be dictated to by you, or any other contemptible Puritan; you are much mistaken if you think so."

"And I say I am not going to stand by and see foul play,"

"Ha, ha! Come on if you dare!"

Stephen Willoughby accepted the challenge. The next instant—Dorothy scarcely knew how it happened,—she saw her persecutor laid prostrate at Dr. Willoughby's feet, felled by a sudden and skillfully-directed blow.

"Now is your opportunity," he hastily said; and thus released Dorothy turned and fled, never pausing until she had reached the shelter of her home, and was safe in Owen's parlor.

Then, panting for breath, she related what had happened.

MR. CRAWFORD WAS FELLED BY A SKILLFULLY-DIRECTED BLOW.

An anxious look came into the other's face, but she did not say much, except to remark what a happy thing it was that Dr. Willoughby should have come along just at that moment.

"I never should have thought he would have fought any one," said Dorothy. "He always looks so quiet and gentle."

"But I should say he has plenty of spirit as well; and when his indignation is aroused, I should think he would be a match for any one. His gentleness does not proceed from want of strength of character."

"Nor want of true courage; for I am sure he showed that plainly enough all through the time of the plague."

"But I fear Mr. Crawford will owe him a grudge for this, and will try to be revenged in some way," remarked Owen.

"Oh, I hope not," said Dorothy fervently, "and now he has had a plain answer, I hope he will let me alone. He seemed to think it impossible I could have meant what I said before; but now he finds I do mean it, surely there will be an end of the matter," she added hopefully.

When the time for the little meeting, which they were going to hold that evening, drew near, Dr. Willoughby presented himself, looking as usual calm and unruffled.

Dorothy tried to thank him for his bold interference on her behalf; but did so rather shamefacedly, vexed that he should have found her in such a situation; and yet she knew, and hoped he knew too, that it was from no fault of hers, except perhaps the imprudence of not having summoned an attendant to accompany her.

"I suppose he was furious with you?" she said.

"Yes; he challenged me to a duel; but I said I did not fight duels, it was against my principles; I only sought to redress wrong, and that having released you I had accomplished my end, and should molest him no more, unless he gave me further cause to do so; whereupon he informed me that I was a miserable, sneaking, cowardly fellow," said Dr. Willoughby with a smile. But he did not add, what Mr. Crawford had added in wrathful tones, that he would have his revenge sooner or later for the insult, as he called it, which had been offered him.

Dorothy's fears and agitation were forgotten as she listened to the glowing words of faith and hope which fell from the preacher's lips as he dwelt on the verse, "God is our refuge and strength, a very present help in time of trouble." And as he spoke his listeners felt that he was not speaking of that which he only knew by hearsay, but of that which he had proved and tried for himself, and found a blessed and living reality.

But the next time they met things were not allowed to terminate so peacefully.

As the little service proceeded, Dorothy with her quick ears fancied more than once that she heard stealthy sounds outside; but each time as soon as the thought had crossed her mind the sounds had ceased. No idea of danger had presented itself to her; she had merely concluded that one of the gardeners was late in finishing his work.

Suddenly, however, she turned pale. She had detected the sound of footsteps and of muffled voices in the hall. In an instant she took in the whole position. Quick as thought she stood at Dr. Willoughby's side.

"They are coming to take you," she said in a whisper. "Follow me, quickly, quickly; it is you they are seeking."

He paused a moment to say in a low clear tone to the little assembly, "It seems we are discovered; save yourselves;" and then turned to follow Dorothy.

She pushed aside the tapestry hanging at the top of the room near where he stood, and opened a door behind, through which they passed, only a few seconds before the door at the lower end of the long room was burst open and several constables entered.

Most of the audience, however, had already escaped through the large bay window, which they had flung hastily open. Thus only Mrs. Willoughby, Owen and old William were left to confront them. As only these three were found actually present, they were safe, as that was under the forbidden number. Besides, they were not the object of pursuit. Behind the constables appeared the lowering visage of Mr. Crawford, and Owen saw at once that her surmises had been correct, that he was seeking thus to be revenged on his late antagonist.

Meanwhile Dorothy was hurrying Dr. Willoughby along the corridor and up the staircase by which Owen had led her towards the secret chamber, imploring him to follow her to a place of safety; for he paused more than once, as if thinking it cowardly thus to flee.

"My mother," he said, "where is she?"

"They are not seeking her, but you. She would rather, I am

sure, that you escaped. What good can you be to her if you get thrown into prison again? Oh, do not run the risk unnecessarily! I can save you if you will let me."

Her common-sense view of the matter prevailed, and he followed her. When safely within the secret chamber she breathed more freely.

"They cannot find you here, search as they may; and I suppose they will search the house. You will stay here for a while, will you not? And will you please promise to keep the secret of this chamber? I only knew of it a short time ago, and I promised to guard it carefully; but I am sure Owen cannot blame me for bringing you here, as it is just for such a purpose that it exists."

"I have to thank you much for your promptitude and quick thought. Your presence of mind has saved me this time."

"Alas, it is all through me that this has happened," she said in tones of regret.

"How so? It was surely through the ill-will of those who hate these irregular meetings and try to put them down."

"Nay, I do not think that was the motive. I believe Mr. Crawford is at the bottom of it. I believe he has done this in revenge for the thrashing you gave him. What mean, contemptible conduct! If only he could be put in prison and kept safely there, what a good thing it would be!" she added laughing.

"Nay, let us not wish him such hard measure as that; for prison is not a pleasant place of abode."

"But he doesn't deserve anything pleasant; just the opposite. And now I will leave you and go and reconnoiter. I wonder if they have gone. I will return again presently or send Owen; and you will wait here patiently, will you not, until it is safe to release you?"

"I will. But is it well for you to venture forth just yet?"

"I shall be very cautious. And I dare say Owen will guess where I have taken you, and will come in search of us as soon as all is safe and clear."

Half an hour later all was quiet again. The disturbers of the peace, baffled in their quest, had been forced to retire without their wished-for victim; Mr. Crawford gnashing his teeth in his vexation at the frustration of his plans, and inwardly vowing to have his revenge some time or other.

"We have to thank Mistress Dorothy for my escape this

time," said Stephen Willoughby, addressing his mother, when after a while, all danger being past for the time, they had assembled in the south parlor. "It is all owing to her quick thought and courage and coolness."

Mrs. Willoughby turned to the girl with words of thanks, but she was conscious herself that they were not as hearty as she would have liked them to be. What was there in her son's words that had jarred upon her, and awakened an uneasy sensation in her mind?

During all this time of her sojourn at Hurstwood she had grown to regard Dorothy with totally different feelings from those which she had once entertained for her, having been won to admiration first by witnessing the girl's noble devotion towards Owen, and then by her attention and kindness to herself. But now something undefined seemed to be lessening that cordial feeling. She could have wished at that moment that the young maiden had been less attractive in her beauty and courage and generosity; for again fears for her son's peace of mind darted across her.

Was it jealousy? she asked herself, taking herself to task. Oh, surely not. She would be ashamed of any such unworthy feeling. And then she told herself she did her son wrong in entertaining any such thoughts with regard to him. Had not all such things come an end with him when Rosamond nearly broke his heart by her falseness; and was not his mind too much set on his work and higher aims to be likely to be brought into captivity to any fair charmer? Moreover the gulf which separated them was too great—Dorothy's position being such that it was impossible she would ever think for a moment of an evicted Presbyterian minister, without any charge, without a fortune, indeed, well-nigh penniless—the mere notion of such a thing was preposterous, and surely he would see it in that light, and never dream of anything so utterly unattainable.

At the other side of the question, whether there might be any risk to Dorothy's peace of mind, she never once glanced; not from lack of due estimation of her son, who in her eyes was without a peer, but from the reasons stated above.

After a little discussion they came to the conclusion that it might be wiser for Dr. Willoughby not to return to the cottage that night, lest his enemies might still be lurking about to annoy him; and so he was prevailed upon to remain at the Hall.

"And, my dear, I think I will return with him tomorrow," said Mrs. Willoughby. "I am now so much better that I see no reason for delaying longer, and my son will be glad to have me. I think I shall succeed in making him more comfortable than he can have been all alone."

Dorothy's countenance expressed regret.

"Must you really leave us? I shall miss you so much. But I am sure you had better wait a little longer. The cottage may be damp or cold, and it may bring back your rheumatism."

"Nay, I must risk that, and not think only of my own ease."

"I don't know how to thank you enough for all the help you gave me in my time of need," said Dorothy frankly and warmly; "and I am very sorry to lose you."

"And I have to thank you, my dear, for all your attention and care of me during my illness. You were unwearied, and showed yourself a skilful nurse."

The question as to whether the little meetings should still be continued from time to time or altogether dropped was discussed, and they came to the conclusion that if they were held it had better be in some other place.

Owen suggested a disused barn that stood among some other outbuildings, and which had the advantage of possessing two means of ingress and egress; the desirability of which had already been made so evident by the facility it had afforded Dr. Willoughby for escaping by one door while his pursuers were entering by the other.

Dr. Willoughby's remark that as long as he had the opportunity he should continue to proclaim his Master's message when and where he could, and that were he no longer to do so at Hurstwood he must elsewhere, made them feel they were relieved from the responsibility of exposing him to danger by begging him to continue the services; and so it was settled that from time to time they should still be held. But the need for caution was to be more than ever impressed on all who should attend.

Dorothy found herself half wondering at her own eagerness for their continuance, when she recalled bygone days, when even to accompany her beloved mother to anything of the sort would have been a weariness to her. What a change had come over her since then! Now she felt these little gatherings and the teaching she there received were to her as a feast of good things, a rich spiritual banquet, as Dr. Willoughby unfolded fresh lessons of truth that were new to her from the Scriptures, and it seemed as if Christ Himself drew near and was verily present in their midst, as He had been in the upper chamber in Jerusalem of old.

The Hall at Hurstwood was situated so far from the church that it was always a matter of difficulty to get there on foot, save in very fine weather. The present rector was a man of a type not uncommon in those days in the country. In towns there was a higher standard, London at that time possessing many first-rate preachers, who were also excellent men. But too often in remote parishes they were not only ignorant, but utterly unsuited to their position; spending their days, not in their study or in visiting their flock, but in pursuits very far from consistent with the clerical office.

Lady Elizabeth had bemoaned the state of affairs, but there was no redress; and the absence of all help in spiritual things at Hurstwood had made her the more value and delight in the teaching she got from Dr. Willoughby when in London, even though her predilections were for the Established Church, to which she belonged.

The habit she had formed during the Commonwealth— when service according to the Church of England was forbidden by law, as well as the use of the Book of Common Prayer— of gathering some of the members of her household about her on the Sabbath for the study of God's Word, and the reading of a few of the Church prayers, she had continued after the Parliament, on the Restoration, had placed the present rector in the living of Hurstwood, which they had done apparently without much regard to his qualifications for such a post, or rather his want of them. It was not only that he was illiterate, but that his personal character was such as to destroy all respect.

Thus the state of things at Hurstwood had been one of spiritual destitution, making it little wonder that souls who were hungering for the Bread of Life should gladly seize the opportunity of listening to such a teacher as Dr. Willoughby when they had the chance, even if there might be a measure of risk attaching to it.

Dorothy was sincerely sorry to lose Mrs. Willoughby, who had won her hearty gratitude by her kindness and valuable

assistance during the time of Owen's illness, when her presence had been such a strength and comfort to the worn-out girl,
who had had so many solitary vigils.

All that time she had seen the better and softer side of the
other's character; and even the Puritan costume, which she
had formerly so much disliked, now had almost ceased to seem
objectionable in her eyes; either because she had grown more
accustomed to it, or that the other surroundings at Hurstwood
toned it down, and made it appear less rigid than it had done
in Knightrider Street.

Still, she could not but think Owen's a more tasteful dress,
consisting as it generally did of some rich shade of handsome
camlet[1] or of tabbinet,[2] which well became her tall and rather
portly figure, while a pretty lace kerchief gave lightness and
softness to the whole.

But Dorothy was beginning to care less for externals, and
more for the heart which beat underneath, which in Mrs.
Willoughby's case she knew was a genuinely kind one, and as
true as steel.

And were not even Dr. Willoughby's straight bands and
plain doublet now far more pleasing in her eyes than all the
gold lace and plumes, and silks and satins of such men as Mr.
Crawford and her brother's other friends? For the one she could
trust, and even revere, looking upon him as she did not only as
a hero but also a saint; while the others she could only shun
and shrink from.

---

1 Camlet—A mixed stuff of wool and silk
2 Tabbinet—A kind of poplin.

CHAPTER XVIII

AN OLD FRIEND

"Nor man nor Nature satisfies whom only God created."
                                        MRS. BROWNING

A FEW days after Mrs. Willoughby's departure the household at Hurstwood was startled by the sudden sound of the trampling of horses' hoofs on the gravel of the drive, followed by a loud knocking at the front door.

Dorothy and Owen were sitting in the south parlor, busy over their embroidery frames. The former started and glanced apprehensively at her companion.

"Who can it be? What can it mean? Is it somebody come to take Dr. Willoughby or any of us?"

"I hope not; I don't see how it can be," said Owen. "Hark! there are footsteps coming across the hall."

Dorothy had risen, and appeared on the point of taking flight, which perhaps had been her first thought; but her second was that such a course would be cowardly and undignified.

At any rate it was now too late, for the old serving man threw open the door at that instant, to usher in the newcomers, whoever they might be. But as he did not announce their names Dorothy was still left in doubt as to what was before her.

A tall, fine-looking, middle-aged gentleman in riding boots and spurs advanced into the room, followed, not by a constable, as Dorothy had half feared in her hurried conjectures, but by a young gentlewoman apparently about her own age, with a fair, gentle face and small, slight figure.

The gentleman glanced towards Owen, who had risen on his entrance, and then paused. Dorothy came forward with a vague feeling that the faces ought to be familiar to her.

"Is this Mistress Dorothy Devereux?" he asked, a little doubtfully.

"Yes, I am Dorothy."

"I thought you must be, and yet you have almost grown out of recollection. This is not the child you used to play with, is it, Mary? but a young gentlewoman grown taller than yourself. Dear me, how time runs on, and what changes it brings!"

"Do you not know me, Dorothy?" asked the young maiden, approaching nearer and coming more into the light.

"Is it Mary Stafford?" cried Dorothy, in accents of astonishment and pleasure.

"Yes; it is Mary," said Colonel Stafford. "She could not be satisfied till I had brought her to Hurstwood to renew the long-interrupted intercourse with her old friends here. We would not let the man announce our names, as we wanted to see whether you would recollect us. But it was scarcely to be expected that you would do so at once, after so long an absence. How long is it, my dear, that we have been abroad?" he added, turning to his daughter.

"Nearly ten years, father."

"And meanwhile you young people have grown out of knowledge. Well, now you must make friends again."

"Have you come to live at home now?" inquired Dorothy, who had given her old playmate a warm embrace. "I had not heard anything of your return, or I should have wanted to go and see you."

"We came back quite unexpectedly at the last, only a week or so ago."

"How glad I am to have you here again! I remember how much I missed you when you first went away, for you were about the only playmate I had of my own age, and you used to be so much with us."

"Yes, and I was always so happy when here. It was so pleasant to have companions, for you know I have ever been the only one at home. And Lady Elizabeth was always so good to me; I loved her like another mother."

Tears started into Dorothy's eyes at this allusion, bringing back as it did so vividly the old joyous sheltered days of childhood.

Mary put her arm round her with a caressing, sympathetic gesture.

"Could we not go and take a turn in the garden?" she said. "I long to look again upon the old spots; and you see they are deep in conversation, so they will not miss us;" indicating with a little motion of her head Colonel Stafford and Owen, whom the former had drawn aside into one of the large bay windows, where in a low voice he was asking her to give him some details of the death of Lady Elizabeth, of which he had only heard the report since his return; and also he wished to know whether the dreadful rumor which had come to his ears as to the fate of Sir Richard were true, or was without foundation.

So the two young people stepped into the sunshine without, and sauntered arm in arm up and down the terrace walk in full talk. Each had so much to say, and so much she wished to hear from the other.

At length the colonel's voice summoned them.

"Come, Mary, my dear; we must be returning homewards now, or your mother will be wondering what has become of us."

"Must you really go? Could you not leave Mary behind?" said Dorothy pleadingly. "Oh, do let her stay; it would be so nice."

Mary's looks seconded the request as plainly as looks could do so.

"What, you want to rob me of my daughter! Is that to be the result of my bringing her to see you?" said Colonel Stafford smiling. "Nay, I can't quite agree to that proposal. We must wait and see what her mother says."

"And if she agrees you will bring her again some day soon, and leave her for a good long visit, will you not? Please promise that much; and do try and win Mrs. Stafford's consent," urged Dorothy in a coaxing manner that Colonel Stafford could not resist.

"Well, well, we will see; we will see. Mary's heart is set on it, that is evident; but it must rest with her mother. I will not say 'No,' if she says 'Yes.'"

With that Dorothy had to be content. She watched them remount their horses and ride off, waving her hand to them till they were out of sight; and then she rejoined Owen in the south parlor.

The visit had brightened her much. "I do so hope Mrs. Stafford will let Mary come and stay here a good while. It would be delightful to have her. I always was so fond of her, and so we all were."

"Yes; it would be very pleasant for you to have such a

companion, and I much hope her parents will consent to her coming."

Dorothy, full of eagerness, began planning which chamber should be given her, and at length decided upon the one next to her own.

"For Mary does not care for grandeur, I am sure, and would rather be near me than away by herself in one of the 'state rooms,' as I call them. Will you tell the maids tomorrow to get it ready, Owen?"

"Yes, Mistress Dorothy, if you like," returned Owen, with a smile at the girl's eagerness; "but you are not yet sure, are you, of her coming?"

"I shall be very disappointed if she doesn't. And at any rate we may as well be ready for her. It will do no harm having the chamber prepared."

Meantime Colonel Stafford and Mary pursued their way to Stoke Manor, the country seat of the Staffords; the former giving his daughter as they rode along the details which he had gleaned from Owen respecting Lady Elizabeth, Sir Richard and Cicely.

"How dreadfully sad it all seems!" she said sorrowfully. "Poor Dorothy! what she must have gone through! It seems to me almost a wonder she could have lived through it."

"Ah, my dear, hearts don't break so easily. They must be tough things, I think, or they could not bear all that some have to endure. But I am heartily sorry for that poor child; and we must try and get your mother to spare you to her for a time."

"I should like to go very much. How handsome Dorothy has grown! Don't you think so, father?"

"Yes, she is a fine creature, and evidently has plenty of spirit and courage in her. There is something very winsome about her. She is getting more like her mother than she used to be."

"Oh, how sweet Lady Elizabeth was!" said Mary, "I don't think any one could ever be like her; I mean, not quite equal to her. I used to love her dearly; in fact, I think I almost worshipped her, she was so good and gentle and gracious."

"She used to win all hearts, I believe; so I am not surprised that my little Mary lost hers. You can't do better than take her for your model, my child."

On dismounting from their horses both father and daughter went at once to the withdrawing room to report themselves to

Mrs. Stafford, half doubting what sort of reception they might meet with, for they were a little late in returning.

Mrs. Stafford was a person of a type as far removed as possible from that of Lady Elizabeth, of whom both Colonel Stafford and Mary had been speaking in such high terms of praise. Imperious and somewhat overbearing, it was she who ruled the household; and as her temper was capricious and uncertain, it was always doubtful whether a request or suggestion would be received favorably or not; as it depended upon the mood of the moment.

Thus Colonel Stafford and Mary both felt a certain amount of trepidation as they approached the subject of the latter's visit to Hurstwood, fearing a decided negative, and conscious that in that case they would both be too cowardly to oppose the decision, or to try and fight for their own way in the matter. They knew by long experience that such a course would only raise a domestic storm, which would descend on their own devoted heads, and of which they would feel the consequences for a long time to come. Thus to keep the peace was always the one thing to be aimed at.

The father and daughter were much attached to one another, and were always happy in each other's company; but they were not allowed to enjoy that happiness too often, the exacting nature of Mrs. Stafford causing her claims upon them to be somewhat heavy, and one or other of them generally had to be in attendance upon her.

She had been a beauty in her youth, and was still a fine-looking woman. In Paris, where Colonel Stafford for some years had held a diplomatic appointment, she had been one of the leaders of fashion, and had led a gay, worldly life. Now that they had returned to England it was not her intention to remain long buried in the country, even at so pleasant a home as Stoke Manor; and she was already beginning to urge her husband to seek some post under government or at court; something that she hoped would involve a residence in London, when she could again be in the centre of the gay world.

Poor Colonel Stafford, who loved his country home, was already gloomily anticipating the time when he would once more be dragged forth from its peaceful retreat.

To Mary's great delight, her mother was in a more gracious mood than usual, and did not oppose the idea of her going to Hurstwood.

"Yes, child, you may go if you choose, as long as you don't ask me to accompany you. If you like to bury yourself there, do so by all means. It must be insufferably dull there, I should think, a great empty house like that;—but that is your affair. Yes, you may go, and I will send for you when I want you back. For the next few weeks I am going to have the house full of company, and then we may be going away ourselves."

Mary, duly grateful for the concession, thanked her mother warmly, and then let the subject drop.

All the next day Dorothy was on the tip-toe of expectation, straining her ears to catch the sounds of horses' hoofs, until she more than once fancied she heard them. It proved a delusive hope, however, and the day closed without the arrival of her friend.

But in the course of the following morning Mary appeared—come with bag and baggage to stay for a while.

Dorothy gave her a hearty welcome, and led her to her chamber. It had the same lovely view from its windows that Dorothy's had, and looked gay with the spring flowers with which the latter had decorated it.

"How did you like living in Paris?" asked Dorothy, a little later on, when they were sauntering round the kitchen garden, whither she had led her friend, that she might admire the blossoms on the apple trees, which were a mass of delicate white and pink blooms.

"Not at all," replied Mary. "I was always wishing to return to dear old England, which I like far the best; and I cannot tell you how glad I am to be at home again. But you see father had to stay; he could not throw up his post; and mother liked the life there. But I am very glad the time has come to an end, for it was always a little like banishment."

"You don't seem to have changed a bit. You are just as simple and nice as ever," remarked Dorothy, surveying her friend with a critical glance. "I was afraid when you went away that you would never come back the same. I thought the French people would spoil you; but they haven't."

Mary smiled, and then said, as she passed her arm through that of her companion, "But you are altered, Dorothy. I don't mean that you are not just as nice and dear as ever, in fact, nicer somehow, but you are older and graver."

"Naturally I am older, how could I help it? And I dare say

I am graver. At one time I thought I never could have laughed or smiled again."

"Poor Dorothy!" said Mary in sympathizing tones. "How dreadful it must have been for you all through that time of the plague!"

"Yes, I shouldn't like to go through it again. But I made it worse by my own stubbornness and discontent."

And then Dorothy went on to tell her friend how Mrs. Willoughby and her son, who had given her a shelter all that time in London, had now come to Hurstwood, driven from London by the Five Mile Act; of the persecution the latter had already endured; of the little meetings he held—though this of course was only divulged under promise of the strictest secrecy—and of the risk attending them.

"We are going to have another tomorrow night."

"I should like to hear this great preacher."

"Oh, but you mustn't come, Mary, dear. Think of the possible risk. I am sure you ought not to be present without your father's consent. What would he say if you got involved in any trouble of that sort while staying here? He would say I was not to be trusted, and I fear would never let you come again."

Mary's was a gentle, clinging nature, with a far less strong will than Dorothy's. Consequently she yielded the point, at any rate for the time being, and allowed the other to decide for her.

By degrees the talk turned again to the old days when they had been children together.

"You have not told me anything about Eugene yet," said Mary at length. "Has he remained the same, or is he altered?"

"Oh, he is so changed," returned Dorothy sadly. "Being at court seems to have ruined him. He may come down here any time to take possession, as now the place belongs to him, and then you will see for yourself."

Not much more was said on the subject then, but Dorothy noticed that Mary from time to time managed to turn the conversation back into the same channel, until she almost began to suspect that her friend must have some secret soft spot in her heart for him whom she remembered as a bright, good-natured boy of about sixteen, before he had left home and become spoiled by evil associations. But the topic was not a pleasant one to the sister, and she always avoided it as much as she could.

The next evening came, and the little company assembled as arranged in the old barn. They were allowed that time to meet without molestation, and departed at the close to their respective homes in peace. And so it was for the next two or three times, until they had become emboldened again, and began to hope that persecution was at an end. But their hopes were to prove delusive.

It was the first evening that Mrs. Willoughby had accompanied her son, for the walk had hitherto been too long a one for her, until she had more fully recovered her strength. This evening, however, she was present, and they were a larger company than usual. Carried away by Dr. Willoughby's eloquence, they were perhaps less on their guard, less watchful for any suspicious sounds that might indicate cause for alarm.

Suddenly the little audience, listening with wrapt attention to the words of the preacher, was startled by the unceremonious bursting open of the door of the barn, and the entrance of the dreaded constables.

"Can you not fly? You know the place of concealment," whispered Dorothy hurriedly to Dr. Willoughby, while all the rest of the party save Mrs. Willoughby and Owen were seeking their own safety by flight in all directions.

But there was no time. The new-comers were too quick. They knew their man now by sight, and in a moment had arrested him in the name of the law. He was their prey; the only one they sought; and the case was clear against him. He had been caught in the act of holding an unlawful service, and of preaching to almost twenty persons.

The foremost man had a low, cunning face, and he was evidently acting, as so many did at that time, from the desire of gain. Numbers of low informers sprang up all over the country who, for the sake of a share in the fine imposed, were ready basely to betray any one without distinction; while others acted, like Mr. Crawford, from personal grudge and hatred. The latter had found a willing tool in this man Hart, who for the sake of Mr. Crawford's gold was prepared to do even worse things than to take to prison one so blameless and inoffensive as Dr. Willoughby.

Dorothy saw that escape for him now was hopeless. Then she must at once carry out another plan, which she had formed in her mind in case things should turn out as they had done.

In the momentary confusion she escaped by the door nearest to the house, and fleeing as if for dear life she hurried on, panting for breath, until she had reached her own chamber. There she hastily unlocked a cabinet, and taking therefrom a little jewel case she chose out of it a certain jewel which she had already in her mind destined for this purpose, should it be needed. For of ready money she had but little, if any; and ten pounds was a larger sum in those days than in these.

Darting down stairs again, she hastened back to the barn.

She had been so quick that she found the little group, of which Dr. Willoughby was the centre still, standing much as she had left them. Hart, with his hand laid on the shoulder of his victim, who was meekly submitting to the indignity, wore a leer on his evil face.

Gliding noiselessly to Mrs. Willoughby's side Dorothy whispered, "You said, did you not, that the penalty for the second offence was imprisonment for six months or a fine of ten pounds?"

"Yes, it is even so; and there is no alternative for us; he must go to prison," returned Mrs. Willoughby in a voice which she tried to steady.

"Nay," said Dorothy, "we will pay the fine. This jewel is worth more than ten pounds, as I happen to know, for I was with my father when he bought it for me in London. Take it and see if that wretch will not gladly accept it."

"But, my dear," began Mrs. Willoughby, in tones of astonishment as well as of remonstrance, "I cannot allow you to do any such thing."

"Oh, you must; indeed you must," pleaded Dorothy. "Do I not owe you far, far more than this? Would not my dearest mother have done the same, and infinitely more, if she could, for one who had been so much to her? I owe the debt she could not pay for all his goodness to her at the last; as well as for all your kindness to myself. Please do not say another word; you must not indeed. And time is going. If you will not give it to that horrid man, I must," she added, with a touch of her old imperiousness.

Too much touched to have a word of thanks ready, but seeing that Dorothy was determined not to be baulked in her generous intentions, Mrs. Willoughby advanced to Hart, as he was about to lead away the young divine, who for the sake of others, and of preventing any disturbance, was making no resistance. She requested a moment's conversation with him.

Leaving his prisoner in charge of the men he had brought with him, he went apart with her to the farther end of the barn. His eye glistened as it fell upon the proffered jewel, which he at once perceived was worth more than the prescribed sum of ten pounds. With greed of gain written on every feature, his hand closed over it; the evil thought darting into his mind that he would be able to make still more out of this business next time, when the fine would be infinitely higher; or failing that—and he knew this was what Mr. Crawford was aiming at—the sentence of transportation for seven years should be carried out. And if he could only bring that about, he knew his employer would reward him handsomely.

The fine having been paid, the disturbers of the peace prepared to depart, and Dr. Willoughby, to his astonishment, found himself at liberty again.

"We have to thank Mistress Dorothy," explained Mrs. Willoughby briefly; for the young maiden had begged her not to enter into particulars as to how the fine had been paid. "Her quick thought has again found a way out of the difficulty; and we owe her many thanks."

"Pray say no more," exclaimed the latter, with heightened color. "But I fear we are not set free from further interference. And the penalty for the next offence is heavier still, is it not?"

"It is," replied Dr. Willoughby gravely.

"Shall you continue to run the risk?" she asked.

"I have no choice, or it seems to me I have none," he promptly answered, his face as calm and unruffled and his manner as quiet as if nothing had occurred calculated to disturb his composure. "I have a message to proclaim, and woe is me if I shrink back from proclaiming it. I must obey God rather than man, and I can leave the consequences with Him. If He has work for me to do in the gaol or the plantations rather than here, I must follow His bidding. My life is His; for I am not my own, but His servant, and He shall have the disposal of me. He can frustrate all designs against me if He sees fit; and if not, it is because I can serve Him better in some other way."

"But still we must use prudence, my son, and not heedlessly run into danger. Does it not say, 'If they persecute you in one city, flee ye to another?'"

"You are right, my mother; and I would desire to use all due precaution. It would not be well to meet here again, now that the place is known to our enemies. Is there any other within our reach?"

"I should think," remarked Owen, "that now that the weather has become warm and genial we might meet in the thickest part of the woods, and there be screened from observation; while if disturbed it would be easy to fly in all directions; easier than to make one's escape from a room, where the moment the door is opened the numbers assembled can be seen at a glance."

"That would be a capital plan surely," cried Dorothy eagerly. "Near the old well, I should say, would be the best spot," she added, with a significant glance towards Owen. And thus it was settled.

Meantime Mary Stafford, left to herself, and feeling sleepy, had retired to rest at an early hour. Consequently it was not till the next morning, when the two girls were sitting together in the wide window seat in Dorothy's room, through the open casement of which the soft May breeze was wafting in the perfume of many a sweet-scented flower, that she heard any details of what had taken place on the previous night. She looked excited as she listened.

"But why do you run such dreadful risks, Dorothy? I should think it would be better to put a stop to these meetings."

"If you were very hungry—starving, in fact—would you not be willing to run a little risk for the sake of obtaining food that you knew was within reach?"

"But that is different," said Mary, not understanding her friend's drift.

"Only inasmuch as that the one is for the body, which anyhow must perish sooner or later, while the other is for that part of us which lives for ever, and therefore surely is of greater importance."

"I see what you mean. Oh, Dorothy, then you too know what it is to be hungry and unsatisfied? Oh, how often during all these years I have been abroad I have wished that I could find something that would satisfy!" cried Mary, forgetting all reserve. "I have longed over and over again for one of the old talks with Lady Elizabeth. She often used to read to Cicely and me when we asked her—you seldom seemed to care to join us—some of the holy words and sayings of Christ, and then she would talk about His life on earth, and His death for us, and all His love until He seemed so real and so gracious and so sweet that I thought I loved Him. But it all seems to have died away during these years abroad. There was no one in Paris that I came across who appeared to care for these things; no one who gave me any help; and I have often felt so weary of all the gaieties and foolish doings that we were mixed up with."

Dorothy put her arm round her friend, feeling drawn more closely to her than ever.

"Let us together seek to know more of Him. He says those 'who seek shall find,' and those who 'hunger and thirst after righteousness shall be filled.' Oh, I wish you could hear Dr. Willoughby preach! He does help one so. But of course you mustn't run the risk without Colonel Stafford's consent."

"And that he would not give, though he is so kind," said Mary sadly. "He has no sympathy with the Puritans or Presbyterians, whichever they call themselves. And if he heard of my being mixed up with these doings, I am afraid he would not let me remain here."

"Then I must tell you all I can recollect of what he says as well as I can. Though of course that won't be a bit like hearing him for yourself."

"But it will be far better than nothing," said Mary, who in her hunger was glad to seize and make the most of a few crumbs, if she could not have a whole loaf.

"I wonder," she remarked a little later, after Dorothy had given her an account of the discourse of the previous evening, "that Mrs. Willoughby can let her son expose himself to such danger."

"She cannot prevent his acting as he thinks fit. But she would not do so if she could. All through the time of the plague she never tried to keep him back from going among the people into the very midst of infection. She is just as brave and fearless as he is, and would not hinder him from doing what he considers his duty for any consideration."

"It is very grand of her," said Mary; "for she must surely think a great deal of such a son as that."

"Of course she does, for he is the only one left to her, and he is everything in the world to her. Yes, it is very unselfish and devoted of her."

CHAPTER XIX

DR. WILLOUGHBY MAKES A DISCOVERY

"Laid on Thine altar, O my Lord Divine,
  Accept my will this day, for Jesu's sake.
I have no jewels to adorn Thy shrine,
  Nor any world-famed sacrifice to make;
But here I bring within my trembling hand,
  This will of mine, a thing that seemeth small;
But Thou, O Lord, alone can'st understand
  How, when I yield Thee this, I yield mine all."

A WEEK or two later the sound of horses' hoofs was again heard on the gravel of the carriage-drive that led to the Hall. The two girls were on the terrace, where they could hear the sound, but could not see who the new-comer might be, as the front entrance was on the other side of the house.

It was Mary's turn now to surmise what the sounds might bode.

"I hope that is not father come to fetch me away," she exclaimed, "I have been so happy here."

"If it is, we will try and persuade him to allow you to remain longer. I wish he would leave you, oh, for ever so long. It is so nice having you here. But let us go and see if it is Colonel Stafford."

They went round by the path leading to the front of the house, and reached the porch just as the new-comer was alighting from his horse.

"Eugene!" was Dorothy's exclamation, not as she could have wished had been possible, in tones of rapturous delight, but in accents expressive of something almost the opposite. However, he did not seem to perceive it.

"Well, Dorothy, I suppose you have been expecting me; but I couldn't come before. However, now I must see to business," he said, with rather a consequential air. "But who have you here?" he added, as his eye fell upon Mary. "Will you introduce me to your friend?"

"You do not need any introduction. This is Mary Stafford."

"You don't remember me?" said Mary advancing.

"I remember a little girl of that name, but I did not know she and the blooming maiden I see before me were the same."

And as he took off his hat he made such a profound bow in recognition of her charms that the plumes nearly swept the ground.

Mary with a smile returned the salutation, conscious at the same time of a feeling of disappointment, as she glanced at the face, which had lost all the old boyish frankness and brightness, and bore traces of the life of dissipation and self-indulgence of the last few years.

They had been great friends as children. He had often playfully called her his little wife, and had ever treated her with kindness and a certain boyish chivalry. And during all these years of absence she had never forgotten her 'young esquire' as he used to call himself. But the look with which he now regarded her made her turn away with the disappointed feeling that this was not the Eugene whom she remembered, but some one quite different, who fell far short of her ideal.

It was a great comfort to Dorothy having Mary with her. It took off some of the awkwardness of this their first meeting after the little episode which had closed her brother's last visit. Not that he seemed at all self-conscious, or in any way abashed; but Dorothy, alas! had lost her confidence in him, as well as all respect for him. Still, he was her brother; nothing could break that tie; and she would gladly have done anything she possibly could to have influenced him in the right direction. Mary's presence, she hoped, would act as some little check upon him, and cause him to exercise more self-restraint than he might otherwise have done.

The family man of business came, and there was a grand hunt for any will that Sir Richard might have left. But none at first appeared to be forthcoming.

At length, however, one day, by the casual touching of a spring, a secret drawer was discovered in an old-fashioned bureau which stood in Sir Richard's closet, and within which lay the will. It had been made shortly before the last visit to London, when he was preparing to go abroad.

THE WILL WAS FOUND IN AN OLD FASHIONED BUREAU.

The lawyer summoned Dorothy and Owen, and in their presence, as well as that of the young baronet, he read it aloud.

Dorothy was mentioned, and provided for with a yearly income out of the estate, in the event of her surviving her mother; and there was also a portion assigned to Cicely, which was to revert to the elder sister, should the younger die first, or *vice versa*. There was also a handsome legacy to Owen, and a smaller one to old William, as well as to two or three others. The rest was left to the only son.

After that there were various matters of business to be gone into, which kept Eugene occupied with the lawyer for some part of each day. When he joined his sister and her friend, it seemed as if the gentle influence of the latter were telling upon him; as if the sight of her were bringing back softer recollections of bygone days and better things. Was his old boyish love reviving? or was he feeling how different he was from what he had been in those days, and how great a gulf separated him from the innocent maiden who no longer looked trustfully into his face, as she had done as a child, but seemed sometimes to wear a reproving air?

At any rate he appeared on his best behavior while with them, to Dorothy's infinite relief; and the oaths with which the young gallants were accustomed to interlard their conversation were in some measure restrained, while his manner was a little less free and easy. So all went tolerably smoothly for the short time he remained at Hurstwood; and, much to his sister's satisfaction, he said nothing about Mr. Crawford, seeming, indeed, to have forgotten the whole affair.

When Dorothy had retired to her chamber on the night after her brother's departure, Owen came to her, as she did sometimes, to render some slight assistance required.

"Then things are to go on just as usual, are they not?" asked Dorothy.

"Yes, for the present. Sir Eugene says he should not dream of living here all the year round, as his father did; he likes London better; but he must have the place kept up and ready for him to come to whenever the whim seizes him. He seems to expect to draw a large income to spend upon his pleasures and luxuries; but I told him the place would scarcely bear it, and it would be bad policy to grudge necessary expense in keeping it up, and so let it go to rack and ruin. But he doesn't seem to have much thought for anything but the gratification of the present hour."

"Still he has behaved better this time, and we will be thankful for that," remarked Dorothy. "And it is a great relief that we can go on as we have been doing. My fear was that when he became master he would be always filling the house with a set of dissipated friends, as he did at Christmas; but I might have remembered that life at court must be to him much more full of excitement and amusement than a quiet country home. Having become accustomed to town, he will not care to bury himself in the country. So I don't expect he will be here much."

Meantime the little meetings were held in the thickest part of the woods. The days were long now, for they had entered on May, and the season was a warm and lovely one. Everything was forward that year, so that the foliage on the trees was already thick enough to form a screen, more especially as there was a rather dense growth of underwood. They made a little clearing in one spot, and at each meeting scouts were set to watch in all directions for the approach of the enemy.

Dr. Willoughby had been shown the stone near the old well which formed a sort of trap door, giving admittance to the underground passage which led to the secret chamber; and it was arranged that he should always take his stand near it, so that should an alarm be suddenly given he could seek refuge there unobserved in the midst of the confusion that would be sure to ensue. Owen and Dorothy, who alone were in the secret, undertook to cover his retreat, as it was most important that the place of concealment should not be discovered by any one.

They did not dare to sing, lest the sounds should betray them; but what they wanted most was to have the Word of God opened up, and that the young preacher did with a freshness and power that were new to them. Such preaching they had never heard in Hurstwood before. Never had they listened to anything like the fervid words which fell from his lips, and which brought conviction and life and healing with them to many, who, having the plan of salvation clearly put before them for the first time in their lives, embraced it with all their hearts in the simplicity of a faith that did not question nor doubt, but gladly received the good news as it was told to them.

No wonder they listened with breathless eagerness and wrapt attention. There were no sleepy hearers, but hearty earnestness characterized the whole of the little assembly; for none who were not in earnest would have run the risk of attending such a meeting.

But there was one face among all those upturned to his which the young divine's eye often sought, perhaps unconsciously to himself—the face of a maiden whose countenance seemed to glow and kindle as she listened, and whose eyes shone with a deep earnest look as some new thought awakened a responsive chord in her heart. For Dorothy had much to learn, and eagerly she drank in each fresh truth, or fresh unfolding of an old one from the lips of one whose teaching came with all the weight of a consistent life and example.

Owen, too, felt it to be a rich spiritual feast, and it gladdened her heart to find that Dorothy, who once had turned so coldly away from anything of the sort, enjoyed it as much as she did herself.

But Hart, backed and incited as he was by Mr. Crawford, was not the man to let the grass grow under his feet, or to lose any opportunity of enriching himself, such as that presented by the chance of again catching Dr. Willoughby infringing the law as laid down by the Conventicle Act.

In some way or other he got scent of the new place of meeting, and one evening one of the scouts suddenly rushed into their midst with the news that the enemy was upon them. They had been descried, through the trunks and branches of the trees, advancing stealthily towards them.

In a moment every one took to flight, Dr. Willoughby, as previously arranged, disappearing through the trap door behind the thick bushes, while Owen and Dorothy carefully screened his movements from observation. Then they turned and hurried towards the house; and by the time Hart arrived on the spot—for he was not quite sure in which direction it lay, so that a little time was lost in that way—the little company had all dispersed; and though he came upon one or two stragglers, that did not afford him sufficient grounds for an accusation of holding an unlawful assembly. Besides his prey, the only one whom Mr. Crawford had directed him to seize, had vanished altogether.

Angry at being thus baffled, Hart ground his teeth with rage and disappointment, inwardly vowing to leave no stone unturned until he had accomplished his purpose.

Meantime Dr. Willoughby, making his way along the underground passage and up the little flight of stairs, found himself in the secret chamber, where he remained until Owen, after a certain interval of time had elapsed, and she thought all was safe, came to release him.

The escape had been managed so easily that they all congratulated themselves upon the advantages presented by this new place of meeting; and again, on the appointed evening, they gathered themselves together as usual, except that perhaps the numbers were a trifle smaller, two or three timid natures fearing to adventure themselves.

But again Hart and his men appeared upon the scene, this time creeping up so stealthily and coming so suddenly upon them, that the scout had only just time to utter a warning note, and Dr. Willoughby barely managed to escape before the men were on his track. Another moment's delay, and he would have been taken. The rest of the company, much alarmed, hurried away helter skelter, some in one direction, some in another.

However, Hart and his men were once more baffled; and once more the former inwardly vowed vengeance, and resolved to accomplish his object sooner or later.

That evening, when Dr. Willoughby reached the cottage, where his mother was awaiting him, for she had not been present at the meeting, he sank wearily into a seat, and the watchful eye of the other saw that his face wore a graver look than usual.

"Have you been disturbed again, my son?"

"Yes; and it was a very narrow escape this time. We were all but caught. Mother, this place seems getting almost too hot to hold me," he said, with a shade of despondency in his tone.

"I fear me it is," she said anxiously; "and the risk you run is a great one."

"Moreover there appears no hope of my getting employment here. I seem to have too many enemies in the place, and they prejudice the minds of those who perhaps would not otherwise be unfavorably disposed towards me. The farmer whose boys I have been teaching, told me today that he should not require my services any longer, and he refused to give me any reason; but I suspect it is that my enemies have been persuading him to dismiss me."

"What can be their motive?"

"Perhaps they wish to starve me out of the place."

"But who is there that can be so bitter against you? What have you ever done to make an enemy here?"

Stephen Willoughby did not reply for a moment, and then briefly and half unwillingly he related the little episode of his encounter with Mr. Crawford; how he had interfered on Dorothy's behalf, and had discomfited his adversary.

"I do not think he has forgiven me," he added, which, was a mild way of putting it; for that Mr. Crawford was his bitter enemy, and at the bottom of all this persecution, he was well aware.

A deepening shade of anxiety came into Mrs. Willoughby's face. This was the first time she had heard of the occurrence; and while she acknowledged to herself that her son could have done no less, she yet felt, from what she knew and had heard of Mr. Crawford, that it was only too probable that implacable hatred, as well as fierce jealousy, had been aroused in his breast; even though, as she told herself, he could have no real cause for the latter feeling. For it was impossible that her son could be in any way his rival. Situated as he was, even if he cared for Dorothy, he must know that she was about as far beyond his reach as one of the stars in the sky above. Yet jealousy, she knew, was often ill-founded and unreasonable; and she had seen enough of human nature to feel that possibly it mingled with other motives, if it did not form the chief one, in causing this unrelenting enmity on the part of Mr. Crawford.

Noticing her son's wearied look, she suddenly started up, exclaiming, "The best thing I can do at the present moment is to get you some supper; and while you are taking it we can discuss this matter further."

The meal she placed on the table was of the plainest and scantiest, revealing their poverty as plainly as did the cottage itself, with its bare walls and homely articles of furniture. The floor was flagged with stones, the walls whitewashed and destitute of any hangings, the rafters showed overhead. The only signs of anything like comfort were presented by a folding screen and an easy chair with cushions, which Dorothy had insisted on sending for Mrs. Willoughby, and which the latter had consented to accept as a loan.

But Dorothy, though she thought it dreadful for them to be so poor, and would gladly have done more to help them had she been able, yet never dreamt of the depth of poverty to which they were being reduced by the melting away of their little store, and the failing to find means of replenishing it. And this was no uncommon case. Numbers of the evicted clergy all over the country suffered as much or more; some of them being driven, through failing to get teaching or other suitable employment, to take the posts of shepherds, or of common laborers on farms, to save themselves and their families from starvation.

No complaint, however, was uttered by the two inmates of the little cottage. They tried to accept their lot unmurmuringly, even cheerfully. Still, that night they came to the conclusion that if they would neither starve nor run into debt, it was time they tried some fresh plan. Would it not be better to make a new start somewhere else, where the same spirit of bitterness and persecution did not exist?

But where to go, and what to do, that was the difficulty. There had been a reason for coming to Hurstwood, and it had appeared to be clearly the best course for them; but now all the wide world lay alike before them, no one place presenting any opening more than another.

"We must spread our difficulty before God," said Stephen. "He can make a way for us out of it, or give us strength to bear whatever may be before us."

After Mrs. Willoughby had retired to her chamber that night her son, who seemed in a restless mood, paced the room several times to and fro; and then, as if he felt the need of more air, opening the cottage door he resumed his walk up and down in front, like a sentinel on his beat. His hands were clasped behind his back, and his head bent with his eyes fixed on the ground in an attitude of deep meditation, as he pondered over many things.

He was earnestly asking direction as to what course to pursue, and willingness to be guided in all things. For as the thought of leaving Hurstwood presented itself to his mind, he found himself strangely loth to entertain the idea. How was it? It would have seemed natural to have been glad to quit a place where he had met with so much persecution, and where, for perhaps the first time in his life, he had made a bitter enemy.

But as the lowering face of the latter rose before him, so also side by side with it arose a pure, frank, girlish face, with truth and honesty and nobility stamped on every feature of it;

a face that though handsome had once looked cold and proud, but which now seemed to wear a new beauty in the expression of rest and peace, of softness and gentleness which had come into it. It had often haunted him of late; he had even seen it in his dreams; but this evening it rose before him more persistently than ever. He tried to turn his thoughts into another channel, but back they went into the same groove.

Now it was a vision of a young maiden tenderly waiting upon his mother in her sick room that arose before him; then it was the same maiden sitting listening with kindling face to preaching in the old barn or under the leafy canopy of the trees; anon the countenance was wearing a look of high courage and resolve, as with quick promptitude she formed a plan for his escape, or with spirit and indignation flashing from her eyes bravely confronted her unmanly persecutor, and refused to listen to his solicitations.

Had he found here the secret of his unwillingness to leave Hurstwood? He almost started as he asked himself the question. Alas, for his peace of mind! He could not honestly deny that therein lay the true reason.

The discovery caused him a shock. Was it possible that he had allowed himself to drift into any sort of personal feeling for this young maiden? Could he indeed have been so foolish, so utterly, inconceivably foolish! He might as well hope to win a princess as to win her, he told himself. It was not for an evicted Presbyterian minister, with no hopes of preferment, but, on the contrary, with the prospect of unmitigated poverty and difficulties of all kinds before him, to dream of lifting his eyes to Mistress Dorothy Devereux of Hurstwood Hall, the daughter of Sir Richard Devereux, the granddaughter of the Earl of Burnham, and the descendant of a long line of Royalist ancestors.

True, he could count back as many ancestors perhaps as she could; but then his had been a family that had come down in the world, and had been shorn of its ancient patrimony, while hers had ever held up their heads, and had allied themselves rather with those above than beneath them in social standing. Unworldly as Stephen Willoughby was, and caring little for earthly dignities as he did, his thoughts being set on things far grander and more enduring, still he could not fail to be aware how these things were estimated by others, and that an impassable gulf separated them, high-souled and generous though the maiden was, and free from all sordidness and covetousness.

Alas, of what folly had he been guilty! He scarcely knew how it had come about, but he had only himself to blame. Never had Dorothy transgressed the bounds of maidenly modesty and propriety; on the contrary, all that time in London she had treated him with reserve and almost disdain; and the ghost of a smile played around his lips as he recalled the scene in Aldersgate Street, when, obeying Lady Elizabeth's directions, he had gone to her door to request her to accompany him whither she knew not. He remembered how he had shrunk in the most cowardly way from confronting the young beauty, and could have wished such a charge had not been laid upon him. And he had no reason to think that she entertained any very different feelings now. Her nature had softened and mellowed under the discipline and trials through which she had passed; she had by degrees emerged into the sunshine of a soul at peace with God, and a new humility and gentleness had given her manner a charm it had previously lacked. But that was all.

Alas, alas! that he had not been more watchful over himself; that insensibly he should have glided into this! Well, only one course remained for him now. He must sever himself as quickly as possible from the scenes connected with her, and try to forget her.

Late into the night Stephen Willoughby still paced up and down, fighting and wrestling with the thoughts and feelings that surged within. His peace of mind was disturbed; he could not rest until he had regained it.

Was he coveting a gift which God had withheld from him? The thought was pain to his guileless spirit. Was he allowing another to usurp the throne of his heart, where Christ had, as he hoped, reigned supreme? Nay, that must not be. The very idea was grief to him. That image must be banished, or at any rate must be thrust into the background. It must not for a moment be allowed the first place.

And so in the silence and darkness of the still summer's night he looked up beyond the stars overhead to Him who sat enthroned above them, and yet had a fellow feeling for every struggling, burdened, sorrowful, human soul. To Him he made his petition for help and strength, for singleness of purpose and purity of motive. And he knew he should not ask in vain. He prayed to be made willing to surrender this the desire of his heart, if it should not be according to God's will and purpose to grant it him. And as to his future he must place it all in his Heavenly Father's hands, and wait the unfolding of His plans. He could not see a single step before him, but his Guide knew the way and would lead him, gently, tenderly, wisely, if he only committed himself to Him.

CHAPTER XX

CONTINUED PERSECUTION

"To be made with Thee one spirit
    Is the boon that I lingering ask.
To have no bar 'twixt my soul and Thine;
    My thoughts to echo Thy will divine;
Myself Thy servant, for any task."—LUCY LARCOM

THE following morning Stephen Willoughby's countenance bore marks of the sleepless night which he had passed; but it also wore a resolute look, as of one determined to conquer, and not to be conquered by circumstances.

When breakfast was over, as he had no longer any pupils to attend to, he sat down to his books, while his mother was busy about her domestic duties, in which she declined his help, though he playfully offered it, saying that if everything else failed he must turn household drudge, as he could not live in idleness. However, as she very decidedly refused his proffered assistance—which she appeared to think would be no assistance at all—he drew his books towards him, and sat down as if to study.

But after his mother had quitted the room, and he felt himself no longer under observation, the leaves of his book remained unturned, as leaning back in his chair, he gave himself up to a profound reverie.

Through the open casement were wafted to him the songs of the birds, and the sweet scent of the honeysuckle and roses growing against the cottage. It was a lovely June morning, and everything in Nature seemed rejoicing in the bright sunshine. But Stephen Willoughby's heart felt heavy as lead; the clouds seemed to have gathered around him more darkly than ever before; even in Newgate he had not been conscious of such deep depression as that which he was now feeling.

And no wonder; for after all he was but human, and in himself possessed of no more strength than others, while his nature was one peculiarly susceptible to suffering, such as that which was now weighing upon him. But the notion of sinking under trial was one which he could not bear to entertain for a moment. Strength and endurance and courage were the qualities that he admired. Was it a necessary part of the discipline that he was now being made to feel his weakness,—his "miserable, abject weakness," as he called it to himself? For he had to confess his utter inability to tear from his heart at once and for ever that image which had unbidden found entrance there, and which in his extreme conscientiousness he deemed it wrong to suffer to remain there.

Yet he was powerless to expel it, and the struggle gave him infinite pain. Well, he must bear the pain, and bear it manfully, he said to himself, as he rose from his seat and again paced the room to and fro, as he had done during the conflict of the previous evening. And now what plan could be thought of for the future? What should be his next step? Whither should he go? For that he must go forth from Hurstwood seemed plain.

While still debating these questions in his mind, a figure passed the window. It was the messenger who brought letters to the village. He went to the open casement, and calling to the man, received from him what he had brought.

It was a letter directed to himself. On opening it he found it was from Mr. Evelyn, who wrote to say that a friend of his, living at his country seat in Kent, was in want of a private secretary for a few months, to help him over some literary work which he had undertaken; and he had applied to him, Mr. Evelyn, to know if he could recommend him any one. It had occurred to him that Stephen Willoughby might like such a post, provided he had not already obtained something better. His friend, Mr. Cavendish, would also like Dr. Willoughby to officiate as private chaplain while under his roof; thus he would be provided with plenty of occupation of a kind that would be congenial to him. After mentioning the salary that would be given, Mr. Evelyn added that if Dr. Willoughby thought further of the matter, he had better write direct to Mr. Cavendish, as time was an object, his services being required at once.

Stephen Willoughby's first impulse was to lift up his heart in gratitude for this unexpected opening in this his hour of need, in which he clearly saw God's good hand. Then going out into the little kitchen at the back, where his mother was at that moment engaged in making a pie for dinner,—wondering as she did so, how much longer they would be able to have any dinner at all,—he imparted to her the good news.

"This makes my path clear and plain," he said. "Instead of seeing you brought to needing even the necessaries of life, I shall be able to send you supplies which will at any rate keep you from want. My only regret is that I shall have to leave you behind, and that I shall be living in ease and abundance, while you, my mother, will still be feeling the stress of poverty."

"My son, I have never sought for a life of ease, nor set my heart on earthly vanities," she replied. "What God appoints, that will I seek to be content with. But while we are in this life, soul and body cannot be kept together on nothing, and to have to go into debt for bread wherewith to support a bare existence would have been grievous, and would have tried my spirit sorely. And we seemed nearly coming to that. So, though this involves separation from each other for a time, I will not complain; nay, I shall rejoice to think that you will be out of reach of your persecutors. And by the time you return their malice may have cooled down, and their thoughts have turned into other channels."

To avoid the risk of delay in the transmission of letters, Stephen Willoughby decided to take a few belongings with him, and present himself in person to Mr. Cavendish.

"If he does not approve of me," he said, "and I do not obtain the post, I shall still be no worse off than I am; for perhaps I might find some other occupation in that neighborhood, as this seems closed to me."

So after they had partaken of an early dinner together he departed on foot, carrying his bag with him, and trusting he might find some conveyance or other to help him over part of the journey.

A couple of hours later Mrs. Willoughby, locking the cottage door behind her, and taking the key with her, bent her steps towards the Hall. She found Dorothy and Mary Stafford sitting out of doors under the spreading chestnuts, which formed a grateful shade from the hot rays of the sun. She made her way towards them.

They rose to meet her on perceiving her, and made her seat herself on the rustic bench between them.

"You must be tired," said Dorothy, "and hot, for it is very warm today."

"Yes; but I thought I would come at once, because I had to let you know that the little meetings cannot be held any longer, and so the people had better be told."

"Not held any longer? But why? Is Dr. Willoughby ill?" asked Dorothy.

An attentive observer might have detected a slight change in her voice as she uttered the last words—a certain undertone of anxiety. But if Mrs. Willoughby noticed it, she did not show that she did so, but went on to explain the reason—that her son had suddenly departed, and would probably be absent for about three months or longer.

"So we can have no more meetings!" said Dorothy in tones of regret. "Oh, I am sorry! How we shall all miss them."

And then she turned away her face, and stooped to pick up a book which was lying on the turf beside her; and for the next few minutes it rested with Mary to carry on the conversation with Mrs. Willoughby.

Suddenly Dorothy interrupted them, for her thoughts having wandered far away, she had not been listening to what they were saying.

"Now you are left all alone at the cottage, will you not come and take up your abode here again while your son is away—or at any rate for a time?" she added, as Mrs. Willoughby seemed to demur.

"Do say 'Yes,'" went on Dorothy. "Would it not be better for you than remaining all by yourself? It would be so lonely."

"You are very kind, my dear, but—"

"Nay," interrupted Dorothy, "do not add any 'buts.' It would be so pleasant to have you. And Mary has to leave tomorrow. Her father and mother have spared her all this time at our entreaties; but now they say they really must have her back. So it would cheer us up to have a visit from you."

Seeing that Dorothy was really sincere in her desire to have her for a guest, Mrs. Willoughby agreed to come on the morrow to pay a visit, the duration of which was left undecided.

The next two or three months slipped away without anything very special to mark them.

The beginning of September brought a flying visit from Robert Hay, who arrived one morning without having previously given any intimation of his coming, as was his habit; for he had appeared two or three times in the same unexpected manner since the day when he had brought Dorothy home.

"You didn't expect to see me turning up again just yet, did you, Dorothy? And I had no idea when I came last that we should be back again at the castle so soon. But the fact is we are burnt out of house and home in London, and so we are driven to seek a shelter in the paternal mansion."

"What has happened?" asked Dorothy. "Have you had a fire?"

"We have indeed. Such a fire as never was heard of. A great part of London has been destroyed; twelve or thirteen thousand houses they say have been burnt down, and eighty-seven churches, as well as St. Paul's Cathedral, the Exchange, Guildhall, and the Custom House."

"How dreadful! I never heard of anything like it!" said Dorothy with a look of dismay.

"Nor any one else," returned Robert. "It went on for three days and three nights. The sky overhead was fiery red, and the night as light as day. Clouds of smoke and the roaring of the flames, which, driven by the east wind, made a sound almost like thunder, with the noise of falling buildings, and the shrieks and cries of the people, made it altogether a dreadful time. At St. Paul's the melted lead ran down the street in a stream, and the pavements became so hot we could not tread on them."

"What a dreadful sight it must have been! Could nothing be done to stop it?"

"They tried everything, but without success, until at last they were obliged to blow up some houses, to make a gap that the flames could not leap over. What made it so much worse was the narrowness of the streets, where in some cases the upper stories project so that they nearly touch the opposite ones. And so many of the houses were built of wood, which of course served as fuel to the flames. It was a terrible time."

"And your house was burnt down among the rest?"

"Yes. A good many things were saved; the plate, and the most valuable pictures, and some of the furniture; but the house itself is a perfect wreck. We, in common with about 200,000 people of all classes and degrees, were forced to take refuge in the fields about Highgate. Many people were rendered

penniless and destitute; and we were all exposed to the great-
est hardships, with no roof over our heads. The exposure, and
perhaps partly the shock as well, has told on my father, and he
has been ill ever since. We managed to bring him home to the
castle; but he has not left his bed since."

"I am sorry to hear that. Then I suppose you will stay with
him?"

"Yes, till he is better. You see he has no one but myself besides servants; for Alicia is as good as lost to us since she married that old wretch, Lord Castleton."

"What a way to speak of your brother-in-law!"

"You would speak of him in the same way if he had married
your sister. I believe they lead a cat and dog life; anyhow, he
and my father are not on speaking terms; and as to my lady, I
don't think she has much affection left for anybody but herself.
Dorothy, I begin to see now why your mother would not let you
go within the precincts of Whitehall, or have anything to do
with the set there. You may thank her she did not suffer you to
run the risk of becoming what Alicia has become."

Dorothy listened to these words from the lips of Robert Hay
with some surprise. He would not once have spoken thus. She
remembered that day when he had tried to tempt her to accompany him to Whitehall, in spite of her mother's prohibition.

But now that she regarded him more attentively she was
struck by a certain alteration in his look and manner; more of
manliness and less of frivolity; an air of thoughtfulness, almost
of gravity, where once there had been only emptiness and good-
natured thoughtlessness. Was he really going to turn into a
man with something in him after all?

"Have you seen much of Eugene lately?" she asked suddenly.

"Not so much as I used to do," he replied.

"How is that?"

"Oh, he is mixed up with some new friends that I don't
much care about."

The words gave Dorothy a pang. Did they indeed mean, as
it seemed to her they did, that her brother was sinking below
even Robert's level, and choosing companions such as even he
did not care to associate with? Sick at heart, she felt she could
not pursue the subject, or at least not just then.

"Owen," said Dorothy, the next day, "suppose we go and
see Mrs. Willoughby, and carry her the news of the great fire

of London? I dare say she has not heard it yet, or not with all the details that my cousin brought us, and she will like to hear all we can tell her. She will be sorry to learn that St. Benedict's was one of the churches burnt down."

It was a beautiful morning, fresh and bright, with just sufficient chilliness in the air to make a little exercise desirable, and Dorothy stepped out briskly.

Mrs. Willoughby, after paying a lengthened visit at the Hall, had now been back in her own quarters for some weeks, and Dorothy, accompanied by Owen, frequently looked in to see how she was getting on.

Today the cottage door was not standing open, as had been the case all through the warm summer weather, but was closed, so Dorothy had to knock and wait for it to be opened. What was her surprise to find the summons answered not by Mrs. Willoughby, as she had expected, but by her son himself!

For the moment both looked a little confused and embarrassed, and in that instant Dr. Willoughby discovered that the absence of all these weeks and months had not been effectual in enabling him to meet with indifference the young maiden who stood before him.

"I did not know you had returned home," said Dorothy, vexed to find her cheeks growing hot.

"I only came back last evening, just to see my mother. I do not know that I shall be remaining long. But will you not come in and see my mother?" said Stephen, a sense of politeness forcing him to give the invitation, though he was feeling that the less he saw of Dorothy the better for himself.

She went in, feeling it would look odd to turn back without fulfilling the purpose of her coming; and she knew Owen would be glad of a rest. But she felt shy and constrained, though she could not tell why, and moreover Dr. Willoughby did not seem himself. There was some undefinable change. He appeared graver and more distant somehow, though perfectly courteous and polite, as indeed it was impossible he could be otherwise. But the change pained her, and she did not make the visit a long one. After telling her news, and discussing the details of the fire, she rose to go.

As soon as it became known that Dr. Willoughby was again in Hurstwood, those who had been wont to attend his meetings at once sent in a petition that they might be resumed; and so earnestly did they desire it that he consented. For indeed he was only too ready to speak when and where he could the message of glad tidings entrusted to him. But he gave them to understand that his stay was uncertain, and that perhaps it would only be for two or three times that they would meet.

It was too cold now, and the days closed in too early to allow of the open air meetings, so it was settled that they should again have recourse to the room in which they had first held them, the large long book-room or library. It was also arranged that Dr. Willoughby should always take his stand at the top of the apartment, near the door by which he had escaped on the first occasion; and as he now knew the way, he was to make straight for the secret chamber, should any disturbance again arise. But after all this interval of time it was hoped that the malice of their enemies might have died out, and that there would be no further molestation from them.

The first two gatherings passed off without any interruption of their tranquility; while every precaution was taken to avoid the possibility of a surprise. But the matter got wind somehow. The fact that Dr. Willoughby was again in Hurstwood of course became known, and it reached Mr. Crawford's ears. His bitter hatred of one whom he was pleased to regard as a rival was in no way diminished, but perhaps had rather grown in intensity through the length of time it had been cherished and suffered to dwell in his heart.

His former tool was again set on the track. But he had to go to work now in a more wily manner. Having wormed out the secret of their place of meeting as well as the day and hour from some unwary dupe, the next thing was to consider how to effect an entrance into the house; for experience having taught caution, the doors were now kept carefully shut and guarded.

On the third occasion of their assembling together an ominous sound was suddenly heard; the bay window opening on the ground, through which so many of them had once escaped, and which was supposed to be bolted, but through the treachery of one of the servants who had been bribed by Hart was really not secured, was pushed open from without, the curtain flung aside, and the evil face of Hart, followed by some more men, showed itself upon the scene.

In an instant Dr. Willoughby disappeared behind the tapestry hanging and effected his escape through the door, which

Dorothy with great presence of mind immediately locked, taking the key out and putting it in a safe hiding-place. If she could do nothing more, she would at any rate delay the pursuers as much as she could.

The rest of the little company fled through the other door, but the harm was done. Hart had it now in his power to swear that he had caught Dr. Willoughby holding an unlawful assembly, and now he was free to take him when and where he could. He might have escaped for the time, but that he would have him sooner or later in his clutches he was quite resolved. The search for him that night proved fruitless, but Hart, though vexed, told himself that he had only to bide his time, and he was sure of his prey.

When they were safely off the premises, which was not for some little while, Owen made her way to the secret chamber, where she found Dr. Willoughby in safety.

"Have you come to release me?" he asked. "Is the coast clear?"

"They seem to have gone for the present; but I think, sir, you should make up your mind to stay here for a while. I believe they mean to lurk about, and I don't think it will be safe for you to stir for some days, until you have tired them out. Because now they have you in their power, having caught you in the very act."

"But, my good Mistress Owen, don't you think maybe you are over cautious?" remonstrated Dr. Willoughby.

"I may be so, sir; but better that than for you to run unnecessary risk. Would it be a great hardship, sir, to stay here quietly for a few days?"

"Nay," he replied with a smile. "Such a chamber as this is certainly preferable to a cell in Newgate, or to being shipped off to the plantations."

"Ah, sir," responded Owen with a serious face, "this seems to me too grave a matter to smile over."

"Nay, why should we look more solemn than we can help? Do you think I fail to perceive the gravity of the situation?"

"I don't know, sir. But it is dreadful to think of such persecution as this, and that any can bear you such bitter malice."

"I grieve certainly to have made an enemy. But on the other hand, if I have been allowed to be of use to any soul, that more than makes up for it all."

"Then, sir, there is plenty to cheer you in that way. I could tell you of several to whom your preaching has been as life from the dead. Many who were in darkness some months ago are now rejoicing in the light. It was only a day or two since that I myself heard this from two of the farm servants, and they said there were others in the village who blessed the day you ever came to the place."

Stephen Willoughby's expressive face shone with a happy light as he said, "Then, my good Owen, is it not worth while for such glorious results to suffer pain or imprisonment, or aught that the malice of my enemies can devise? To have been allowed to lead another sheep into the fold, to pluck out of the mire another jewel for my Savior's crown, is compensation enough for aught that can befall me."

For two or three days word continued to be brought by those who were friendly to Dr. Willoughby that his enemies were still on the watch, waiting to entrap him. Then they appeared to grow tired and to relax their vigilance; and it seemed as if for the present they had given up the pursuit.

But, as Owen said, it was perhaps done in the hope of decoying him from his hiding-place.

CHAPTER XXI

REVELATIONS

"Wounded, faint, bleeding, never yield the strife.
Stunned, fallen—awake, arise and fight again.
Before you victory stands with shining train."

GEO. MACDONALD

DOROTHY, I have brought sad tidings with me, this time, said Robert Hay, a day or two later, as he came to her in the south parlor, where she was sitting.

She looked up quickly. "Is Uncle Robert dead?" she asked in a low voice.

"Yes. He went off very suddenly at the last. I had no idea the end was so near. It was yesterday afternoon."

Dorothy expressed her sympathy and sorrow; though the latter could not be expected to be so very keen, as she had not seen a great deal of her uncle, her mother not having cared for her to visit at the Castle, or to be thrown much with her cousins, as the gay manner in which they were brought up was so different from the simplicity which Lady Elizabeth desired for her own girls. Besides which, Lord Burnham and his family had always spent more of their time in London than at their country seat.

While Robert was giving some further details, claiming Dorothy's sympathy, which was sweet to him, Owen put her head in at the door, and said in rather a mysterious manner, "Can I speak with you, Mistress Dorothy?"

Asking her cousin to excuse her, Dorothy followed Owen who led the way into an adjoining room, and closed the door.

Then without preamble she said, "Mistress Dorothy, they have taken him."

"Who? Dr. Willoughby?" asked the girl, in startled tones.

"Yes, it is even so."

"But how did it happen?"

"Well, thinking that at last it must be safe, he ventured out with the intention of going to the cottage. But they must have been lying in wait. He had not gone far before they caught him; and they have brought him back to the house, to see if the fine is going to be paid. If not, of course they will take him away."

"How can the fine be paid?" cried Dorothy in despairing tones, and with looks of utter dismay. "It is a hundred pounds! Oh dear! oh dear! and if it isn't paid the penalty is transportation for seven years! What can be done to save him from that?"

"It is a dreadful sentence. But I am sure I don't see how we are to raise a hundred pounds. It is a very large sum, and you are not worth that, Mistress Dorothy," added Owen with a half smile.

"No, indeed; I am scarcely worth anything at all at present."

"I see no way out of the difficulty," said Owen despondingly.

Dorothy stood with a grave, pondering look on her face.

"Poor Mrs. Willoughby!" she said. "What a dreadful blow it will be to her! Oh! we must do something for her sake to save him from being sent out of the country. But what a wicked, iniquitous Act this is!" she went on, with a sudden burst of indignation. "To persecute and banish some of the best men in the kingdom, while they pamper all those depraved and debased fellows about the court. Don't you call it a disgraceful state of things?"

"I do indeed. I think it is most unjust; but our opinion of it will not alter it, or reverse the law."

"No, something must be done. Oh, I know what I will do," she cried suddenly, as if an inspiration had come to her. "You wait for me here. I will come back to you."

And without any explanation of her intentions she darted out of the room like a shot.

Owen, left thus in ignorance of her intentions, remained standing near the window, wearing a look of perplexity on her usually placid face, and striving to devise some plan for delivering Dr. Willoughby. But the thing appeared quite hopeless, she thought.

Returning to the south parlor, Dorothy hurriedly began, "Robert, will you do me a favor?"

"Certainly, my fair cousin," he cried with alacrity. "In what manner can I serve you?"

"Can you lend me a hundred pounds?" asked Dorothy abruptly.

Even Robert looked a little taken aback. The demand was such a very unexpected one.

Dorothy perceived his hesitation. "Is it too much to ask? You must be a rich man now."

"Yes; but ready money is not always forthcoming on the instant. Do you want it at once?"

"Yes, this very moment," returned Dorothy impetuously.

"But you don't think I go about in such times as these with a hundred pounds in my pockets, do you?" said Robert with a smile.

"I don't know; I hadn't thought about it. But I want this money so very much. Couldn't you give a written promise to pay it, and I dare say that would do as well."

Robert sat down at the table, and drew pen, ink, and paper towards him.

"Yes, I can do that, if that will suffice."

"Thank you; oh, thank you so much," And Dorothy flew off with the paper in her hand, leaving the young earl, for such he now was, a good deal mystified by her proceedings.

"Whatever can she want, with all that money?" he said to himself. "And in such a hurry too. Young maidens don't generally deal in such large sums. They can't have bailiffs in the house, surely. I wonder if Eugene has been getting into some dreadful scrape again."

Meantime Dorothy returned to Owen, triumphantly bearing the paper with her.

"I have found a way out of the difficulty!" she exclaimed joyously. "See, Lord Hay, or rather Lord Burnham as he is now, has given me this promise. You show it to that man Hart, and see if it will not be all right. He can have the money on presenting that paper."

Owen's face expressed extreme astonishment, as she glanced at the paper put into her hand.

"And now, Owen, will you manage the rest? Don't let either Dr. or Mrs. Willoughby know or guess how the affair has been arranged; or if they must know something, say that the Earl of Burnham settled the matter. And now I must go back to him."

On re-entering the south parlor Dorothy's face wore a look of relief and satisfaction.

"I am so much obliged to you, Robert. It was very good of you to do this thing. But—" she paused, while the satisfied look suddenly changed to one of consternation.

"Well, what is it?"

"Oh, Robert, I didn't think what I was doing. I don't know how I am going to repay you, at least not for a long time. Will that matter? I hope you are not in a hurry?"

"Nay, I don't want the money back. You shall repay me in another way," he said impulsively, while a deep earnest look came into his face, which made him seem more manly and more worthy of respect than Dorothy had ever before thought him. He had risen from his seat, and crossed the room to where she stood.

"What do you mean?" she said, looking up into his face questioningly and unsuspectingly.

"I mean that I want you to give me yourself, Dorothy. Nay, hear me out," said Robert, as she seemed about to stop him. "This is no sudden idea. You have long been more to me than any one else; the only one I have ever truly loved, and I want you to give me a helping hand to lift me out of the mire," he went on rapidly. "I scarce know how it is, but of late Lady Elizabeth's words have been haunting me,—those words she spoke to Eugene and me that day in Aldersgate Street, when she talked of that other King, and of taking service under Him. I have never forgotten them; and all this time of my father's illness I have had leisure for thinking,—there was little to do but to think; and I want to know more of that service. I am tired of the service of the king I have served hitherto, and of all the emptiness and hollowness, ay, and vice too of the court of Charles II. Dorothy, won't you come and be mine, and help me to find what I believe you have already found? You know more of these things than I do. Come and carry on the work that your mother began; for it is to her it is all due. I never had a thought in my life of serious things until she put it there. Oh, Dorothy, say you will be mine!" he pleaded. "My heart has long been given to you, and to you alone."

He had spoken so rapidly and so impetuously that Dorothy had had no opportunity of putting in a word; but she had turned her face away from his ardent gaze, and had tried to withdraw the hand he had seized.

"I can't," she now returned, almost sorrowfully; for never

had she liked him half so well as at that moment, when, the outer covering of frivolity, which had for so long concealed the better nature below, having been dropped, the real worth that lay underneath was allowed to appear.

Robert had pleaded his cause well. That reference to her beloved mother had touched her much. Moreover he was offering her a coronet, wealth and position, and a heart that she could not fail to see was a true and honest one. He had always been kind to her, and now it was evident that he was altogether in earnest; no longer the shallow, vain young gallant she had once thought him, but a man, with aspirations after that which is noblest and highest.

Then why could she not say "Yes"? She could scarcely have answered the question even to herself; for she did not dislike him—nay, she liked him, but still the thing seemed impossible.

"Let us go on being cousins," she said; "let us still be friends, great friends."

"Nay, I want something more. That will not content me. Oh, Dorothy, have you no other answer for me? Say you will at any rate think about it."

"It is no use," she said gently, "I am very sorry you wish for what I cannot give," she added meekly, with a deprecating look, as if she thought herself to blame in the matter. "Oh, if only you wouldn't have wanted this, we could have been such friends."

The words were spoken with an artlessness and simplicity that almost forced Robert to smile in spite of his disappointment, and made him long more than ever to call her his.

He looked sorrowfully at her. She looked sweeter than ever as she stood there with drooping mien, as if feeling almost guilty in refusing anything to one who thought nothing too much to do for her. "Dorothy, is there any one else?" he asked abruptly.

"Because if there is not I shall still hope."

"No; oh no!" she answered promptly.

But the words had scarcely left her lips when a crimson flush suddenly dyed her cheeks, and she hung her head as if from very shame.

Robert noticed it, and drew his conclusions as in silence he watched her.

For some moments neither spoke. She seemed to have forgotten his presence as she stood gazing into the fire, recognizing with dismay a fact of which she had been unconscious until that moment. Robert's question had revealed to her as with a flash of lightning the truth to which she had hitherto been blind—that there *was* some one else; that her heart was no longer free; that the reason she could not say "Yes" to Robert's proposal was that the image of one who, in her estimation, was all that was noble and pure and good rose above and dwarfed all others; and nothing less than the highest could satisfy her. She could not content herself with anything that fell short of her ideal. And she had found her ideal in him to whom, all innocently and unconsciously, her affections had gone forth.

The discovery was a bitter shock to her maidenly pride. For in her low estimate of herself it did not seem to her as a thing within the bounds of possibility that one so far above her in every way, as Dr. Willoughby could ever give a thought to her, whose failings and shortcomings he knew too well, and who was as far inferior to him, so she thought, as a glow-worm is inferior to a bright star in the heavens.

And then she felt as if she must sink into the earth, as in this new light, which had brought with it such startling revelations, she perceived that what she had been doing all along as she thought for Mrs. Willoughby's sake had in fact, been for his sake; that her anxiety that the fine should be paid was perhaps not altogether that the mother might be spared the pain of having her son banished from her for so long, but partly at least on the son's account as well.

Suddenly she looked up and saw Robert standing before her. The color deepened in her cheeks, if that were possible, and her eyes fell before his glance. Was he reading her through and through, and finding out her bitter secret—that she had given her heart to one who had not even asked for it, or desired it, as far as she knew?

Feeling she would like to hide herself from everybody, she moved as if to leave the room. Then another impulse made her turn back.

"Robert, forgive me," she said vaguely. And then, impelled thereto by her love of candor and hatred of any concealments, she added, "I think perhaps I ought to have let you know for what purpose I wanted that money."

"Nay; say no more about it. It is enough that you wished for it. You are welcome to it."

"But I must repay you when I can."

"I will only accept one sort of payment. Oh, Dorothy, do not say me nay!" he urged in pleading tones.

She shook her head sorrowfully, but decidedly. "It can never be. I am very sorry to pain you, but I cannot help it. But, Robert—I do not like concealments—and perhaps you would wish you had not given me that money if you knew what it was wanted for."

"I would give you that and far more, merely because you wished for it," he exclaimed impetuously. "I would gladly give you all I possess if you would have it. I would lay myself and all I have at your feet if you would let me."

For a moment, just one moment, she wavered. Here was a true heart offering her honest love and a home where under the shelter of a husband's protection, she could be at peace. Rank and dignities he offered also; but they had not now the charm for her they once had. But she might, so he had said, lend him a helping hand in seeking higher things, and there was something attractive in that thought. While that other love was an utterly hopeless thing, and must be expelled from her heart and thoughts at any cost. Should she then say "Yes"?

Ah! no. She must be true to herself. She knew now that Robert did not hold the first place in her affections. She would not be a wife at all if she could not be a loyal and faithful one. She would live and die a single woman rather than stoop to what she considered an unworthy course.

Her mind was made up, the question settled once and for ever.

"It is very generous of you," she said, referring to the money. "And very trustful of you to ask me no questions. But I feel as if it would be more honest to tell you, in case you might wish to withdraw your promise. I ought to have told you in the first instance. Only will you please keep it a secret? It was for the purpose," and again her eyes sought the fire, "of paying a fine to save Mrs. Willoughby's son from being transported for seven years."

Robert made a half-smothered exclamation, while a dark flush mounted into his cheek and brow. It was his turn to be silent for a moment; while Dorothy felt she had inadvertently put herself in a peculiar situation. Had she been wrong? Had she acted too impulsively? Had she done anything unmaidenly, and not according to the correct usages of society? She did not know. She was too ignorant of the world. She had just followed the impulses of her heart, and of her honest nature, which hated subterfuge of any kind. But what if that flush on Robert's face meant that he too would henceforth be among Dr. Willoughby's enemies? Oh dear, what a world it was! Everything seemed going wrong.

"Robert, are you vexed?" she asked. "I mean at the purpose to which your money was applied?"

"Nay," he answered slowly, renouncing at that moment, as he recognized its hopelessness, that which had for some time past been the desire of his heart. "Nay, I am glad to serve you in *any* way; glad to have something that I can place at your disposal, and I pray you accept it without another word. Suffer me to render you that little service.

"And now I must be going," he added sadly. "Good-bye, Dorothy."

His tone and manner were so sad and hopeless that Dorothy felt quite miserable. She longed to comfort him, but was powerless to do so. So she had to let him depart,—back to his solitude at the Castle; back to his closed house, and to his dead; back to his lonely musings, but, oh! she trusted not back to the old frivolous life. He had begun to seek better things; he had asked her to aid him in the search. He had said she could do so. But she had refused; and the thought of it pained her to the heart.

On the other hand, how nobly had he acted! She believed, she feared, he had read her secret, or at least had suspected it; and yet he had not withdrawn his gift, had not even appeared to grudge the use that was being made of it. How generous it was of him! How noble!

Poor Robert! What could she do for him! she asked herself. It seemed to her that all she could do was to pray for him, and pray she did,—that he might be comforted; that the Giver of all strength would strengthen him to be true to his better self; to follow on in his quest until he found, not a mere abstraction, but Him whom to know is life eternal.

CHAPTER XXII

TARDY REPENTANCE

"Guilty, forgive me, Lord, I cry;
    Pursued by foes, I come;
A sinner, save me, or I die,
    An outcast, take me home."—E. H. BICKERSTETH

IT was a beautiful evening about a week later. The sky at sunset had been brilliant with crimson and purple and golden clouds, which floated in the clear expanse of heaven, hovering over the departing orb like a gorgeous canopy. And even after he had set and disappeared from view there remained for a long time a soft beautiful glow in the heavens, which lingered, as if loth to fade away.

In the twilight Stephen Willoughby was returning from the sick-bed of a poor man whom he had been visiting. His way back to his home lay through a corner of an extensive wood, the farther end of which stretched as far as to the Hall.

He was walking slowly, and meditating over many things as he walked. What his future movements were to be was one subject that was occupying his thoughts.

So abstracted was he that he scarcely noticed where he was going, until suddenly he was startled by the report of a gun. The sound did not appear far distant, and he fancied it was succeeded by a groan. He paused and looked about him. What did it mean? that one solitary shot followed by this silence and stillness. Where was the individual who had fired the shot? Was he in hiding? Was it some poacher, or was there some foul play going forward?

He turned to go in the direction whence the sound proceeded. It was quite dusk now, and considerably darker in the wood than it was outside, where the thick foliage of the trees no longer intercepted the light.

HE PERCEIVED A MAN LYING WITH A GUN BY HIS SIDE.

As he followed the narrow path through the brushwood, he stumbled upon something on the ground. Stooping, he perceived the figure of a man lying there insensible, with a gun by his side, the report from which had doubtless been the sound which he had heard. Had the miserable man been trying to take his own life, or was it an accident? In either case it was evident that it was his own hand which had stretched him there.

Who was he? A glance sufficed to show that he was a Cavalier, but his face could not be seen. Going down on his knees and stooping over the prostrate figure, he removed the broad-brimmed hat, which had fallen over and screened the countenance from view, and with a start of surprise and dismay he recognized Mr. Crawford.

His face looked ghastly in the dim light. Was he mortally wounded? Stephen Willoughby did not waste time in surmises, nor in deliberating as to his own course of action. Here lay his enemy—one who had done him grievous wrong, and was seeking to injure him yet further. But the words were ringing in his ears, "Love your enemies; do good to them that hate you;" and the command must be obeyed. His duty was clear and plain.

Hastily quitting the shelter of the wood and seeking the open highway, he hailed a laborer whom he saw leisurely making his way homewards after his day's toil in the fields, and requested his help. The man, signifying his readiness to do what was required of him, followed Dr. Willoughby to the spot where Mr. Crawford lay. Between them they raised the insensible form and bore it to the humble dwelling of the young divine, which was the nearest habitation at hand.

Mrs. Willoughby was startled as she heard the trampling of feet approaching, and on going to the door perceived the prostrate form being borne along. But she was a person of good nerve and ready resource. She took in the state of things at a glance, and at once directed them where to lay the wounded man. Then she set about adopting the usual remedies for restoring him to consciousness, and proceeded to dress his wounds. But still Mr. Crawford lay without showing any signs of life.

"You must go for the doctor, Stephen," she said quietly.

By this time the laborer who had given his assistance had departed; thus there was no one else to send.

"Shall you mind being left alone, my mother? It is growing

dark, and it will take me some time to reach Mr. Wood's, and get back to you. It will be a solitary time for you in this lonely place. I wonder if I could fetch anyone to come to your help."

"Nay, my son, you need not think of anything of the sort for a moment. I should be a poor creature if I couldn't keep watch for a couple of hours or so over a sick man alone; even though he I have to watch over is my son's bitterest enemy, and one from whom I naturally shrink. But our duty in the matter is plain, and that is enough. Now leave me, and hasten on your way."

Mrs. Willoughby turned to re-enter the darkened chamber and to watch beside the mute form, while her son started on his long walk in quest of the doctor. He returned with him in a few hours' time.

Mr. Wood looked grave as he examined his patient, who still lay unconscious.

"His injuries are serious," he said, when they had withdrawn from the room for a moment to hear the doctor's opinion. "I cannot yet tell how it may end, but I am very doubtful. He must on no account be moved, for it might prove fatal. But he is in good hands, as I know by experience," he added, turning to Mrs. Willoughby with a smile. "I found out your capabilities at the Hall during Mistress Owen's illness."

It was an anxious watch that the mother and son kept through that night.

Fever set in, and soon ran high. It was after Dr. Willoughby had come to relieve his mother, whom he insisted on sending to rest, and had taken his place by the sick-bed, that the patient grew delirious.

In his delirium he kept on muttering words to which Stephen at first paid no attention, but by degrees they became louder and more audible, until he could not help hearing them.

"I'll have him—the scoundrel! He is sure to go through the wood on his way back. Where is the gun? Is it all right? Yes. Now—there he goes. Who goes? Why, that miserable fellow Willoughby, of course—See—take good aim. But I can't! What is this? It is all darkness and blackness. Oh, this is too dreadful!"

And so the refrain went on, as the sick man tossed restlessly from side to side, muttering words partially incoherent, and yet his listener seemed to have a clue to their meaning.

But he tried not to dwell on the thought. If he were right in his surmises; if Mr. Crawford had in very deed been lying in wait for him;—well—God had mercifully preserved him, and that command about forgiveness of injuries still held good. "Even until seventy times seven" were the words that ran in his mind; and he asked for grace to obey them.

And as he sat there in the stillness of the midnight hour the chief thought in his mind was not the enormity of Mr. Crawford's conduct towards himself, but how solemn a thing it was to see a soul hovering between life and death, with perhaps only a few more days or hours before him in this world, and yet all unprepared for a summons into the next.

They nursed him unweariedly, and as carefully as if he had been one of themselves. It soon became evident that his days were numbered; that he was slowly sinking. Many a prayer was put up for him, by him whom he had so relentlessly persecuted and sought to injure. As the fever somewhat subsided, and the patient became more himself, the young minister sought to lead his thoughts to the Savior of the lost and perishing. But the sick man seemed at first too restless to allow of his attending to the tender, earnest words.

When he had first recovered consciousness, and found who his nurses were, he had peremptorily demanded to be taken home; but Mr. Wood as steadily refused to allow him to be moved, saying that he would probably die on the road. So he had been forced to submit, which he did very ungraciously.

All the first day of recovered consciousness he lay chiefly with his face turned to the wall, in what seemed a morose and sullen silence. But though silent he was not unobservant. His eye followed Stephen Willoughby's every movement with a peculiar expression in it, as if pent up within were concentrated feelings of dislike and hatred; of bitter humiliation at being thus in his adversary's power; of intense surprise at the behavior of the other, as well as of fierce rebellion against the fate which had laid him low. These seemed to be some of the conflicting sentiments which tortured him, and would allow him no repose.

But Stephen took no notice of all this. He was one of those men who possess the qualities needed to make a good nurse. His watchful eye and quiet manner, his innate gentleness and tenderness,—which were now drawn out to the full towards his prostrate foe, whom he pitied from his soul,—his soft touch and earnest desire to soothe and help, all made him invaluable in the sick-room, and Mr. Crawford could not have been in better hands. More and more Mrs. Willoughby left the patient in his charge, thinking he would probably do him more good than she could.

But a fierce battle was raging within the sick man's soul; and perhaps Stephen Willoughby felt it must be so, for he left him pretty much to himself, carefully ministering to his wants, but doing so with few words.

When night came he insisted upon undertaking the watch, for he feared the return of the fever and delirium, and felt he could not leave his mother to cope with it alone.

But though the patient passed a restless night, he was conscious throughout, and every time Dr. Willoughby stirred to render any service he found those bright wide-open eyes watching him intently. If he sat down to read, and inadvertently glanced up from his book, there they were fixed on him with a look something like that of a caged tiger at bay; a look that seemed to say that were not their owner chained to his bed by weakness, he might probably have felt inclined to spring at the other's throat. If he rose to attend to the fire, they followed him; if he approached the bed with medicine or nourishment or a cooling drink, the strange look in them intensified; and but for the resolute manner of Stephen Willoughby, which had an air of quiet command in it, it might have been doubtful whether the patient would not have flung what he brought him back in his face.

But something in Dr. Willoughby's calm bearing seemed to exercise a strange constraint over him; and he would receive what he handed to him in a sort of dogged way, as if forced to do so in spite of himself.

Wishing to get out of range of those eyes which never closed, Stephen as morning dawned turned his back upon the patient, and drawing a seat near the window opened his Bible, and for a little while read on in the dim light. Then, perhaps forgetting for the moment the presence of the other, he fell upon his knees, and long and earnestly he prayed that this wanderer might be brought back to Him from whom he had strayed; that the rebel might be pardoned; that light might break in upon his soul and dispel the darkness. He had but one thought, for

personal feeling had entirely been put aside, and now the longing of his heart was that, ere it should be too late, this erring
one might be brought to knock at heaven's door, and seek for
admission there through the merits of Him who had died for
him. In his intense earnestness he was perhaps unconscious
that he uttered many of his petitions aloud.

As he rose from his knees a glance at the clock showed him
that it was again time to give the cooling draught that Mr.
Wood had sent; and as he held it to the lips of the patient he
thought the eyes no longer glared upon him quite as they had
done, but seemed to wear a softer look.

Encouraged by this, he sat down by the bedside, and in
gentle tones repeated a few verses of Scripture. He got no response, but that he did not expect.

As it grew to be broad daylight his mother came to relieve
him of his watch for a time. When he again returned to his
post, which was some hours later, Mr. Crawford seemed qui-
eter, and he again endeavored, in a few simple words, to lead
the dying man's thoughts upwards.

But as the day wore on, though the fierce glitter in the eyes
was gone, he grew more restless. Mr. Wood had paid his second
visit, and had plainly told him, in answer to his inquiries, that
he had not very long to live.

In the dusk Stephen Willoughby had been sitting for a
while meditatively near the fire. But now he had begun to de-
bate whether it would be more cheerful to light up, or whether
the semi-darkness might be soothing to the patient, when a
voice from the bed spoke his name in a hollow tone.

He was at the other's side in a moment.

"I want you to do something for me, Willoughby," he said,
with an evident effort.

"Gladly, only tell me what it is."

"Will you hire a horse at my charge, and ride over to
Wharton Park the first thing tomorrow morning?"

The request astonished Dr. Willoughby. It was not what he
had expected.

"Certainly," he replied. "What can I do for you there?"

Mr. Crawford explained that he wished him to go into his
own private closet, and there open a certain drawer, which he
described, the key of which he told him how to find. He wanted
him to take therefrom a sealed document, which he would find

lying underneath and hidden by a mass of other papers.

"You may have to hunt a long time, because it has been purposely thus concealed; and you may find the key hard to turn in the lock, because it has only once been opened since I have been in possession at the Park, and then it seemed rusty. But do not be deterred by any little difficulty. And you will say nothing to anybody?" he added. "The affair is a secret between you and me."

Stephen Willoughby promised to attend scrupulously to his directions, and continued to minister to him through the night, as he had done on the previous one.

On his return from Wharton Park on the following morning, he at once repaired to the sick-chamber, with the paper concealed among the folds of his doublet; for Mrs. Willoughby had met him with the information that Mr. Crawford was impatiently awaiting his coming.

"He seems as if he couldn't rest. He certainly has something on his mind. I believe if he were to confess it he would feel better. But I have no doubt he has a great many things on his mind that he ought to confess," remarked Mrs. Willoughby.

"He may have been confessing them to God, for aught we know," said Stephen. "At least let us hope so. We cannot tell what has been passing in his mind."

As he entered the chamber the sick man stretched out his hand with feverish impatience for the document. He had just strength to tear it open, and then he held it out to the other, saying in a hoarse voice, "Read that. I know I am at your mercy, but you have shown me that you are not one to take advantage of it. Hate and despise me, I suppose you must; but I shall soon be beyond reach of it, and at least you will know that I tried to make some tardy reparation, such as it is, for the wrong I have done you."

Stephen Willoughby read while Mr. Crawford watched him, this time with a half-deprecatory look on his face, as he scanned attentively each passing expression on that of the other man.

The chief feeling depicted on Stephen's countenance as he read was utter and undisguised astonishment. Mr. Crawford had expected to see burning indignation and resentment towards himself, as well as unmitigated contempt written there; or rather he would have expected it from any other man; but Stephen Willoughby was so different from any whom he had hitherto known that he could not tell how he would act or feel; and so he waited in suspense, with an inquiring gaze fixed upon his companion.

Dr. Willoughby might well look surprised. It was a will of old Mr. Crawford's that he was reading; and in it he found his own father,—or, in the event of the latter's death, himself, Stephen Willoughby, named as the heir to the old man's property.

The reason for such a bequest was stated; namely, that his son having turned out a scoundrel, as he expressed it, he had made up his mind to disinherit him, and leave his property to his old friend James Willoughby, or failing him, to his son Stephen; the aforesaid James Willoughby having earned his gratitude by signal services rendered in former years, and being moreover the one person in the world whom he most esteemed, and who would make the best use of the wealth entrusted to him. A certain annual sum was to be paid to his son out of the estate; a sum sufficient to keep him in comfort, but that was all.

Having read and re-read it, to make sure that he had fully taken in its meaning, Stephen looked towards Mr. Crawford for an explanation,

"Do you not understand?" he said, a dark flush overspreading his face. "I found, as well as this, another will, an earlier one, made many years before, and which no doubt my father, who was rather a careless man, thought he had destroyed; for it was among litters of papers and other things in an old cabinet that did not appear to have been opened for years. In that earlier will he left the property to me, his only son.

"And though I also found this one," he went on, "which you see is dated only a short time before he died, I suppressed it and produced the other. Why I did not destroy this one I know not; it could scarcely have been that I thought it too great a depth of villainy," he said bitterly, "but somehow I always seemed to be withheld from doing so. But it was put away in a safe place, as you know, and no eye has seen it but yours and mine.

"My father was in London," further explained Mr. Crawford, "at the time he made this last will, and called in some strange lawyer. So that the fellow in this neighborhood whom he was accustomed to employ knew nothing about this second will. Thus it was easy to carry out the fraud I committed. But many had heard my father say he meant to disinherit me, and therefore were surprised to find me in possession of the property. But I kept my own counsel. Perhaps the London lawyer might have got wind of the affair and exposed me, but he was dead, as I found out."

All this had been said not without difficulty, and with several pauses between; but the other had listened without once interrupting him.

After he had ceased Stephen did not at once speak, but turning to the window stood looking out for a few minutes. He was thinking of all the straits and privations to which he and his mother had been reduced; of the bitter struggle with poverty which even a small portion of this wealth would have prevented. A conflict went on in his breast, a battle, short if sharp, in which, however, he proved victorious in the strength which he knew so well where to seek. But he saw now that Mr. Crawford had had a double motive in his wish to drive him from Hurstwood.

"I do not ask you to forgive me," said the sick man after a time, breaking in upon Stephen's reverie; "that would be too much to expect. But I ask whether you think such a wretch as I can be forgiven by God. You have prayed for me,—I heard you. Do you think He has heard your petitions?"

"I cannot doubt it; and do not you doubt it either," answered Stephen earnestly. "Ah, yes; He is ever ready to forgive and to receive each repentant sinner. But do not think for a moment," he added, "that I do not also forgive;" and he held out his hand with a frank smile that quite vanquished the other. He took the proffered hand in his for a moment, and then a strange mist seemed to dim his eyes. He turned away his face and did not speak again for a time.

Stephen Willoughby respected his silence, and waited for him to break it.

"You have conquered me," he said at last. "I never believed in anybody's goodness before. I always thought they had some base or sordid motive in all they did. But I see you are no sham. You are as different from myself as light from darkness. How you can forgive all my injuries I know not; but you have shown that you do so by treating me as you have. You could not have done more for your dearest friend,—and I hated you for it at first. But you have tried to save my life, though, in a fit of madness, I was ready to take yours."

The last words were uttered in a low tone, so low as to be only just audible. It was the only allusion he ever made to that fateful evening in the wood.

"I cannot understand it," he went on, "but so it is. And now, in addition to all, you forgive me this grievous wrong of keeping you out of your inheritance?" he said interrogatively.

"Yes, fully and freely," answered Stephen heartily.

The other lay looking at him for a few moments with a new expression on his face.

"No wonder she preferred you to me," he murmured faintly. "Take her and be happy."

There was no need to mention any name. The quick color that mounted into Stephen's face showed that he well understood to whom the words referred. A glad light flashed into his eye for a moment. Then it went out and he shook his head.

"Nay, it is not for me to win such a prize."

"But it is. Try."

Stephen shook his head, as if he considered any such hope would be utterly vain.

"You will not be a poor man now," said Mr. Crawford. "Even if you had been, I would have given a good deal for your chances."

And then another silence fell upon them. The sick man was exhausted, and not equal to any more conversation. As he lay and dozed Stephen Willoughby sat apparently looking out of the window, but in reality contemplating visions of bliss that floated before him and almost dazzled him. Was it possible that such joy as that of winning Dorothy lay within his grasp? Might he indeed venture to hope? Had Mr. Crawford good grounds for what he had said? The conduct of the latter had touched him much, showing such a total change of feeling towards himself. How thankful he felt that they were now at peace with one another!

And then his thoughts went back to Dorothy, and very radiant was the look his face wore for a time. But then apparently some doubt again returned and damped the new-born hope, for the countenance clouded somewhat.

But when after a while his patient stirred and moved uneasily he was at his side in a moment, his own hopes or fears forgotten as he gave his whole attention to soothing the sick man's restlessness.

Mr. Crawford lingered through another night and day, wonderfully altered and subdued, and expressing more than once his gratitude for the kindness shown him and his sorrow for the past. He seemed as if he could scarcely bear to have Stephen out of his sight for a moment, and evidently listened with attention to the words of Scripture he repeated from time to time or the earnest petitions he put up by the bedside.

It was towards sunset that his sun went down. Stephen, bending over him, had asked if he was looking to the crucified Savior for pardon, and the words that came in reply were,— "May I?—dare I?—one who has sinned so deeply—worse than others!"

"Trust Him. He never yet turned away any who came to Him," said Stephen earnestly.

The dying man gave a glance upward, and a few moments later passed away.

Two or three hours afterwards Stephen followed his mother into the little front room downstairs, and told her of the strange change in their fortunes. It seemed difficult for either of them to believe in it; it appeared so like a dream, so unreal, so improbable.

"We must put the matter into the hands of a lawyer and see what he says. Until we find that I am honestly entitled to claim the property, we will say nothing about it to others."

"I have not seen anything of Mistress Dorothy or Mistress Owen all these days since the accident happened," said Mrs. Willoughby. "I don't think they can know anything about it. Perhaps it would be well for me to walk up to the Hall tomorrow morning and tell them all that has occurred. In some ways it cannot fail to be a great relief to Mistress Dorothy;—I mean to know that all persecution both of herself and others is at an end."

"Poor Crawford!" said Stephen, with a tender and sorrowful intonation in his voice. "I quite believe that even for him the Arms of Mercy, have opened wide, and have received him, though at the eleventh hour. Yes; tell Mistress Dorothy all, and how changed he seemed, that she may not cherish any bitter memories of his past conduct. Let it all be forgotten."

CHAPTER XXIII

CONCLUSION

"Happy are they who learn at last,—
  Though silent suffering teach
The secret of enduring strength,
  And praise too deep for speech,—
Peace that no pressure from without,
  No storm within, can reach."—A. L. WARING

IT was a beautiful autumn afternoon. In the bright sunshine the old Hall at Hurstwood was looking its best. Where the sunbeams glinted on the red brick of the picturesque pile of buildings, they imparted a rich warm tone; where they fell upon the smooth well-kept lawn, they made the turf a more vivid shade of green.

Dorothy and Mary Stafford, who, to the former's great satisfaction, had again come on a visit to Hurstwood, were pacing up and down the terrace walk arm in arm, deep in conversation.

Mary had been with her parents in London for a time, and had just returned from thence. After talking about many things connected with her visit there, Dorothy suddenly asked, "Did you ever happen to come across Eugene?"

"Yes," replied Mary quietly; "we saw him two or three times."

"And how did he look? I mean," added Dorothy with a sense of shame, "how does he seem to be going on?"

"Not very well, I fear," returned Mary sadly.

Something in the unconscious tone of her voice made Dorothy glance at her friend's countenance. It looked very sweet, and yet sorrowful, as if she were feeling much as Dorothy felt about this young life which was being so wasted and thrown away.

"Oh, Mary, can't you do something for him?" cried Dorothy impulsively. "I don't seem to have any influence: besides, I see so little of him; but if you are going to be a good deal in London, you may often come across him; and I believe he would listen to you. I believe he would give more heed to you than anybody. He would always do anything for you in the old days."

A soft flush came into Mary's cheek, and an earnest thoughtful look into her face, as if she were pondering this new idea, and mentally forming some secret resolve. But all she replied was, "I would gladly do anything I could for the playfellow of old days. But I fear there is very little I can do."

* * * * * * *

"There appears to be no difficulty in the way of my taking possession of the property, according to old Mr. Crawford's will," said Stephen Willoughby, as he entered the room where his mother was sitting, on his return from an interview with the lawyer, a few days later. "And that will mean no more battling with poverty for you, my mother; no more of the privations and hardships which, you have endured so bravely and cheerfully."

"It is a wonderful change of fortune. But it will bring its own cares and responsibilities with it," said Mrs. Willoughby gravely. "We must remember the words, 'If riches increase, set not your heart upon them.'"

"I hope I shall ever look upon it as a talent entrusted to me by God, and for the use of which I shall have to give an account to Him. I pray that I may be found a faithful steward!"

"God has indeed been good to us," said Mrs. Willoughby with a softened light in her eye. "In our darkest hour He has never forgotten or forsaken us. We have proved how faithful He is to those who trust in Him."

"And now," said Stephen, after a little pause, as he rose and paced the room, "I have begun to wonder whether He may not be going to grant me the crowning joy of all, the fulfillment of my heart's desire, as regards earthly things. It once seemed a vain idle dream, utterly unattainable; but now—sometimes I hope—and then again I fear. Perhaps you can guess what my desire is."

"I think I can," replied Mrs. Willoughby calmly; and if her son's words had stirred any conflicting emotions within her she did not allow it to appear.

"Do you think there is any hope for me? At one time I felt there was absolutely none, and perhaps so it may still be. But at any rate I am in a better position to speak. I could not have gone to her as a penniless man, unless she had been penniless too, and then perhaps it would scarcely have been a wise thing," added Stephen with a smile.

"But still," he continued more despondingly, "I fear I have no ground for hope."

"I do not say so. I would advise you to try,"

Stephen's face kindled.

"You bid me hope?" he asked almost incredulously.

"I bid you try. And—I think she will not say you nay."

"Mother, you can give me your good wishes for my success?" he asked, stopping in his walk and standing in front of her. "I would fain feel I had your sympathy and approval. I have had the former all my life long, and given in full measure too."

"And you have it still, my son," she returned, looking up lovingly into his eager face, and without any shadow on her own. "And my approval too," she added frankly. "I could not have felt so at one time with regard to her; but sorrow and discipline, and above all the grace of God, have molded and chastened the once wayward nature; the Refiner's fire through which she has passed has been hot, but it has done much in purifying the gold. If you can win her you will be a happy man."

"The happiest man on the face of the earth," thought Stephen to himself.

"But I almost fear to hope," he said aloud.

"Then I would put myself out of suspense as soon as possible," said Mrs. Willoughby, in her common-sense, matter-of-fact way.

And her son resolved to act upon her advice.

* * * * * * *

Dr. Willoughby was returning from the Hall; walking with a light step, and looking as if not a single cloud remained on his horizon. Sunshine such as he had not known for many a day, if ever before, was flooding his path. His eyes shone with a soft tender light in them, while a new look of intense, quiet happiness illumined his face.

He had started on his mission with many misgivings, with such grave doubts as to his success that he had been on the point of turning back more than once.

But his fears had soon been dissipated. Dorothy, too frank and candid to dissemble, had not kept him in suspense. When once she understood—what she was slow to believe could indeed be true—that he was actually declaring his love for her, and asking if she could give him hers in return, there was scarcely any need for her to reply in words; the radiant look that overspread her face might have been answer sufficient, as well as the confiding gesture with which she put her hand in his.

But when he repeated his question, "Can you love me, Dorothy?" she answered unhesitatingly, though shyly and with a rosy blush,—"Yes, with all my heart."

He had not told her yet of the change in his fortunes, but now he did so. It all seemed very strange to Dorothy, and perhaps she scarcely took in the whole significance of it just then. To her it was sufficient for the present to rest in this new joy of learning that Stephen Willoughby cared for her, that he belonged to her henceforth, and she belonged to him; that life would now be spent beside him and under the shelter of his love and protection; that she would have the right to love him freely, to care for him, to minister to him. What were poverty or riches compared with the priceless treasure of such a heart as his? Having him, did she not possess all that her utmost dreams of earthly happiness had ever conceived?

Her cup of joy was full and overflowing. Afterwards she might find the question of ways and means a necessary one to consider, but for the present she felt that poverty with him would have been infinitely preferable to wealth without him; and bravely would she have gone forth, her hand in his, to meet privation and hardship, had it been so ordered.

Very warm and heartfelt were the congratulations of the faithful Owen, when Dorothy imparted to her the news of the wonderful change in her prospects which had been wrought within the last few hours, of the new and exceeding great joy that had come into her life. The intelligence caused Owen the most boundless satisfaction, and she almost shed tears of joy at the thought of her darling having found such a protector, at her happy lot in being chosen by such a man, one who held as high a place in her estimation as Dorothy did in her affections.

"And I don't think there is any one in all the world to whom my dear Lady Elizabeth would so willingly have given you." she remarked.

"No. It is sweet to think I should have had her full approval. Oh, I wonder if she knows what is going on, if she is rejoicing in my joy, as she would have done had she been here!"

And a yearning look passed over the fair young face, as she thought how sweet would have been that beloved mother's sympathy at this crisis of her life.

And then Mary Stafford had to be taken into the secret; and in the warmth and fervor of her delight she almost suffocated Dorothy by the vehement embrace she gave her.

"Oh, I am so glad for you, Dorothy. For you seemed to stand so alone. You have had so much sorrow to pass through. And now,—oh, how happy you will be with such a man as Dr. Willoughby—and I am rejoiced to think of your living at Wharton Park, which is nearer to us than Hurstwood. If you had gone away from the neighborhood, I should have missed you dreadfully. For you have been such a help to me; you know in what way I mean."

"You must come and pay us long visits," said Dorothy, "and then you can have good long talks with Stephen,"—the name was uttered very shyly—"and you will find how he can help one."

"It will be delightful, oh, so delightful! But, Dorothy, dear,"— Mary paused for a moment, and then went on in a low voice, "I am learning that God does keep His promise, that promise you reminded me of once, 'Seek, and ye shall find.'"

When Dorothy lay down to rest that night, sleep was long in coming to her; she felt too happy to sleep. As her thoughts roamed from one subject to another, they turned more than once to Robert, and her heart felt sore for him. She found herself hoping that he too might some day experience joy such as that which she was now tasting; and earnestly she asked that he might persevere in the search on which he had set out until he, like Mary, might end by saying, "He that seeketh findeth."

Printed in Great Britain
by Amazon